# MONSTER BLOOD COLLECTION

### MONSTER BLOOD

### MONSTER BLOOD II

### MONSTER BLOOD III

# R. L. STINE

SCHOLASTIC INC.

New York   Toronto   London   Auckland   Sydney
Mexico City   New Delhi   Hong Kong   Buenos Aires

# Goosebumps®

## MONSTER BLOOD

"I don't want to stay here. Please don't leave me here."

Evan Ross tugged his mother's hand, trying to pull her away from the front stoop of the small, gray-shingled house. Mrs. Ross turned to him, an impatient frown on her face.

"Evan — you're twelve years old. Don't act like an infant," she said, freeing her hand from his grasp.

"I *hate* when you say that!" Evan exclaimed angrily, crossing his arms in front of his chest.

Softening her expression, she reached out and ran her hand tenderly through Evan's curly, carrot-colored hair. "And I *hate* when you do that!" he cried, backing away from her, nearly stumbling over a broken flagstone in the walk. "Don't touch my hair. I hate it!"

"Okay, so you hate me," his mother said with a shrug. She climbed up the two steps and knocked

1

on the front door. "You still have to stay here till I get back."

"Why can't I come with you?" Evan demanded, keeping his arms crossed. "Just give me one good reason."

"Your sneaker is untied," his mother replied.

"So?" Evan replied unhappily. "I like 'em untied."

"You'll trip," she warned.

"Mom," Evan said, rolling his eyes in exasperation, "have you ever seen *anyone* trip over his sneakers because they were untied?"

"Well, no," his mother admitted, a smile slowly forming on her pretty face.

"You just want to change the subject," Evan said, not smiling back. "You're going to leave me here for weeks with a horrible old woman and — "

"Evan — that's *enough!*" Mrs. Ross snapped, tossing back her straight blonde hair. "Kathryn is not a horrible old woman. She's your father's aunt. Your great-aunt. And she's — "

"She's a total stranger," Evan cried. He knew he was losing control, but he didn't care. How could his mother do this to him? How could she leave him with some old lady he hadn't seen since he was two? What was he supposed to do here all by himself until his mother got back?

"Evan, we've discussed this a thousand times,"

his mother said impatiently, pounding on his aunt's front door again. "This is a family emergency. I really expect you to cooperate a little better."

Her next words were drowned out by Trigger, Evan's cocker spaniel, who stuck his tan head out of the back window of the rented car and began barking and howling.

"Now *he's* giving me a hard time, too!" Mrs. Ross exclaimed.

"Can I let him out?" Evan asked eagerly.

"I guess you'd better," his mother replied. "Trigger's so old, we don't want him to have a heart attack in there. I just hope he doesn't terrify Kathryn."

"I'm coming, Trigger!" Evan called.

He jogged to the gravel driveway and pulled open the car door. With an excited yip, Trigger leapt out and began running in wide circles around Kathryn's small, rectangular front yard.

"He doesn't *look* like he's twelve," Evan said, watching the dog run, and smiling for the first time that day.

"See. You'll have Trigger for company," Mrs. Ross said, turning back to the front door. "I'll be back from Atlanta in no time. A couple of weeks at the most. I'm sure your dad and I can find a house in that time. And then we'll be back before you even notice we're gone."

"Yeah. Sure," Evan said sarcastically.

The sun dipped behind a large cloud. A shadow fell over the small front yard.

Trigger wore himself out quickly and came panting up the walk, his tongue hanging nearly to the ground. Evan bent down and petted the dog's back.

He looked up at the gray house as his mother knocked on the front door again. It looked dark and uninviting. There were curtains drawn over the upstairs windows. One of the shutters had come loose and was resting at an odd angle.

"Mom — why are you knocking?" he asked, shoving his hands into his jeans pockets. "You said Aunt Kathryn was totally deaf."

"Oh." His mother's face reddened. "You got me so upset, Evan, with all your complaining, I completely forgot. Of *course* she can't hear us."

How am I going to spend two weeks with a strange old lady who can't even hear me? Evan wondered glumly.

He remembered eavesdropping on his parents two weeks earlier when they had made the plan. They were seated across from each other at the kitchen table. They thought Evan was out in the backyard. But he was in the hallway, his back pressed against the wall, listening.

His father, he learned, was reluctant to leave Evan with Kathryn. "She's a very stubborn old woman," Mr. Ross had said. "Look at her. Deaf

4

for twenty years, and she's refused to learn sign language or to lip-read. How's she going to take care of Evan?"

"She took good care of you when *you* were a boy," Mrs. Ross had argued.

"That was thirty years ago," Mr. Ross protested.

"Well, we have no choice," Evan heard his mother say. "There's no one else to leave him with. Everyone else is away on vacation. You know, August is just the worst month for you to be transferred to Atlanta."

"Well, excuuuuse me!" Mr. Ross said sarcastically. "Okay, okay. Discussion closed. You're absolutely right, dear. We have no choice. Kathryn it is. You'll drive Evan there and then fly down to Atlanta."

"It'll be a good experience for him," Evan heard his mother say. "He needs to learn how to get along under difficult circumstances. You know, moving to Atlanta, leaving all his friends behind — that isn't going to be easy on Evan either."

"Okay. I said okay," Mr. Ross said impatiently. "It's settled. Evan will be fine. Kathryn is a bit weird, but she's perfectly harmless."

Evan heard the kitchen chairs scraping across the linoleum, indicating that his parents were getting up, their discussion ended.

His fate was sealed. Silently, he had made his

way out the front door and around to the backyard to think about what he had just overheard.

He leaned against the trunk of the big maple tree, which hid him from the house. It was his favorite place to think.

Why didn't his parents ever include *him* in their discussions? he wondered. If they were going to discuss leaving him with some old aunt he'd never seen before, shouldn't he at least have a say? He learned all the big family news by eavesdropping from the hallway. It just wasn't right.

Evan pulled a small twig off the ground and tapped it against the broad tree trunk.

Aunt Kathryn was weird. That's what his dad had said. She was so weird, his father didn't want to leave Evan with her.

But they had no choice. No choice.

Maybe they'll change their minds and take me to Atlanta with them, Evan thought. Maybe they'll realize they can't *do* this to me.

But now, two weeks later, he was standing in front of Aunt Kathryn's gray house, feeling very nervous, staring at the brown suitcase filled with his belongings, which stood beside his mother on the stoop.

There's nothing to be scared of, he assured himself.

It's only for two weeks. Maybe less.

But then the words popped out before he'd even

had a chance to think about them: "Mom — what if Aunt Kathryn is mean?"

"Huh?" The question caught his mother by surprise. "Mean? Why would she be mean, Evan?"

And as she said this, facing Evan with her back to the house, the front door was pulled open, and Aunt Kathryn, a large woman with startling black hair, filled the doorway.

Staring past his mother, Evan saw the knife in Kathryn's hand. And he saw that the blade of the knife was dripping with blood.

# 2

Trigger raised his head and began to bark, hopping backward on his hind legs with each bark.

Startled, Evan's mother spun around, nearly stumbling off the small stoop.

Evan gaped in silent horror at the knife.

A smile formed on Kathryn's face, and she pushed open the screen door with her free hand.

She wasn't anything like Evan had pictured. He had pictured a small, frail-looking, white-haired old lady. But Kathryn was a large woman, very robust, broad-shouldered, and tall.

She wore a peach-colored housedress and had straight black hair, pulled back and tied behind her head in a long ponytail that flowed down the back of the dress. She wore no makeup, and her pale face seemed to disappear under the striking black hair, except for her eyes, which were large and round, and steely blue.

"I was slicing beef," she said in a surprisingly deep voice, waving the blood-stained kitchen knife. She stared at Evan. "You like beef?"

"Uh . . . yeah," he managed to reply, his chest still fluttery from the shock of seeing her appear with the raised knife.

Kathryn held open the screen door, but neither Evan nor his mother made any move to go inside. "He's big," Kathryn said to Mrs. Ross. "A big boy. Not like his father. I used to call his father Chicken. Because he was no bigger than a chicken." She laughed as if she had cracked a funny joke.

Mrs. Ross, picking up Evan's suitcase, glanced uncomfortably back at him. "Yeah . . . he's big," she said.

Actually, Evan was one of the shortest kids in his class. And no matter how much he ate, he remained "as skinny as a spaghetti noodle," as his dad liked to say.

"You don't have to answer me," Kathryn said, stepping aside so that Mrs. Ross could get inside the house with the suitcase. "I can't hear you." Her voice was deep, as deep as a man's, and she spoke clearly, without the indistinct pronunciation that some deaf people have.

Evan followed his mother into the front hall-way, Trigger yapping at his heels. "Can't you get that dog quiet?" his mother snapped.

"It doesn't matter. She can't hear it," Evan replied, gesturing toward his aunt, who was heading to the kitchen to put down the knife.

Kathryn returned a few seconds later, her blue eyes locked on Evan, her lips pursed, as if she were studying him. "So, you like beef?" she repeated.

He nodded.

"Good," she said, her expression still serious. "I always fixed beef for your father. But he only wanted pie."

"What kind of pie?" Evan asked, and then blushed when he remembered Kathryn couldn't hear him.

"So he's a good boy? Not a troublemaker?" Kathryn asked Evan's mother.

Mrs. Ross nodded, looking at Evan. "Where shall we put his suitcase?" she asked.

"I can tell by looking he's a good boy," Kathryn said. She reached out and grabbed Evan's face, her big hand holding him under the chin, her eyes examining him closely. "Good-looking boy," she said, giving his chin a hard squeeze. "He likes the girls?"

Still holding his chin, she lowered her face to his. "You've got a girlfriend?" she asked, her pale face right above his, so close he could smell her breath, which was sour.

Evan took a step back, an embarrassed grin crossing his face. "No. Not really."

"Yes?" Kathryn cried, bellowing in his ear. "Yes? I *knew* it!" She laughed heartily, turning her gaze to Evan's mother.

"The suitcase?" Mrs. Ross asked, picking up the bag.

"He likes the girls, huh?" Kathryn repeated, still chuckling. "I could tell. Just like his father. His father always liked the girls."

Evan turned desperately to his mother. "Mom, I can't stay here," he said, whispering even though he knew Kathryn couldn't hear. "Please — don't make me."

"Hush," his mother replied, also whispering. "She'll leave you alone. I promise. She's just trying to be friendly."

"He likes the girls," Kathryn repeated, leering at him with her cold blue eyes, again lowering her face close to Evan's.

"Mom — her breath smells like Trigger's!" Evan exclaimed miserably.

"Evan!" Mrs. Ross shouted angrily. "Stop it! I expect you to cooperate."

"I'm going to bake you a pie," Kathryn said, tugging at her black ponytail with one of her huge hands. "Would you like to roll out the dough? I'll bet you would. What did your father tell you about me, Evan?" She winked at Mrs. Ross. "Did he tell you I was a scary old witch?"

"No," Evan protested, looking at his mother.

"Well, I am!" Kathryn declared, and once again burst into her deep-throated laugh.

Trigger took this moment to begin barking ferociously and jumping on Evan's great-aunt. She

11

glared down at the dog, her eyes narrowing, her expression becoming stern. "Look out or we'll put *you* in the pie, doggie!" she exclaimed.

Trigger barked even harder, darting boldly toward the tall, hovering woman, then quickly retreating, his stub of a tail whipping back and forth in a frenzy.

"We'll put him in the pie, won't we, Evan?" Kathryn repeated, putting a big hand on Evan's shoulder and squeezing it till Evan flinched in pain.

"Mom — " he pleaded when his aunt finally let go and, smiling, made her way to the kitchen. "Mom — please."

"It's just her sense of humor, Evan," Mrs. Ross said uncertainly. "She means well. Really. She's going to bake you a pie."

"But I don't want pie!" Evan wailed. "I don't like it here, Mom! She hurt me. She squeezed my shoulder so hard — "

"Evan, I'm sure she didn't mean to. She's just trying to joke with you. She wants you to like her. Give her a chance — okay?"

Evan started to protest, but thought better of it.

"I'm counting on you," his mother continued, turning her eyes to the kitchen. They could both see Kathryn at the counter, her broad back to them, hacking away at something with the big kitchen knife.

"But she's . . . weird!" Evan protested.

"Listen, Evan, I understand how you're feeling," his mother said. "But you won't have to spend all your time with her. There are a lot of kids in this neighborhood. Take Trigger for a walk. I'll bet you'll make some friends your age. She's an old woman, Evan. She won't want you hanging around all the time."

"I guess," Evan muttered.

His mother bent down suddenly and gave him a hug, pressing her cheek against his. The hug, he knew, was supposed to cheer him up. But it only made him feel worse.

"I'm counting on you," his mother repeated in his ear.

Evan decided to try and be braver about this. "I'll help you carry the suitcase up to my room," he said.

They carried it up the narrow staircase. His room was actually a study. The walls were lined with bookshelves filled with old hardcover books. A large mahogany desk stood in the center of the room. A narrow cot had been made up under the single, curtained window.

The window faced out onto the backyard, a long green rectangle with the gray-shingled garage to the left, a tall picket fence to the right. A small, fenced-in area stretched across the back of the yard. It looked like some sort of dog run.

The room smelled musty. The sharp aroma of mothballs invaded Evan's nose.

Trigger sneezed. He rolled onto his back, his legs racing in the air.

Trigger can't stand this place either, Evan thought. But he kept his thought to himself, smiling bravely at his mother, who quickly unpacked his suitcase, nervously checking her watch.

"I'm late. Don't want to miss my plane," she said. She gave him another hug, longer this time. Then she took a ten-dollar bill from her pocketbook and stuffed it into his shirt pocket. "Buy yourself a treat. Be good. I'll hurry back as fast as I can."

"Okay. Bye," he said, his chest feeling fluttery, his throat as dry as cotton. The smell of her perfume momentarily drowned out the mothballs.

He didn't want her to leave. He had such a bad feeling.

You're just scared, he scolded himself.

"I'll call you from Atlanta," she shouted as she disappeared down the stairs to say good-bye to Kathryn.

Her perfume disappeared.

The mothballs returned.

Trigger uttered a low, sad howl, as if he knew what was happening, as if he knew they were being abandoned here in this strange house with the strange old woman.

Evan picked Trigger up and nose-kissed his cold, black nose. Putting the dog back down on the worn carpet, he made his way to the window.

He stood there for a long while, one hand holding the curtains aside, staring down at the small, green yard, trying to calm the fluttering in his chest. After a few minutes, he heard his mother's car back down the gravel drive. Then he heard it roll away.

When he could no longer hear it, he sighed and plopped down on the cot. "It's just you and me now, Trigger," he said glumly.

Trigger was busily sniffing behind the door.

Evan stared up at the walls of old books.

What am I going to do here all day? he asked himself, propping his head in his hands. No Nintendo. No computer. He hadn't even seen a TV in his great-aunt's small living room. What am I going to do?

Sighing again, he picked himself up and walked along the bookshelves, his eyes scanning the titles. There were lots of science books and textbooks, he saw. Books on biology and astronomy, ancient Egypt, chemistry texts, and medical books. Several shelves were filled with dusty, yellowed books. Maybe Kathryn's husband, Evan's great-uncle, had been some sort of scientist.

Nothing here for me to read, he thought glumly.

He pulled open the closet door.

"Oh!"

He cried out as something leapt out at him.

"Help! Please — help!"

Everything went black.

"Help! I can't see!" Evan screamed.

## 3

Evan staggered back in fear as the warm blackness crept over him.

It took him a few seconds to realize what it was. His heart still thudding in his chest, he reached up and pulled the screeching black cat off his face.

The cat dropped silently to the ground and padded to the doorway. Evan turned and saw Kathryn standing there, an amused grin on her face.

How long had she been standing there? he wondered.

"Sarabeth, how did you get in there?" she asked in a playfully scolding tone, bending down to speak to the cat. "You must have given the boy a fright."

The cat mewed and rubbed against Kathryn's bare leg.

"Did Sarabeth scare you?" Kathryn asked Evan, still smiling. "That cat has a strange sense of humor. She's evil. Pure evil." She chuckled as if she'd said something funny.

"I'm okay," Evan said uncertainly.

"Watch out for Sarabeth. She's evil," Kathryn repeated, bending down and picking the cat up by the scruff of the neck, holding her up in the air in front of her. "Evil, evil, evil."

Seeing the cat suspended in the air, Trigger uttered an unhappy howl. His stubby tail went into motion, and he leapt up at the cat, barking and yipping, missed, and leapt again, snapping at Sarabeth's tail.

"Down, Trigger! Get down!" Evan cried.

Struggling to get out of Kathryn's arms, the cat swiped a clawed black paw at her, screeching in anger and fear. Trigger barked and howled as Evan struggled to pull the excited cocker spaniel away.

Evan grabbed hold of Trigger as the cat swung to the floor and disappeared out the door. "Bad dog. Bad dog," Evan whispered. But he didn't really mean it. He was glad Trigger had scared the cat away.

He looked up to see Kathryn still filling the doorway, staring down at him sternly. "Bring the dog," she said in a low voice, her eyes narrowed, her pale lips pursed tightly.

"Huh?" Evan gripped Trigger in a tight hug.

"Bring the dog," Kathryn repeated coldly. "We can't have animals fighting in this house."

"But Aunt Kathryn — " Evan started to plead, then remembered she couldn't hear him.

"Sarabeth is a bad one," Kathryn said, not softening her expression. "We can't get her riled, can we?" She turned and started down the stairs. "Bring the dog, Evan."

Holding Trigger tightly by the shoulders with both hands, Evan hesitated.

"I have to take care of the dog," Kathryn said sternly. "Come."

Evan was suddenly filled with dread. What did she mean, *take care* of the dog?

A picture flashed into his mind of Kathryn standing at the doorway with the bloody kitchen knife in her hand.

"Bring the dog," Kathryn insisted.

Evan gasped. What was she going to *do* to Trigger?

"I will take care of you, doggie," Kathryn repeated, frowning at Trigger. The dog whimpered in reply.

"Come, Evan. Follow me," she said impatiently.

Seeing that he had no choice, Evan obediently carried Trigger down the stairs and followed his aunt to the backyard. "I'm prepared," she said, turning to make sure he was following.

Despite her age — she was at least eighty — she walked with long, steady strides. "I knew you were bringing a dog, so I made sure I was prepared."

Trigger licked Evan's hand as they walked across the yard to the long, fenced-in area at the back. "It's a special place for your dog," Kathryn said, reaching up to grab one end of the rope that stretched across the run. "Attach this to the collar, Evan. Your dog will have fun here." She frowned disapprovingly at Trigger. "And there will be no problems with Sarabeth."

Evan felt very relieved that this was all Kathryn wanted to do to Trigger. But he didn't want to leave Trigger tied up in this prison in the back of the yard. Trigger was a house dog. He wouldn't be happy by himself out here.

But Evan knew he had no way of arguing with his aunt. Kathryn is smart in a way, he thought bitterly as he hooked Trigger's collar to the rope. Since she won't learn sign language and won't lip-read, it means she gets to do whatever she wants, and no one can tell her no.

He bent down and gave Trigger's warm head a pat and looked up at the old woman. She had her arms crossed in front of her chest, her blue eyes glowing brightly in the sunlight, a cold smile of triumph on her face.

"That's a good boy," she said, waiting for Evan to get up before starting back to the house. "I knew when I looked at you. Come to the house, Evan. I have cookies and milk. You'll enjoy them." Her words were kind, but her voice was hard and cold.

Trigger sent up an unhappy howl as Evan followed Kathryn to the house. Evan turned, intending to go back and comfort the dog. But Kathryn grabbed his hand in an iron grip, and, staring straight ahead, led him to the kitchen door.

The kitchen was small and cluttered and very

21

warm. Kathryn motioned for him to sit at a small table against the wall. The table was covered with a plastic, checkered tablecloth. She frowned, her eyes studying him, as she brought over his snack.

He downed the oatmeal raisin cookies and milk, listening to Trigger howl in the backyard. Oatmeal raisin wasn't his favorite, but he was surprised to find that he was hungry. As he gobbled them down, Kathryn stood at the doorway, staring intently at him, a stern expression on her face.

"I'm going to take Trigger for a walk," he announced, wiping the milk mustache off his upper lip with the paper napkin she had given him.

Kathryn shrugged and wrinkled up her face.

Oh. Right. She can't hear me, Evan thought. Standing at the kitchen window, he pointed to Trigger, then made a walking motion with two fingers. Kathryn nodded.

Whew, he thought. This is going to be hard.

He waved good-bye and hurried to free Trigger from his backyard prison.

A few minutes later, Trigger was tugging at the leash, sniffing the flowers along the curb as Evan made his way up the block. The other houses on the street were about the same size as Kathryn's, he saw. And they all had small, neatly trimmed, square front yards.

He saw some little kids chasing each other around a birch tree. And he saw a middle-aged man in bright orange bathing trunks washing his

22

car with a garden hose in his driveway. But he didn't see any kids his age.

Trigger barked at a squirrel and tugged the leash out of Evan's hand. "Hey — come back!" Evan called. Trigger, disobedient as always, took off after the squirrel.

The squirrel wisely climbed a tree. But Trigger, his eyesight not what it once was, continued the chase.

Running at full speed, calling the dog's name, Evan followed him around a corner and halfway down the block before Trigger finally realized he had lost the race.

Breathing hard, Evan grabbed the leash handle. "Gotcha," he said. He gave the leash a tug, trying to lead the panting dog back to Kathryn's street.

Trigger, sniffing around a dark tree trunk, pulled the other way. Evan was about to pick up the stubborn dog when he was startled by a hand grabbing his shoulder.

"Hey — who are *you?*" a voice demanded.

# 5

Evan spun around to find a girl standing behind him, staring at him with dark brown eyes. "Why'd you grab my shoulder like that?" he asked, his heart still pounding.

"To scare you," she said simply.

"Yeah. Well . . ." Evan shrugged. Trigger gave a hard tug at the leash and nearly pulled him over.

The girl laughed.

She was pretty, he thought. She had short, wavy brown hair, almost black, and flashing brown eyes, and a playful, teasing smile. She was wearing an oversized yellow T-shirt over black spandex leggings, and bright yellow Nikes.

"So who *are* you?" she demanded again.

She wasn't the shy type, he decided. "I'm me," he said, letting Trigger lead him around the tree.

"Did you move into the Winterhalter house?" she asked, following him.

He shook his head. "No. I'm just visiting."

She frowned in disappointment.

"For a couple of weeks," Evan added. "I'm staying with my aunt. Actually, she's my great-aunt."

"What's so great about her?" the girl cracked.

"Nothing," Evan replied without laughing. "For sure."

Trigger sniffed at a bug on a fat brown leaf.

"Is that your bike?" Evan asked, pointing to the red BMX bike lying on the grass behind her.

"Yeah," she replied.

"It's cool," he said. "I have one like it."

"I like your dog," she said, eyeing Trigger. "He looks real stupid. I like stupid dogs."

"Me, too. I guess." Evan laughed.

"What's his name? Does he have a stupid name?" She bent down and tried to pet Trigger's back, but he moved away.

"His name's Trigger," Evan said, and waited for her reaction.

"Yeah. That's pretty stupid," she said thoughtfully. "Especially for a cocker spaniel."

"Thanks," Evan said uncertainly.

Trigger turned to sniff the girl's hands, his tail wagging furiously, his tongue hanging down to the ground.

"I have a stupid name, too," the girl admitted. She waited for Evan to ask.

"What is it?" he said finally.

"Andrea," she said.

"That's not a stupid name."

"I hate it," she said, pulling a blade of grass off

her leggings. "Annndreeea." She stretched the name out in a deep, cultured voice. "It sounds so stuck up, like I should be wearing a corduroy jumper with a prim, white blouse, walking a toy poodle. So I make everyone call me Andy."

"Hi, Andy," Evan said, petting Trigger. "My name is — "

"Don't tell me!" she interrupted, clamping a hot hand over his mouth.

She certainly *isn't* shy, he thought.

"Let me guess," she said. "Is it a stupid name, too?"

"Yeah," he nodded. "It's Evan. Evan Stupid."

She laughed. "That's *really* a stupid name."

He felt glad that he made her laugh. She was cheering him up, he realized. A lot of the girls back home didn't appreciate his sense of humor. They thought he was silly.

"What are you doing?" she asked.

"Walking Trigger. You know. Exploring the neighborhood."

"It's pretty boring," she said. "Just a lot of houses. Want to go into town? It's only a few blocks away." She pointed down the street.

Evan hesitated. He hadn't told his aunt he was going into town. But, what the heck, he thought. She wouldn't care.

Besides, what could possibly happen?

26

## 6

"Okay," Evan said. "Let's check out the town."

"I have to go to a toy store and look for a present for my cousin," Andy said, hoisting her bike up by the handlebars.

"How old are you?" Evan asked, tugging Trigger toward the street.

"Twelve."

"Me, too," he said. "Can I try your bike?"

She shook her head as she climbed onto the narrow seat. "No, but I'll let you run alongside." She laughed.

"You're a riot," he said sarcastically, hurrying to keep up as she began to pedal.

"And you're stupid," she called back playfully.

"Hey, *Annnndreeeea* — wait up!" he called, stretching the name out to annoy her.

A few blocks later, the houses ended and they entered town, a three-block stretch of low two-story shops and offices. Evan saw a small brick post office, a barbershop with an old-fashioned barber pole out front, a grocery, a drive-through bank, and a hardware store with a large sign in the window proclaiming a sale on birdseed.

"The toy store is in the next block," Andy said, walking her bike along the sidewalk. Evan tugged Trigger's leash, encouraging him to keep up the pace. "Actually there are two toy stores, an old one and a new one. I like the old one best."

"Let's check it out," Evan said, examining the cluttered window display of the video store on the corner.

I wonder if Aunt Kathryn has a VCR, he thought. He quickly dismissed the idea. No way. . . .

The toy store was in an old clapboard building that hadn't been painted in many years. A small, hand-painted sign in the dust-smeared window proclaimed: WAGNER'S NOVELTIES & SUNDRIES. There were no toys on display.

Andy leaned her bike against the front of the building. "Sometimes the owner can be a little mean. I don't know if he'll let you bring your dog in."

"Well, let's give it a try," Evan said, pulling open the door. Tugging hard on his leash, Trigger led the way into the store.

Evan found himself in a dark, low-ceilinged, narrow room. It took awhile for his eyes to adjust to the dim light.

Wagner's looked more like a warehouse than a

store. There were floor-to-ceiling shelves against both walls, jammed with boxes of toys, and a long display counter that ran through the center of the store, leaving narrow aisles that even someone as skinny as Evan had to squeeze through.

At the front of the store, slumped on a tall stool behind an old-fashioned wooden cash register, sat a grumpy-looking man with a single tuft of white hair in the center of a red, bald head. He had a drooping white mustache that seemed to frown at Evan and Andy as they entered.

"Hi," Andy said timidly, giving the man a wave.

He grunted in reply and turned back to the newspaper he was reading.

Trigger sniffed the low shelves excitedly. Evan looked around at the stacks of toys. It appeared from the thick layer of dust that they'd been sitting there for a hundred years. Everything seemed tossed together, dolls next to building sets, art supplies mixed in with old action figures Evan didn't even recognize, a toy drum set underneath a pile of footballs.

He and Andy were the only customers in the store.

"Do they have Nintendo games?" Evan asked her, whispering, afraid to break the still silence.

"I don't think so," Andy whispered back. "I'll ask." She shouted up to the front, "Do you have Nintendo games?"

It took awhile for the man to answer. He

scratched his ear. "Don't carry them," he grunted finally, sounding annoyed by the interruption.

Andy and Evan wandered toward the back of the store. "Why do you like this place?" Evan whispered, picking up an old cap pistol with a cowboy holster.

"I just think it's neat," Andy replied. "You can find some real treasures here. It's not like other toy stores."

"That's for sure," Evan said sarcastically. "Hey — look!" He picked up a lunchbox with a cowboy dressed in black emblazoned on its side. "Hopalong Cassidy," he read. "Who's Hopalong Cassidy?"

"A cowboy with a stupid name," Andy said, taking the old lunchbox from him and examining it. "Look — it's made of metal, not plastic. Wonder if my cousin would like it. He likes stupid names, too."

"It's a pretty weird present," Evan said.

"He's a pretty weird cousin," Andy cracked. "Hey, look at this." She set down the old lunchbox and picked up an enormous box. "It's a magic set. 'Astound your friends. Perform one hundred amazing tricks,' " she read.

"That's a lot of amazing tricks," Evan said.

He wandered farther back into the dimly lit store, Trigger leading the way, sniffing furiously. "Hey — " To Evan's surprise, a narrow doorway led into a small back room.

30

This room, Evan saw, was even darker and dustier. Stepping inside, he saw worn-looking stuffed animals tossed into cartons, games in faded, yellowed boxes, baseball gloves with the leather worn thin and cracked.

Who would want this junk? he thought.

He was about to leave when something caught his eye. It was a blue can, about the size of a can of soup. He picked it up, surprised by how heavy it was.

Bringing it close to his face to examine it in the dim light, he read the faded label: MONSTER BLOOD. Below that, in smaller type, it read: SURPRISING MIRACLE SUBSTANCE.

Hey, this looks cool, he thought, turning the can around in his hand.

He suddenly remembered the ten dollars his mother had stuffed into his shirt pocket.

He turned to see the store owner standing in the doorway, his dark eyes wide with anger. "What are you *doing* back here?" he bellowed.

# 7

Trigger yipped loudly, startled by the man's booming voice.

Evan gripped the leash, pulled Trigger close. "Uh . . . how much is this?" he asked, holding up the can of Monster Blood.

"Not for sale," the owner said, lowering his voice, his mustache seeming to frown unpleasantly with the rest of his face.

"Huh? It was on the shelf here," Evan said, pointing.

"It's too old," the man insisted. "Probably no good anymore."

"Well, I'll take it, anyway," Evan said. "Can I have it for less since it's so old?"

"What is it?" Andy asked, appearing in the doorway.

"I don't know," Evan told her. "It looks cool. It's called Monster Blood."

"It's not for sale," the man insisted.

Andy pushed past him and took the can from Evan's hand. "Ooh, I want one, too," she said, turning the can around in her hand.

"There's only one," Evan told her.

"You sure?" She began searching the shelves.

"It's no good, I'm telling you," the owner insisted, sounding exasperated.

"I need one, too," Andy said to Evan.

"Sorry," Evan replied, taking the can back. "I saw it first."

"I'll buy it from you," Andy said.

"Why don't you two *share* it?" the owner suggested.

"You mean you'll sell it to us?" Evan asked eagerly.

The man shrugged and scratched his ear.

"How much?" Evan asked.

"You sure you don't have another one?" Andy demanded, going back to the shelf, pushing a pile of stuffed pandas out of her way. "Or maybe two? I could keep one and give one to my cousin."

"Two dollars, I guess," the man told Evan. "But I'm telling you, it's no good. It's too old."

"I don't care," Evan said, reaching into his shirt pocket for the ten-dollar bill.

"Well, don't bring it back to me complaining," the man said grumpily, and headed toward the cash register at the front of the store.

A few minutes later, Evan walked out into the bright daylight carrying the blue can. Trigger

33

panted excitedly, wagging his stubby tail, pleased to be out of the dark, dusty store. Andy followed them out, an unhappy expression on her face.

"You didn't buy the lunchbox?" Evan asked.

"Don't change the subject," she snapped. "I'll pay you five dollars for it." She reached for the can of Monster Blood.

"No way," Evan replied. He laughed. "You really like to get your way, don't you!"

"I'm an only child," she said. "What can I tell you? I'm spoiled."

"Me, too," Evan said.

"I have an idea," Andy said, pulling her bike off the storefront wall. "Let's share it."

"Share it?" Evan said, shaking his head. "For sure. I'll share it the way you shared your bike."

"You want to ride the bike home? Here." She shoved it at him.

"No way," he said, pushing it back toward her. "I wouldn't ride your stupid bike now. It's a girl's bike, anyway."

"It is not," she insisted. "How is it a girl's bike?"

Evan ignored the question and, pulling at Trigger's leash to keep the old dog moving, started walking back toward his aunt's.

"How is it a girl's bike?" Andy repeated, walking the bike beside him.

"Tell you what," Evan said. "Let's go back to my aunt's house and open up the can. I'll let you mess with it for a while."

"Gee, swell," Andy said sarcastically. "You're a great guy, Evan."

"I know," he said, grinning.

Kathryn was seated in the big armchair in the living room when Evan and Andy arrived. Who is she talking to? he wondered, hearing her voice. She seemed to be arguing excitedly with someone.

Leading Andy into the room, Evan saw that it was just Sarabeth, the black cat. As Evan entered, the cat turned and haughtily walked out of the room.

Kathryn stared at Evan and Andy, a look of surprise on her face. "This is Andy," Evan said, gesturing to his new friend.

"What have you got there?" Kathryn asked, ignoring Andy and reaching a large hand out for the blue can of Monster Blood.

Evan reluctantly handed it to her. Frowning, she rolled it around in her hand, stopping to read the label, moving her lips as she read. She held the can for the longest time, seeming to study it carefully, then finally handed it back to Evan.

As Evan took it back and started to his room with Andy, he heard Kathryn say something to him in a low whisper. He couldn't quite hear what she had said. It sounded like, "Be careful." But he wasn't sure.

He turned to see Sarabeth staring at him from the doorway, her yellow eyes glowing in the dim light.

"My aunt is completely deaf," Evan explained to Andy as they climbed the stairs.

"Does that mean you can play your stereo as loud as you want?" Andy asked.

"I don't think Aunt Kathryn has a stereo," Evan said.

"That's too bad," Andy said, walking around Evan's room, pulling back the window curtains and looking down on Trigger, huddled unhappily in his pen.

"Is she really your great-aunt?" Andy asked. "She doesn't look very old."

"It's the black hair," Evan replied, setting the can of Monster Blood on the desk in the center of the room. "It makes her look young."

"Hey — look at all these old books on magic stuff!" Andy exclaimed. "I wonder why your aunt has all these."

She pulled one of the heavy, old volumes from the shelf and blew away a layer of dust from the top. "Maybe your aunt plans to come up here and cast a spell on you while you're sleeping, and turn you into a newt."

"Maybe," Evan replied, grinning. "What *is* a newt, anyway?"

Andy shrugged. "Some kind of lizard, I think." She flipped through the yellowed pages of the old book. "I thought you said there was nothing to do here," she told Evan. "You could read all these cool books."

"Thrills and chills," Evan said sarcastically.

Replacing the book on the shelf, Andy came over to the desk and stood next to Evan, her eyes on the can of Monster Blood. "Open it up. It's so old. It's probably all disgusting and rotten."

"I hope so," Evan said. He picked up the can and studied it. "No instructions."

"Just pull the top off," she said impatiently.

He tugged at it. It wouldn't budge.

"Maybe you need a can opener or something," she said.

"Very helpful," he muttered, studying the label again. "Look at this. No instructions. No ingredients. Nothing."

"Of course not. It's Monster Blood!" she exclaimed, imitating Count Dracula. She grabbed Evan's neck and pretended to strangle him.

He laughed. "Stop! You're not helping."

He slammed the can down on the desktop — and the lid popped off.

"Hey — look!" he cried.

She let go of his neck, and they both peered inside the can.

## 8

The substance inside the can was bright green. It shimmered like Jell-O in the light from the ceiling fixture.

"Touch it," Andy said.

But before Evan had a chance, she reached a finger in and poked it. "It's cold," she said. "Touch it. It's really cold."

Evan poked it with his finger. It was cold, thicker than Jell-O, heavier.

He pushed his finger beneath the surface. When he pulled his finger out, it made a loud sucking noise.

"Gross," Andy said.

Evan shrugged. "I've seen worse."

"I'll bet it glows in the dark," Andy said, hurrying over to the light switch by the door. "It looks like the green that glows in the dark."

She turned off the ceiling light, but late afternoon sunlight still poured in through the window curtains. "Try the closet," she instructed excitedly.

Evan carried the can into the closet. Andy followed and closed the door. "Yuck. Mothballs," she cried. "I can't breathe."

The Monster Blood definitely glowed in the dark. A circular ray of green light seemed to shine from the can.

"Wow. That's way cool," Andy said, holding her nose to keep out the pungent aroma of the mothballs.

"I've had other stuff that did this," Evan said, more than a little disappointed. "It was called Alien Stuff or Yucky Glop, something like that."

"Well, if you don't want it, I'll take it," Andy replied.

"I didn't say I didn't want it," Evan said quickly.

"Let's get out of here," Andy begged.

Evan pushed open the door and they rushed out of the closet, slamming the door shut behind them. Both of them sucked in fresh air for a few seconds.

"Whew, I hate that smell!" Evan declared. He looked around to see that Andy had taken a handful of Monster Blood from the can.

She squeezed it in her palm. "It feels even colder outside the can," she said, grinning at him. "Look. When you squeeze it flat, it pops right back."

"Yeah. It probably bounces, too," Evan said,

unimpressed. "Try bouncing it against the floor. All those things bounce like rubber."

Andy rolled the glob of Monster Blood into a ball and dropped it to the floor. It bounced back up into her hand. She bounced it a little harder. This time it rebounded against the wall and went flying out the bedroom door.

"It bounces really well," she said, chasing it out into the hall. "Let's see if it stretches." She grabbed it with both hands and pulled, stretching it into a long string. "Yep. It stretches, too."

"Big deal," Evan said. "The stuff I had before bounced and stretched really well, too. I thought this stuff was going to be different."

"It stays cold, even after it's been in your hand," Andy said, returning to the room.

Evan glanced at the wall and noticed a dark, round stain by the floorboard. "Uh-oh. Look, Andy. That stuff stains."

"Let's take it outside and toss it around," she suggested.

"Okay," he agreed. "We'll go out back. That way, Trigger won't be so lonely."

Evan held out the can, and Andy replaced the ball of Monster Blood. Then they headed downstairs and out to the backyard, where they were greeted by Trigger, who acted as if they'd been away for at least twenty years.

The dog finally calmed down, and sat down in the shade of a tree, panting noisily. "Good boy,"

Evan said softly. "Take it easy. Take it easy, old fella."

Andy reached into the can and pulled out a green glob. Then Evan did the same. They rolled the stuff in their hands until they had two ball-shaped globs. Then they began to play catch with them.

"It's amazing how they don't lose their shape," Andy said, tossing a green ball high in the air.

Evan shielded his eyes from the late afternoon sun and caught the ball with one hand. "All this stuff is the same," he said. "It isn't so special."

"Well, I think it's cool," Andy said defensively.

Evan's next toss was too high. The green ball of gunk sailed over Andy's outstretched hands.

"Whoa!" Andy cried.

"Sorry," Evan called.

They both stared as the ball bounced once, twice, then landed right in front of Trigger.

Startled, the dog jumped to his feet and lowered his nose to sniff it.

"No, boy!" Evan called. "Leave it alone. Leave it alone, boy!"

As disobedient as ever, Trigger lowered his head and licked the glowing green ball.

"No, boy! Drop! Drop!" Evan called, alarmed.

He and Andy both lunged toward the dog.

But they were too slow.

Trigger picked up the ball of Monster Blood in his teeth and began chewing it.

"No, Trigger!" Evan shouted. "Don't swallow it. Don't swallow!"

Trigger swallowed it.

"Oh, no!" Andy cried, balling her hands into fists at her sides. "Now there isn't enough left for us to share!"

But that wasn't what was troubling Evan. He bent down and pried apart the dog's jaws. The green blob was gone. Swallowed.

"Stupid dog," Evan said softly, releasing the dog's mouth.

He shook his head as troubling thoughts poured into his mind.

What if the stuff makes Trigger sick? Evan wondered.

What if the stuff is poison?

# 9

"Are we going to bake that pie today?" Evan asked his aunt, writing the question on a pad of lined yellow paper he had found on the desk in his room.

Kathryn read the question while adjusting her black ponytail. Her face was as white as cake flour in the morning sunlight filtering through the kitchen window.

"Pie? What pie?" she replied coldly.

Evan's mouth dropped open. He decided not to remind her.

"Go play with your friends," Kathryn said, still coldly, petting Sarabeth's head as the black cat walked by the breakfast table. "Why do you want to stay inside with an old witch?"

It was three days later. Evan had tried to be friendly with his aunt. But the more he tried, the colder she had become.

She's mean. She's really mean, he thought, as he ate the last spoonful of cereal from his bowl of shredded wheat. That was the only cereal she had. Evan struggled to choke it down every morning. Even with milk, the cereal was so dry and she wouldn't even let him put sugar on it.

"Looks like it might rain," Kathryn said, and took a long sip of the strong tea she had brewed. Her teeth clicked noisily as she drank.

Evan turned his eyes to the bright sunlight outside the window. What made her think it was going to rain?

He glanced back at her, seated across from him at the small kitchen table. For the first time, he noticed the pendant around her neck. It was cream-colored and sort of bone-shaped.

It *is* a bone, Evan decided.

He stared hard at it, trying to decide if it was a real bone, from some animal maybe, or a bone carved out of ivory. Catching his stare, Kathryn reached up with a large hand and tucked the pendant inside her blouse.

"Go see your girlfriend. She's a pretty one," Kathryn said. She took another long sip of tea, again clicking her teeth as she swallowed.

Yes. I've *got* to get out of here, Evan thought. He pushed his chair back, stood up, and carried his bowl to the sink.

I can't take much more of this, Evan thought miserably. She hates me. She really does.

He hurried up the stairs to his room, where he brushed his curly red hair. Staring into the mirror, he thought of the call he had received from his mother the night before.

She had called right after dinner, and he could tell immediately from her voice that things weren't going well down in Atlanta.

"How's it going, Mom?" he had asked, so happy to hear her voice, even though she was nearly a thousand miles away.

"Slowly," his mother had replied hesitantly.

"What do you mean? How's Dad? Did you find a house?" The questions seemed to pour out of him like air escaping a balloon.

"Whoa. Slow down," Mrs. Ross had replied. She sounded tired. "We're both fine, but it's taking a little longer to find a house than we thought. We just haven't found anything we like."

"Does that mean — " Evan started.

"We found one really nice house, very big, very pretty," his mother interrupted. "But the school you'd go to wasn't very good."

"Oh, that's okay. I don't have to go to school," Evan joked.

He could hear his father saying something in the background. His mother covered the receiver to reply.

"When are you coming to pick me up?" Evan asked eagerly.

It took his mother awhile to answer. "Well . . . that's the problem," she said finally. "We may need a few more days down here than we thought.

How's it going up there, Evan? Are you okay?"

Hearing the bad news that he'd have to stay even longer with Kathryn had made Evan feel like screaming and kicking the wall. But he didn't want to upset his mother. He told her he was fine and that he'd made a new friend.

His father had taken the phone and offered a few encouraging words. "Hang in there," he had said just before ending the conversation.

I'm hanging in, Evan had thought glumly.

But hearing his parents' voices had made him even more homesick.

Now it was the next morning. Putting down his hairbrush, he examined himself quickly in his dresser mirror. He was wearing denim cutoffs and a red Gap T-shirt.

Downstairs, he hurried through the kitchen, where Kathryn appeared to be arguing with Sarabeth, ran out the back door, then jogged to the backyard to get Trigger. "Hey, Trigger!"

But the dog was asleep, lying on his side in the center of his run, gently snoring.

"Don't you want to go to Andy's house?" Evan asked quietly.

Trigger stirred, but didn't open his eyes.

"Okay. See you later," Evan said. He made sure Trigger's water bowl was filled, then headed to the front of the house.

He was halfway down the next block, walking slowly, thinking about his parents so far away in

Atlanta, when a boy's voice called, "Hey — you!" And two boys stepped onto the sidewalk in front of him, blocking his way.

Startled, Evan stared from one boy to the other. They were twins. Identical twins. Both were big, beefy guys, with short, white-blond hair and round, red faces. They were both wearing dark T-shirts with the names of heavy-metal bands on the front, baggy shorts, and high-top sneakers, untied, without socks. Evan guessed they were about fourteen or fifteen.

"Who are *you*?" one of them asked menacingly, narrowing his pale gray eyes, trying to act tough. Both twins moved closer, forcing Evan to take a big step back.

These guys are twice my size, Evan realized, feeling a wave of fear sweep over him.

Are they just acting tough? Or do they really mean to give me trouble?

"I — I'm staying with my aunt," he stammered, shoving his hands into his pockets and taking another step back.

The twins flashed each other quick grins. "You can't walk on this block," one of them said, hovering over Evan.

"Yeah. You're not a resident," the other added.

"That's a big word," Evan cracked, then immediately wished he hadn't said it.

Why can't I ever keep my big mouth shut? he asked himself. His eyes surveyed the neighborhood, searching for someone who might come to his aid in case the twins decided to get rough.

But there was no one in sight. Front doors were closed. Yards were empty. Way down the block, he could see a mailman, heading the other way, too far away to shout to.

No one around. No one to help him.

And the two boys, their faces set, their eyes still menacing, began to move in on him.

# 10

"Where do you think you're going?" one of the twins asked. His hands were balled into fists at his sides. He stepped closer until he was just an inch or two from Evan, forcing Evan to take a few steps back.

"To see a friend," Evan replied uncertainly. Maybe these guys were just bluffing.

"Not allowed," the twin said quickly, grinning at his brother.

They both snickered and moved toward Evan, forcing him to back off the curb onto the street.

"You're not a resident," the other one repeated. He narrowed his eyes, trying to look tough.

"Hey, give me a break, guys," Evan said. He tried moving to the side, walking on the street, to get around them. But they both moved quickly to keep him from getting away.

"Maybe you could pay a toll," one of them said.

"Yeah," the other one quickly chimed in. "You could pay the nonresident toll. You know, to get temporary permission for walking on this block."

"I don't have any money," Evan said, feeling his fear grow.

He suddenly remembered he had eight dollars in his pocket. Were they going to rob him? Would they beat him up and *then* rob him?

"You have to pay the toll," one of them said, leering at him. "Let's just see what you've got."

They both moved quickly forward, making a grab for him.

He backed away. His legs suddenly felt heavy from fear.

Suddenly a voice cried out from down the sidewalk. "Hey — what's going on?"

Evan raised his eyes past the two hulking boys to see Andy speeding toward them on her bike along the curb. "Evan — hi!" she called.

The twins turned away from Evan to greet the new arrival. "Hi, Andy," one of them said in a mocking tone.

"How's it going, Andy?" the other one asked, imitating his brother.

Andy braked her bike and dropped both feet to the ground. She was wearing bright pink shorts and a yellow sleeveless undershirt top. Her face was red, her forehead beaded with perspiration from pedaling so hard.

"You two," she said, and made an unpleasant face. "Rick and Tony." She turned to Evan. "Were they getting on your case?"

"Well . . ." Evan started hesitantly.

"We were welcoming him to the neighborhood," the one named Rick said, grinning at his brother.

Tony started to add something, but Andy interrupted. "Well, leave him alone."

"Are you his *mother*?" Tony asked, snickering. He turned to Evan and made goo-goo baby noises.

"We'll leave him alone," Rick said, stepping toward Andy. "We'll borrow your bike and leave him alone."

"No way," Andy said heatedly.

But before Andy could move, Rick grabbed the handlebars. "Let go!" Andy cried, trying to pull the bike from his grasp.

Rick held tight. Tony shoved Andy hard.

She lost her balance and fell, and the bike toppled over on top of her.

"Ohhh."

Andy uttered a low cry as she hit her head on the concrete curb. She lay sprawled on the curb, her hands flailing, the bike on top of her.

Before she could get up, Tony reached down and grabbed the bike away. He swung his legs over the seat and began to pedal furiously. "Wait up!" his brother called, laughing as he ran alongside.

In seconds, the twins had disappeared around the corner with Andy's bike.

"Andy — are you okay?" Evan cried, hurrying to the curb. "Are you okay?"

He grabbed Andy's hand and pulled her to her feet. She stood up groggily, rubbing the back of her head. "I hate those creeps," she said. She brushed the dirt and grass off her shorts and legs. "Ow. That hurt."

"Who *are* they?" Evan asked.

"The Beymer twins," she answered, making a disgusted face. "Real heavy-duty dudes," she added sarcastically. She checked her leg to see if it was cut. It was just scraped. "They think they're so cool, but they're total creeps."

"What about your bike? Should we call the police or something?" Evan asked.

"No need," she said quietly, brushing back her dark hair. "I'll get it back. They've done this before. They'll leave it somewhere when they're finished."

"But shouldn't we — " Evan started.

"They just run wild," Andy interrupted. "There's no one home to check up on them. They live with their grandmother, but she's never around. Did they give you a hard time?"

Evan nodded. "I was afraid I was going to have to pound them," he joked.

Andy didn't laugh. "I'd like to pound them," she said angrily. "Just once. I'd like to pay them back. They pick on all the kids in the neighborhood. They think they can do whatever they want because they're so big, and because there are two of them."

"Your knee is cut," Evan said, pointing.

"I'd better go home and clean it up," she replied, rolling her eyes disgustedly. "See you later, okay? I have to go somewhere this afternoon, but maybe we can do something tomorrow."

She headed back to her house, rubbing the back of her head.

Evan returned to Kathryn's, walking slowly, thinking about the Beymer twins, daydreaming about fighting them, imagining himself beating them to a pulp in a fight as Andy watched, cheering him on.

Kathryn was dusting the front room as Evan entered. She didn't look up. He headed quickly up the stairs to his room.

Now what am I going to do? he wondered, pacing back and forth. The blue container of Monster Blood caught his eye. He walked over to the bookshelf and picked up the can from the middle shelf.

He pulled off the lid. The can was nearly full.

I guess Trigger didn't eat that much, he thought, feeling a little relieved.

Trigger!

He'd forgotten all about him. The poor dog must be hungry.

Putting down the Monster Blood, Evan bombed down the stairs, leaning against the banister and taking the stairs three at a time. Then, running full-out, he practically flew to the dog run at the back of the yard.

"Trigger! Hey — Trigger!" he called.

Halfway across the backyard, Evan could see that something was wrong.

Trigger's eyes were bulging. His mouth was wide open, his tongue flailing rapidly from side to side, white spittle running down his chin hair onto the ground.

"Trigger!"

The dog was gasping hoarsely, each breath a desperate, difficult struggle.

He's choking! Evan realized.

As Evan reached the dog run, Trigger's eyes rolled back, and the dog's legs collapsed under him, his stomach still heaving, the air filled with his loud, hideous gasps.

# 11

"Trigger — no!"

Evan dived to his knees beside the dog and began to tug at Trigger's collar. The collar, Evan saw, had become way too tight.

The dog's chest heaved. Thick white spittle flowed from his open mouth.

"Hold on, boy. Hold on!" Evan cried.

The dog's eyes rolled wildly in his head. He didn't seem to see or hear Evan.

"Hold on, fella! Just *hold on!*"

The collar wouldn't budge. It was buried tightly under the dog's fur.

His hands shaking, Evan struggled to pull the collar over Trigger's head.

Come loose, come loose, come *loose*, he begged. Yes!

Trigger uttered a pained whimper as Evan finally managed to pull the collar away.

"Trigger — it's off! Are you okay?"

Still panting hard, the dog jumped immediately

to his feet. He licked Evan's face appreciatively, covering Evan's cheek with his thick saliva, whimpering as if he understood that Evan had just saved his life.

"Easy, boy! Easy, fella!" Evan repeated, but the dog continued to lick him gratefully.

Evan hugged the excited dog. This had been a close call, he knew. If he hadn't come along just then . . .

Well, he didn't want to think about it.

When Trigger finally calmed down, Evan examined the collar. "What made this collar shrink like that, boy?" he asked Trigger.

The dog had walked over to the fence and was frantically slurping water from his bowl.

This is plain weird, Evan thought. The collar couldn't have shrunk. It's made of leather. There was no reason for it to shrink.

Then why did it suddenly start choking Trigger?

Evan turned to Trigger, studying him as the dog lapped greedily at the water, breathing hard. He turned and glanced back at Evan for a second, then returned to his frantic water slurping.

He's *bigger*, Evan decided.

He's definitely bigger.

But Trigger was twelve years old, eighty-four in human years. Older than Aunt Kathryn.

Trigger was too old for a late growth spurt.

It must be my eyes, Evan decided, tossing the collar to the ground. This place must be making me see things.

Kathryn was at the kitchen door, calling Evan to lunch. He poured out a bowl of dry food, shouted good-bye to Trigger, who didn't look up from the water dish, and hurried to the house.

The next morning, an overcast morning with an autumn chill in the air, Evan made his way to Andy's house. He found her huddled under a big maple tree in the neighbor's front yard. "What's going on?" he called.

Then he saw that she was leaning over something, her hands working quickly. "Come help me!" she cried, not looking up.

Evan came jogging over. "Whoa!" he cried out when he saw that Andy was struggling to free a calico cat that had been tied to the tree trunk.

The cat screeched and swiped its paw at Andy. Andy dodged the claws and continued to pull at the big knots in the rope.

"The Beymer twins did this. I know it," she said loudly, over the shrilly protesting cat. "This poor cat was probably tied up here all night."

The cat, in a panic, shrieked with amazingly human-sounding cries.

"Stand still, cat," Evan said as the terrified cat

swiped its claws at Andy again. "Can I help?"

"No. I've almost got it," she replied, tugging at the knot. "I'd like to tie Rick and Tony to this tree."

"Poor, frightened cat," Evan said quietly.

"There," Andy said triumphantly, pulling the rope loose.

The cat gave one last cry of protest, its tail standing straight up. Then it darted away, running at full speed, and disappeared under a tall hedge without looking back.

"Not very polite," Evan muttered.

Andy stood up and sighed. She was wearing faded denim jeans and a pale green, oversized T-shirt that came down nearly to her knees. She lifted the bottom of the shirt to examine a hole the cat had managed to snag in it.

"I can't believe those two creeps," she said, shaking her head.

"Maybe we should call the police or the ASPCA or something," Evan suggested.

"The twins would just deny it," Andy said glumly, shaking her head. Then she added, "And the cat's not a very good witness."

They both laughed.

Evan led the way back to his aunt's house. All the way back, they talked about how they'd like to teach the Beymer twins a lesson. But neither of them had any good ideas.

They found Kathryn concentrating on a jigsaw puzzle at the dining room table.

She looked up when they entered, squinting at them. "You like jigsaw puzzles? I like to keep my mind active, you know. That's why I like puzzles. Your mind can get flabby when you get to be my age. A hundred and twelve."

She slapped the table gleefully at her own wit. Evan and Andy both flashed her agreeable smiles. Then she returned to her puzzle without waiting for a reply.

"She's going to drive me bananas!" Evan exclaimed.

"Evan — she'll hear you!" Andy protested, cupping a hand over his mouth.

"I told you, she's completely deaf. She can't hear me. She doesn't *want* to hear anyone. She *hates* everyone."

"I think she's sweet," Andy said. "Why does she wear a bone around her neck?"

"Probably thinks it's cool," Evan cracked.

"Let's go upstairs," Andy urged, pushing him toward the stairs. "I still feel weird talking about your aunt right in front of her."

"You're a crazy old coot," Evan called to Kathryn, a big smile on his face.

Kathryn looked up from her puzzle pieces to cast a cold stare his way.

"She heard you!" Andy cried, horrified.

"Don't be dumb," Evan said, and started up the stairs, nearly tripping over Sarabeth.

Up in Evan's room, Andy paced uncomfortably. "What do you want to do?"

"Well . . . we could read some of these great books," Evan said sarcastically, pointing to the dusty old books that lined the walls. "Maybe find a spell to cast on the Beymer twins. You know. Turn them into newts."

"Forget about newts," Andy said dryly. "Hey — where's the Monster Blood?" Before Evan could answer, she spotted it on one of the shelves.

They raced across the room for it. Andy got there first and grabbed the can. "Evan — look," she said, her eyes growing wide with surprise. "What's going on?"

She held up the can. The green gunk had pushed up the lid and was flowing up out of the can.

# 12

"Huh? Did the top break or something?" Evan asked.

He took the can from her and examined it. Sure enough, the lid had popped off. The gooey green substance was pushing up out of the can.

Evan pulled out a handful of the green gunk. "Weird," he exclaimed. "It's expanding," he said, squeezing it in his hand. "It's definitely growing."

"I guess so!" Andy exclaimed. "It grew right out of the can!"

"Hey — it's not cold anymore," Evan said. He balled it up and tossed it to Andy.

"It's really warm," she agreed. "Weird!"

She tried to toss it back to him, but it stuck to her palm. "It's getting sticky," she reported. "Are you sure this is the same stuff?"

"Of course," Evan replied.

"But it wasn't sticky before, remember?" she said.

He pulled another warm hunk of it from the

can. "I guess it just changes after the can has been opened."

He squeezed the stuff into a ball shape and tossed it to the floor. "Look — it stuck to the floor. It didn't bounce."

"Weird!" Andy repeated.

"Maybe I should throw it in the trash," Evan said, prying the sticky glob from the floor. "I mean, what good is it if it doesn't bounce?"

"Hey — no way," Andy said. "We've got to see what it does next."

A soft mewing sound made them both turn toward the door.

Evan was surprised to see Sarabeth standing there, her head cocked, her yellow eyes staring at him.

Or was she staring at the glob of Monster Blood in his hand?

"That cat looks so intelligent," Andy said.

"It's as stupid as every other cat," Evan muttered. "Look. She wants to play ball with the Monster Blood."

"Sorry, cat," Andy said. "It doesn't bounce."

As if she understood, Sarabeth mewed unhappily, turned, and padded silently from the room.

"Now where am I going to keep this stuff?" Evan asked. "It's too big for its can."

"Here. How about this?" Andy asked. She reached down to a low shelf and came up with an empty coffee can.

"Yeah. Okay." Evan tossed his hunk into the coffee can.

Andy squeezed hers into a flat pancake. "Look. It isn't glowing the way it used to, either," she said, holding the pancake up for Evan to see. "But it sure is warm. Almost hot."

"It's *alive!*" Evan screamed playfully. "Run for your life! It's *alive!*"

Andy laughed and began to chase Evan, menacing him with the flat, green pancake. "Come get your Monster Blood! Come and get it!"

He dodged away, then grabbed it from her hand. He squeezed it together, balling it up in one hand, then tossed it into the coffee can.

They both peered into the can. The green substance filled it up a little more than halfway.

"Go ahead. Taste it," Andy urged, poking the can in his face. "I dare you."

"Huh? No way. I double-dare you," Evan said, pushing the coffee can back to her.

"Double-darers have to go first," Andy insisted, grinning. "Go ahead. Taste it."

Evan made a disgusted face and shook his head. Then he grabbed a big hunk of it and heaved it at Andy. Laughing, she picked it up off the carpet and tossed it at his face. She threw high, and the green glob stuck to the wall.

Evan reached for another hunk.

They had a messy, hilarious Monster Blood battle till dinnertime. Then, as they tried to clean up, they both heard Trigger through the open window. He was barking loudly out in his pen.

Evan reached the window first. The sky was still gray and overcast. Trigger was leaning on the wooden fence, standing on his hind legs, barking his head off.

"Whoa, Trigger," Evan called, "chill out!"

"Hey — what's with Trigger?" Andy asked. "Is your dog still growing? He looks so big!"

Evan's mouth dropped open and he uttered a silent gasp, realizing that Andy was right.

Trigger had nearly doubled in size.

# 13

"Trigger — come back! Come *back!*"

The big dog continued to run, its giant paws thundering against the concrete.

*"Come back!"* Evan screamed, running with long, desperate strides, his heart thudding, his legs aching with each step as he tried to catch up with the galloping dog.

The night was dark and starless. The street glistened as if it had recently rained.

Trigger's paws hit the pavement, each step a loud thunderclap that seemed to echo forever. His giant ears flapped like wings, twin pennants caught on the wind. His big head bobbed up and down, but he didn't look back.

"Trigger! *Trigger!*"

Evan's voice seemed muffled by the gusting wind, pushed back in his face. He tried shouting louder, but no sound came out at all.

He knew he had to stop the dog from running away. He had to catch the dog and then get help.

Trigger was growing so fast, completely out of control. He was already the size of a pony, and getting larger by the minute.

"Trigger! Trigger! Stop, boy!"

Trigger didn't seem to hear him. Evan's voice didn't seem to carry beyond the gusting, swirling wind.

And still Evan ran, his chest pounding, every muscle aching. And as he ran, he suddenly realized there were others running, too.

Two large figures in front of the stampeding dog.

Two large figures Evan recognized as they fled at full speed, trying to get away from the onrushing animal.

The Beymer twins. Rick and Tony.

Trigger was chasing them, Evan suddenly realized.

The boys turned a corner, onto an even darker street. Trigger followed, bounding after them. Evan continued to run, bringing up the rear of this dark, mysterious parade.

All was silent now, except for the steady, rhythmic thunder of Trigger's enormous padded paws.

Except for the *clapclapclap* of the Beymer twins' sneakers as they darted along the glistening pavement.

Except for the gasp of Evan's breathing as he struggled to keep up.

Suddenly, as Evan watched in horror, the dog raised up on his hind legs. He tilted his head to the sky and let out an ear-piercing howl. Not the howl of a dog. A creature howl.

And then Trigger's features began to transform. His forehead burst forward and enlarged. His eyes grew wide and round before sinking under the protruding forehead. Fangs slid from his gaping mouth, and he uttered another howl to the sky, louder and more chilling than the first.

"He's a monster! A monster!" Evan cried.

And woke up.

Woke up from his frightening dream.

And realized he was in bed, in the study upstairs in Kathryn's house.

It had all been a dream, a frightening, wild chase of a dream.

A harmless dream. Except that something still wasn't right.

The bed. It felt so uncomfortable. So cramped.

Evan sat up, alert, wide awake now.

And stared down at his giant feet. His giant hands. And realized how tiny the bed seemed beneath him.

Because he was a giant now.

Because he had grown so huge, so monstrously huge.

And when he saw how big he had become, he opened his mouth wide and began to scream.

# 14

His screams woke him up.

This time he really woke up.

And realized that, the first time, he had only dreamed that he was awake. Had only dreamed that he had become a giant.

Dreams upon dreams.

Was he really awake now?

He sat up, blinked, rubbed his eyes, struggled to focus.

Dripping with sweat.

His blankets tossed to the floor.

His pajamas damp, clinging to his prickly skin.

Nothing seemed familiar. It took awhile to shake off the dream, to remember where he was. That he was in his room at Kathryn's. Awake now. His normal size.

Tossed by the wind, the curtains brushed over him, then were noisily sucked out the window.

Evan sat up and, still feeling shaky, peered out the window.

Wisps of gray clouds floated over a pale half-moon. Trees tossed and whispered in the cool night wind.

Only a dream.

A frightening dream. A dream on top of a dream.

He could see Trigger sound asleep, curled up on himself, pressed against the fence wall.

Trigger wasn't a monster. But he was definitely bigger, Evan saw.

Maybe there's something wrong with him. The troubling thought pushed its way into Evan's mind as he stared down at the sleeping dog.

Maybe it's glands or something.

Maybe he's eating too much. Or maybe . . .

Evan yawned. He realized he was too sleepy to think clearly. Maybe the next morning he'd see if there was a vet in town.

Yawning again, he started to settle back into bed. But something caught his eye.

The coffee can on the bookshelf. The can where he had stored the Monster Blood.

"Hey — " he cried aloud.

The green gunk was bubbling, quivering up over the top of the coffee can.

# 15

"Your dog seems to be quite healthy for his age." Dr. Forrest scratched Trigger gently under the chin. "Look at all the white hairs," he said, bringing his face down close to the dog's. "You're a good old dog, aren't you?"

Trigger licked the doctor's hand appreciatively.

Dr. Forrest grinned, pushing his black eyeglasses up on his narrow nose, the ceiling light reflecting off his shiny forehead. He wiped his hand on the front of his white lab coat.

Evan and Andy stood across from Trigger in the small, brightly lit office. They had both been tense during the long examination the vet had given the dog. But now, hearing the doctor's verdict, they had relaxed expressions on their faces.

"So you think it's just a late growth spurt?" Evan repeated.

Dr. Forrest nodded, returning to his desk in the corner. "Highly unusual," he said softly, leaning over the desk to write a note on a pad. "Highly unusual. We'll get a lab report in three or four days. It may tell us more. But the dog seems very healthy to me. I really wouldn't be alarmed."

"But do cocker spaniels usually get this big?" Evan asked, leaning down to scratch Trigger under the chin, the leash looped loosely in his hand.

Trigger wanted to leave. He pulled toward the door. Evan stood up and tugged hard at the leash to keep the dog in place. It took all of his strength. Trigger was not only bigger; he was much stronger than he had been a few days before.

"No. Not usually," the vet replied. "That's why I took the hormone tests and the blood and glandular samples. Maybe the lab will have an answer for us."

He finished writing and tore the sheet off the pad. "Here," he said, handing the paper to Evan. "I wrote down the name of a good dog food. Put Trigger on this, and see that he cuts down on his between-meal snacks." He chuckled at his own joke.

Evan thanked the doctor and allowed Trigger to pull him out of the office. Andy jogged after them. In the waiting room outside, a tiny Chihuahua cowered behind the couch, whimpering at the sight of the big cocker spaniel.

"I'm glad to be out of there," Evan exclaimed as they stepped out to the sidewalk.

"Trigger got a very good report," Andy said reassuringly, petting Trigger's head. "Hey, look

— his head is wider than my hand!"

"He's nearly as big as a sheepdog!" Evan said miserably. "And Dr. Forrest says he's perfectly okay."

"Don't exaggerate," Andy scolded. She glanced at her watch. "Oh, no! I don't believe it. Late for my piano lesson. Again! Mom'll *kill* me!"

She waved good-bye, turned, and ran full speed down the sidewalk, nearly colliding with an elderly couple coming slowly out of the small grocery store on the corner.

"Let's go, boy," Evan said, thinking about what Dr. Forrest had said. Tugging the leash, he headed out of the small, three-block town. Despite the vet's assurances, Evan was still plenty worried about Trigger.

He stopped outside the grocery. "Maybe an ice cream pop will help cheer me up." He tied Trigger's leash to the red fire hydrant across from the grocery's door. "Stay," he instructed.

Trigger, ignoring Evan, struggled to pull free.

"I'll only be a second," Evan said, and hurried into the store.

There were three or four people in the store, and it took a bit longer than Evan had expected. When he returned to the sidewalk ten minutes later, he discovered the Beymer twins busily untying Trigger.

"Hey — let go!" he cried angrily.

They both turned toward him, identical grins

on their beefy faces. "Look what we found," one of them teased. The other one successfully untied the leash from the hydrant.

"Hand me that," Evan insisted, holding his chocolate ice cream bar in one hand, reaching for the leash handle with the other.

The Beymer twin held the leash handle out to Evan — then quickly snapped it back out of his reach. "Gotcha!"

The brothers laughed gleefully and slapped each other a high five.

"Stop fooling around," Evan insisted. "Hand me the leash."

"Finders, keepers," one of them said. "Isn't that right, Tony?"

"Yeah," Tony replied, grinning. "It's an ugly dog. But it's *our* ugly dog now."

"Get your own dog, wimp," Rick said nastily. He stepped forward and punched the ice cream bar out of Evan's hand. It landed on the sidewalk with a *plop*.

The brothers started to laugh, but their laughter was cut short as Trigger suddenly uttered a low, warning growl. Pulling back his lips, he bared his teeth, and his growl became a snarl.

"Hey — " Rick cried, dropping the leash.

With a loud, angry roar, Trigger reared up and pounced on Rick, forcing him to stagger backward to the curb.

Tony had already started to run, his sneakers

73

pounding the pavement noisily as he headed at full speed past the vet's office, past the post office, and kept going.

"Wait up! Hey, Tony — wait up!" Rick stumbled, stood up, and took off after his brother.

Evan grabbed for Trigger's leash — and missed.

"Trigger — whoa! Stop!"

The dog took off after the fleeing twins, barking angrily, his enormous paws thudding loudly on the pavement, picking up speed as he closed in on them.

No, Evan thought, finding himself frozen there on the corner in front of the grocery.

No. No. No.

This *can't* be happening!

It's my dream.

Is it coming true?

Evan shuddered, remembering the rest of his dream, remembering how he, too, grew until he was twice his size.

Would that part of the dream also come true?

# 16

That afternoon, about an hour before dinnertime, Evan called Andy. "Can I come over?" he asked. "I have a small problem."

"Sounds like a big problem," Andy said.

"Yeah. Okay. A big problem," Evan snapped impatiently. "I'm not in the mood to kid around, okay?"

"Okay. Sorry," Andy replied quickly. "Any sign of Rick and Tony? They're not your problem, are they?"

"Not at the moment," he told her. "I told you, they were gone by the time I caught up with Trigger. Disappeared. Vanished. Trigger was still barking his head off. Somehow I dragged him home and got him in his pen."

"So what's your problem?" she asked.

"I can't tell you. I have to show you," he said. "I'll be right there. Bye."

He hung up the phone and hurried down the

stairs, carrying the bucket. Kathryn was in the kitchen, her back to him, chopping away at something with her big butcher knife. Evan hurried past and darted out the door.

Andy's house was a modern, redwood ranch style, with a low hedge of evergreens running along the front. Her dad, she said, was a fanatic about the lawn. It was clipped a perfect inch and a half above the ground, smooth as a carpet. A flower garden stretched along the front of the house, tall orange and yellow tiger lilies bobbing in the gentle breeze.

The front door was open. Evan knocked on the screen door.

"What's with the bucket?" was Andy's greeting as she let him in.

"Look," he said, out of breath from running all the way to her house. He held up the aluminum bucket he had taken from Kathryn's garage.

"Oh, wow," Andy exclaimed, raising her hands to her face as she stared into it wide-eyed.

"Yeah. Wow," he repeated sarcastically. "The Monster Blood. It's grown again. Look. It's almost filled this big bucket. What are we going to do?"

"What do you mean *we*?" Andy teased, leading him into the den.

"Not funny," he muttered.

"You didn't want to share it," she insisted.

"I'll share it now," he said eagerly. "In fact

76

. . . do you want it? I'll give it to you for a bargain price — free." He held the bucket toward her.

"Huh-uh." Andy shook her head, crossing her arms in front of her chest. "Put it down, will you?" She pointed to the corner behind the red leather couch. "Put it over there. It's giving me the creeps."

"Giving *you* the creeps!?" Evan cried. "What am I going to do? Every time I turn around, it grows some more. It's growing faster than Trigger!"

"Hey!" they both cried at once.

Both had the same thought, the same frightening memory. Both suddenly remembered that Trigger had eaten a ball of the green gunk.

"Do you think . . ." Evan started.

"Maybe . . ." Andy replied, not waiting for him to finish his thought. "Maybe Trigger's growing because he ate the Monster Blood."

"What am I going to *do*?" Evan wailed, pacing the room nervously, his hands shoved into his jeans pockets. "The stuff is getting bigger and bigger, and so is poor Trigger. I'm all alone here. There's no one who can help me. No one."

"What about your aunt?" Andy suggested, staring at the bucket on the floor in the corner. "Maybe Kathryn can think of something — "

"Are you kidding? She can't hear me. She doesn't *want* to hear me. She *hates* me. She just sits at her jigsaw puzzle and argues

77

with that horrible black cat all day."

"Okay. Forget the aunt," Andy said, making a dispirited face.

"Perhaps if you told Dr. Forrest — "

"Oh, yeah. For sure," Evan snapped. "He'd really believe that Trigger is turning into a giant because I let him eat Monster Blood."

He threw himself down on the couch. "I'm all alone here, Andy. There's no one to help me. No one I can even talk to about this."

"Except me?"

"Yeah," he said, locking his eyes on hers. "Except you."

She plopped down on the other end of the couch. "Well, what can I do?" she asked hesitantly.

He jumped up and carried the bucket over. "Take some of this. Let's split it up."

"Huh? Why don't we just toss it in the trash?" she asked, staring down at it. The green gunk was pushing up near the top of the bucket.

"Toss it? We can't," he said.

"Sure, we can. Come on. I'll show you." She reached for the bucket handle, but he shoved it out of her reach.

"What if it outgrows the trash can?" he asked. "What if it just keeps growing?"

Andy shrugged. "I don't know."

"Also, I *have* to save it," Evan continued excitedly. "If it's really the thing that's causing Trigger to grow, I'll need it as proof. You know. To show the doctors or whatever. So they can cure Trigger."

"Maybe we should call the police," Andy said thoughtfully, tugging at a strand of hair.

"Oh. Sure," Evan replied, rolling his eyes. "They'll really believe us. For sure. 'We bought this stuff in a toy store, officer, and now it's growing bigger and bigger and it's turning my dog into a giant monster.' "

"Okay, okay. You're right," Andy said. "We can't call the police."

"So, are you going to help me?" Evan demanded. "Will you take some of this stuff?"

"I guess," she said reluctantly. "But just a little." She climbed to her feet, carefully stepping around the bucket. "I'll be right back."

She left the room, then quickly returned, carrying an empty coffee can. "Fill 'er up," she said, smiling.

Evan stared at the coffee can. "That's *all* you're going to take?" he complained. Then he immediately softened his tone. "Okay. Okay. It's a help."

Andy crouched down and dipped the coffee can into the middle of the bucket. "Hey!" she cried out. Her hands flew up and she tumbled back onto the floor.

"What's wrong?" Evan hurried over to her.

"It was pulling the coffee can in," she said, her features tight with fear and surprise. "Sucking it. Look."

Evan peered into the bucket. The coffee can had disappeared under the surface. "Huh?"

"I could feel it pulling," Andy said shakily. She regained her perch over the bucket.

"Let's see," Evan said, and plunged both hands into the middle of the Monster Blood.

"Yuck," Andy said. "This is really gross."

"It's pulling. You're right," Evan agreed. "It feels like it's pulling my hands down. Wow. It's so warm. As if it's alive."

*"Don't say that!"* Andy cried with a shudder. "Just get the can out, okay?"

Evan had to tug hard, but he managed to pull up the coffee can, filled to the top with the quivering green substance. "Yuck."

"You sure I have to take this?" Andy asked, not reaching for it even though he was holding it out to her.

"Just for a little while," he said. "Till we think of a better plan."

"Maybe we could feed it to the Beymer twins," Andy suggested, finally taking the can.

"Then we'd have *giant* Beymer twins," Evan joked. "No, thank you."

"Seriously, you'd better watch out for them," Andy warned. "If Trigger scared them away this morning, they'll be looking to get back at you. They really think they're tough dudes, Evan. They can be vicious. They could really hurt you."

"Thanks for trying to cheer me up," Evan said

glumly. He was still pulling tiny, clinging clumps of the Monster Blood off his hands and tossing them into the bucket.

"I was watching a video before you came over. The first Indiana Jones movie. Want to watch it?"

Evan shook his head. "No. I'd better go. Aunt Kathryn was busy making dinner when I left. Chopping up some kind of meat. Another great dinner, sitting there in silence, being stared at by Aunt Kathryn and her cat."

"Poor Evan," Andy said, half teasing, half sympathetic.

He picked up the bucket, now only two-thirds full, and let her walk him to the front door. "Call me later, okay?" she asked.

He nodded and stepped outside. She closed the door behind him.

He was halfway to the sidewalk when the Beymer twins slipped out from behind the evergreen hedge, their hands balled into red, beefy fists.

# 17

The brothers stepped out of the shadows of the hedge. Their short blond hair caught the late afternoon sunlight. They were both grinning gleefully.

Evan stood frozen in place, staring from one to the other.

No one said a word.

One of the Beymers grabbed the bucket from Evan's hand and tossed it to the ground. The bucket hit with a heavy *thud*, and its thick, green contents oozed onto the grass, making disgusting sucking sounds.

"Hey — " Evan cried, breaking the tense silence.

He didn't have a chance to say more.

The other twin punched him hard in the stomach.

Evan felt the pain radiate through his body. The punch took his breath away. He gasped for air.

He didn't see the next punch. It landed on his cheek just below his right eye.

He howled in pain, and his hands flailed the air helplessly.

Both brothers were hitting him now. And then one of them gave Evan's shoulders a hard shove, and he went sprawling onto the cool, damp grass.

The pain swept over him, blanketing him, followed by a wave of nausea. He closed his eyes, gasping noisily, waiting for the sharp ache in his stomach to fade.

The ground seemed to tilt. He reached out and grabbed it, and held on tightly so he wouldn't fall off.

When he finally managed to raise his head, Andy was standing over him, her eyes wide with alarm. "Evan — "

He groaned and, pushing with both hands, tried to sit up. The dizziness, the spinning, tilting grass, forced him to lie back down.

"Are they gone?" he asked, closing his eyes, willing the dizziness away.

"Rick and Tony? I saw them run away," Andy said, kneeling beside him. "Are you okay? Should I call my mom?"

He opened his eyes. "Yeah. No. I don't know."

"What *happened*?" she demanded.

He raised a hand to his cheek. "Ow!" It was already swollen, too painful to touch.

"They beat you up?"

"Either that or I was hit by a truck," he groaned.

A few minutes later — it seemed like hours — he was back on his feet, breathing normally, rubbing his swollen cheek. "I've never been in a fight before," he told Andy, shaking his head. "Never."

"It doesn't look like it was much of a fight," she said, her expression still tight with concern.

He started to laugh, but it made his stomach hurt.

"We'll pay them back," Andy said bitterly. "We'll find a way to pay them back. The creeps."

"Oh. Look. The Monster Blood." Evan hurried over to it.

The bucket lay on its side. The green gunk had oozed onto the grass, forming a wide, thick puddle.

"I'll help you get it back in the bucket," Andy said, leaning over to stand the bucket up. "Hope it doesn't kill the grass. My dad'll have a cow if his precious lawn is hurt!"

"It's so heavy," Evan said, groaning as he tried to push the glob into the bucket. "It doesn't want to move."

"Let's try picking up handfuls," Andy suggested.

"Whoa. It doesn't want to come apart," Evan said in surprise. "Look. It sticks together."

"It's like taffy," Andy said. "Ever see them

make taffy in those taffy machines? The stuff just sticks together in one big glob."

"This isn't taffy," Evan muttered. "It's disgusting."

Working together, they managed to lift the entire green ball and drop it into the bucket. The stuff made a sickening sucking sound as it filled the bucket, and both Evan and Andy had trouble pulling their hands out of it.

"It's so sticky," Andy said, making a disgusted face.

"And warm," Evan added. He finally managed to free his hands from it. "It's like it's trying to swallow my hands," he said, wiping his hands on his T-shirt. "Sucking them in."

"Take it home," Andy said. She looked up to the house to see her mother motioning to her from the front window. "Uh-oh. Dinnertime. I've got to go." Her eyes stopped at his swollen cheek. "Wait till your aunt sees you."

"She probably won't even notice," Evan said glumly. He picked up the bucket by the handle. "What are we going to do with this stuff?"

"We'll take it back to the toy store tomorrow," Andy replied, taking long strides across the lawn to the house.

"Huh?"

"That's what we'll do. We'll simply take it back."

Evan didn't think it was such a hot idea. But he didn't have the strength to argue about it now. He watched Andy disappear into the house. Then he headed slowly back to Kathryn's, his head throbbing, his stomach aching.

Creeping along the wall of the house, he slipped into the garage through the side door to hide the bucket of Monster Blood. Sliding it behind an overturned wheelbarrow, he realized that the bucket was full to the top.

But I gave Andy a big hunk of it, he thought. The bucket had been only two-thirds full.

I'll have to find a bigger place to put it, he decided. Tonight. Maybe there's a box or something in the basement.

He crept into the house, determined to clean himself up before seeing Kathryn. She was still busy in the kitchen, he saw, leaning over the stove, putting the last touches on dinner. He tiptoed up the stairs and washed up. Unable to do much about his swollen, red cheek, he changed into a clean pair of baggy shorts and a fresh T-shirt, and carefully brushed his hair.

As they sat down at the dining room table, Kathryn's eyes fell on Evan's swollen cheek. "You been in a fight?" she asked, squinting suspiciously at him. "You're a little roughneck, aren't you? Just like your father. Chicken was always getting into scrapes, always picking on boys twice his size."

"I wasn't exactly picking on them," Evan muttered, spearing a chunk of beef from his stew with his fork.

All through dinner, Kathryn stared at his swollen cheek. But she didn't say another word.

She doesn't care if I'm hurt or not, Evan thought miserably.

She really doesn't care.

She didn't even ask if it hurts.

In a way, he was grateful. He didn't need her getting all upset, making a fuss because he was in a fight, maybe calling his parents in Atlanta and telling them.

Well . . . she couldn't call his parents. She couldn't use the phone, since she couldn't hear.

Evan downed his big plate of beef stew. It was pretty good, except for the vegetables.

The silence seemed so *loud*. He began thinking about his problem — the Monster Blood.

Should he tell Kathryn about it?

He could write down the whole problem on the yellow pad and hand it to her to read. It would feel so good to tell someone, to have an adult take over the problem and handle it.

But not his Aunt Kathryn, he decided.

She was too weird.

She wouldn't understand.

She wouldn't know what to do.

And she wouldn't care.

Andy was right. They had to carry the stuff back to the toy store. Give it back. Just get rid of it.

But in the meantime, he had to find something to keep it in.

Evan waited in his room until he heard Kathryn go to bed, a little after ten o'clock. Then he crept down the stairs and headed out to the garage.

# 18

It was a cool, clear night. Crickets sent up a relentless curtain of noise. The black sky glittered with tiny specks of stars.

The round beam of light from the flashlight in his hand darted across the driveway, leading Evan to the dark garage. As he entered, something scuttled across the floor near the back wall.

Maybe it was just a dead leaf, blown by the wind when I opened the door, he thought hopefully.

He moved the flashlight unsteadily, beaming it onto the overturned wheelbarrow. Then the light darted across the garage ceiling as he bent down, reached behind the wheelbarrow, and pulled out the bucket of Monster Blood.

He moved the light to the center of the bucket, and gasped.

The green substance was quivering up over the top.

It's growing much faster than before, he thought.

I've *got* to find something bigger to hide it in — just for tonight.

The bucket was too heavy to carry with one hand. Tucking the flashlight into his armpit, he gripped the bucket handle with both hands and hoisted the bucket off the floor.

Struggling to keep from spilling it, he made his way into the dark house. He paused at the door to the basement steps, silently setting the heavy bucket down on the linoleum floor.

He clicked the light switch on the wall. Somewhere downstairs a dim light flickered on, casting a wash of pale yellow light over the concrete floor.

There's got to be something to put this stuff in down there, Evan thought. Hoisting up the bucket, he made his way slowly, carefully down the steep, dark stairway, leaning his shoulder against the wall to steady himself.

Waiting for his eyes to adjust to the pale light, he saw that the basement was one large room, low-ceilinged and damp. It was cluttered with cartons, stacks of old newspapers and magazines, and old furniture and appliances covered in stained, yellowed bed sheets.

Something brushed his face as he stepped away from the stairs.

He uttered a silent cry and, dropping the bucket, raised his hands to swipe at the thick cobwebs that seemed to reach out for him. They clung to his skin, dry and scratchy, as he frantically pulled at them.

He suddenly realized it wasn't the web that was moving against his cheek.

It was a spider.

With a sharp intake of breath, he brushed it away. But even after he saw the insect scuttle across the floor, he could still feel its prickly feet moving on his face.

Moving quickly away from the wall, his heart pounding now, his eyes searching the open wooden shelves hidden in shadow against the far wall, he stumbled over something on the floor.

"Oh!" He fell headfirst over it, throwing his hands forward to break his fall.

A human body!

Someone lying there under him!

No.

Calm down, Evan. Calm down, he instructed himself.

He pulled himself shakily to his feet.

It was a dressmaker's dummy he had stumbled over. Probably a model of Kathryn when she was younger.

He rolled it out of the way as his eyes searched the shadowy room for a container to store the Monster Blood. What was that long, low object in front of the worktable?

Moving closer, he saw that it was an old bathtub, the insides stained and peeling. It's big enough, he realized, and quickly decided to store the green gunk inside it.

With a loud groan, he hoisted the bucket onto the side of the old tub. His stomach muscles were still sore from the punch he had taken, and the pain shot through his body.

He waited for the aching to fade, then tilted the bucket. The thick green substance rolled out of the bucket and hit the tub bottom with a sickening soft *plop*.

Evan set the bucket aside and stared down at the Monster Blood, watching it ooze, spreading thickly over the bottom of the bathtub. To his surprise, the tub appeared nearly half full.

How fast was this stuff growing?!

He was leaning over the tub, about to make his way back upstairs, when he heard the cat screech.

Startled, he let go of the side of the tub just as Sarabeth leapt onto his back. Evan didn't have time to cry out as he toppled forward, over the edge of the tub and into the thick, green gunk.

# 19

Evan landed hard on his elbows, but the thick Monster Blood softened the fall. He heard the cat screech again and pad away.

He sank into the ooze, his arms and legs flailing, trying to lift himself away. But the sticky substance was sucking him down, pulling him with surprising force.

His whole body seemed to be held by it, stuck as if in cement, and now it was quivering up, bubbling silently, rising up to his face. I'm going to suffocate, he realized.

It's trying to choke me.

The warmth of it spread across his body, invaded his chest, his legs, his throat.

I can't move.

I'm stuck.

It's trying to choke me.

No!

He pulled his head up just as the green gunk began to cover his face.

Then he struggled to twist his body, to twist himself around in it. With great effort, panting loudly, hoarse cries escaping his open lips, he pulled himself up into a sitting position.

The green substance rose up even higher, as if it were reaching up to him, reaching to drag him back down into it.

Evan gripped the side of the tub with both hands, held on to it tightly, and began to force himself up. Up, up from the clinging, pulling ooze. Up from the strange force that seemed to be drawing him back with renewed power.

Up. Up.

"No!" he managed to scream as the warm, green ooze slid over his shoulders.

"No!"

It was gripping his shoulders now, sliding around his neck, sucking him down, pulling him back into its sticky depths.

Down. Down.

It's got me, he realized.

It's got me now.

# 20

"No!" Evan screamed aloud as the green gunk bubbled up to his neck.

Pulling him. Pulling him down.

"No!"

Try again. Up.

Try again.

Up. Up.

Yes!

Gripping the sides of the tub, he was moving upward, pulling himself, hoisting himself, straining with all of his strength.

Yes! Yes! He was beating it.

He was stronger than it was. One more tug and he would be free.

With a relieved sigh, he dropped over the side of the tub onto the cool basement floor.

And lay there, pressed against the damp concrete, waiting to catch his breath.

When he looked up, Sarabeth stood a few feet away, her head cocked to one side, her yellow eyes peering into his, an expression of supreme satisfaction on her dark feline face.

The next morning, after a fitful, restless sleep, Evan brought the pad of yellow lined paper and a marker to the breakfast table.

"Well, well," Kathryn greeted him, placing a bowl of shredded wheat in front of him, "you certainly look like something the cat dragged in!" She laughed, shaking her head.

"Don't mention *cat* to me," Evan muttered. He shoved the bowl of cereal aside and pointed to the pad in his hand.

"Don't let your cereal get soggy," Kathryn scolded, reaching to push the bowl back to him. "You get more of the vitamins that way. And it's good roughage."

"I don't care about your stupid roughage," Evan said moodily, knowing she couldn't hear him. He pointed to the pad again, and then began to write, scribbling quickly in big, black letters.

His writing caught her interest. She moved around the table and stood behind him, her eyes on the pad as he wrote his desperate message.

I HAVE A PROBLEM, he wrote. I NEED YOUR HELP. THE BATHTUB DOWNSTAIRS IS OVERFLOWING WITH GREEN MONSTER BLOOD AND I CAN'T STOP IT.

He put down the marker and held the pad up close to her face.

Looking up at her from the chair, seeing her pale face in the morning sunlight as she leaned over him in her gray flannel bathrobe, Kathryn suddenly looked very old to him. Only her eyes, those vibrant, blue eyes running quickly over his words, seemed youthful and alive.

Her lips were pursed tightly in concentration as she read what he had written. Then, as Evan stared eagerly up at her, her mouth spread into a wide smile. She tossed back her head and laughed.

Completely bewildered by her reaction, Evan slid his chair back and jumped up. She rested a hand on his shoulder and gave him a playful shove.

"Don't kid an old woman!" she exclaimed, shaking her head. She turned and headed back to her side of the table. "I thought you were serious. I guess you're not like your father at all. He never played any dumb jokes or tricks. Chicken was always such a serious boy."

*"I don't care about Chicken!"* Evan shouted, losing control, and tossed the pad angrily onto the breakfast table.

His aunt burst out laughing. She didn't seem to notice that Evan was glaring at her in frustration, his hands tightened into fists at his sides.

"Monster Blood! What an imagination!" She wiped tears of laughter from her eyes with her fingers. Then suddenly, her expression turned serious. She grabbed his earlobe and squeezed it.

"I warned you," she whispered. "I warned you to be careful."

"Ow!"

When he cried out in pain, she let go of his ear, her eyes glowing like blue jewels.

I've got to get out of here, Evan thought, rubbing his tender earlobe. He turned and strode quickly from the kitchen and up to his room.

I knew she wouldn't be any help, he thought bitterly.

She's just a crazy old lady.

I should pull her down to the basement and *show* her the disgusting stuff, he thought, angrily tossing the clothes he had worn yesterday onto the floor.

But what's the point? She'd probably laugh at that, too.

She isn't going to help me.

He had only one person he could rely on, he knew.

Andy.

He called her, punching in her number with trembling fingers.

"Hi. You're right," he said, not giving her a chance to say anything. "We have to take the stuff back to the store."

"*If* we can carry it," Andy replied, sounding worried. "That hunk of Monster Blood you gave me — it outgrew the coffee can. I put it in my parents' ice bucket, but it's outgrowing that."

"How about a plastic garbage bag?" Evan suggested. "You know. One of the really big lawn bags? We can probably carry it in a couple of those."

"It's worth a try," Andy said. "This stuff is so disgusting. It's making all these sick noises, and it's really sticky."

"Tell me about it," Evan replied gloomily, remembering the night before. "I took a *swim* in it."

"Huh? You can explain later," she said impatiently. "The toy store opens at ten, I think. I can meet you on the corner in twenty minutes."

"Good deal." Evan hung up the phone and headed to the garage to get a plastic lawn bag.

Andy showed up with her plastic bag wrapped around the handlebars of her BMX bike. Once again, Evan had to go along beside her on foot. His plastic bag was bulging, and so heavy he had to drag it over the sidewalk. He couldn't lift it.

"The tub was nearly full to the top," he told Andy, groaning as he struggled to pull the bag over the curb. "I'm afraid it's going to burst out of this bag."

"Only two blocks to go," she said, trying to sound reassuring. A car rolled by slowly. The driver, a teenager with long black hair, stuck his head out the window, grinning. "What's in the bag? A dead body?"

"Just garbage," Evan told him.

"That's for sure," Andy muttered as the car rolled away.

Several people stopped to stare at them as they entered town. "Hi, Mrs. Winslow," Andy called to a friend of her mother's.

Mrs. Winslow waved, then gave Andy a curious stare, and headed into the grocery.

Andy climbed off her bike and walked it. Evan continued to drag his bulging bag behind him.

They made their way to the next block, then started to cross the street to the toy store.

But they both stopped short in the middle of the street.

And gaped in shock.

The door and window of the store were boarded up. A small, hand-printed sign tacked to the top of the door read: OUT OF BUSINESS.

# 21

Desperate to get rid of the disgusting contents of the garbage bags, Evan pounded on the door anyway.

"Come on — somebody! Somebody, open up!"

No reply.

He pounded with both fists.

Silence.

Finally, Andy had to pull him away.

"The store is closed," a young woman called from across the street. "It closed a few days ago. See? It's all boarded up and everything."

"Very helpful," Evan muttered under his breath. He slammed his hand angrily against the door.

"Evan — stop. You'll hurt yourself," Andy warned.

"Now what?" Evan demanded. "Got any more fantastic ideas, Andy?"

She shrugged. "It's your turn to come up with something brilliant."

Evan sighed miserably. "Maybe I could give it to Kathryn and tell her it's beef. Then she'd chop it up with that knife she's always carrying around."

"I don't think you're thinking too clearly right now," Andy said, putting a sympathetic hand on his shoulder.

They both stared down at the garbage bags. They appeared to be moving — expanding and contracting, as if the green globs inside were *breathing!*

"Let's go back to Kathryn's," Evan said, his voice trembling. "Maybe we'll think of something on the way."

Somehow they managed to drag the Monster Blood back to Kathryn's house. The sun had gotten high in the sky. As they headed to the backyard, Evan was drenched with sweat. His arms ached. His head throbbed.

"Now what?" he asked weakly, letting go of the bulging lawn bag.

Andy leaned her bike against the side of the garage. She pointed to the big aluminum trash can next to the garage door. "How about that? It looks pretty sturdy." She walked over to it to investigate. "And look — the lid clamps down."

"Okay," Evan agreed, wiping his forehead with the sleeve of his T-shirt.

Andy pulled off the lid of the big can. Then she

dumped in the contents of her bag. It hit the bottom with a sick, squishy sound. Then she hurried to help Evan.

"It's so heavy," Evan groaned, struggling to pull the bag up.

"We can do it," Andy insisted.

Working together, they managed to slide the Monster Blood from the plastic bag. It rolled out like a tidal wave, sloshing noisily against the sides of the can, raising up as if trying to escape.

With a loud sigh of relief, Evan slammed the metal lid down on top of it and clamped the handles down.

"Whoa!" Andy cried.

They both stared at the can for a long moment, as if expecting it to explode or burst apart. "Now what?" Evan asked, his features tight with fear.

Before Andy could reply, they saw Kathryn step out of the kitchen door. Her eyes searched the backyard until she spotted them. "Evan — good news!" she called.

Glancing back at the trash can, Evan and Andy came hurrying over. Kathryn was holding a yellow piece of paper in her hand. A telegram.

"Your mother is coming to pick you up this afternoon," Kathryn said, a wide smile on her face.

I think Kathryn is glad to get rid of me, was Evan's first thought.

And then, dismissing that thought, he leapt up and whooped for joy. It was the best news he'd ever received.

"I'm outta here!" he exclaimed after his aunt had returned to the house. "I'm outta here! I can't wait!"

Andy didn't appear to share his joy. "You're leaving your aunt a nice little surprise over there," she said, pointing to the trash can.

"I don't care! I'm outta here!" Evan repeated, raising his hand for Andy to slap him a high five.

She didn't cooperate. "Don't you think we have to tell someone about the Monster Blood? Or do something about it — before you leave?"

But Evan was too excited to think about that now. "Hey, Trigger!" he called, running to the dog's pen at the back of the yard. "Trigger — we're going home, boy!"

Evan pulled open the gate — and gasped.

# 22

"Trigger!"

The dog that came bounding toward him *looked* like Trigger. But the cocker spaniel was the size of a pony! He had *doubled* in size since the day before!

"No!" Evan had to hit the dirt as Trigger excitedly tried to jump on him. "Hey — wait!"

Before Evan could get up, Trigger began barking ferociously. The huge dog was already past the gate and thundering across the backyard toward the street.

"I don't believe it!" Andy cried, raising her hands to her face, staring in shock as the enormous creature bounded around the side of the house and out of sight. "He's so — big!"

"We've got to stop him! He might hurt someone!" Evan cried.

"Trigger! Trigger — come back!" Still off balance, Evan started to run, calling frantically. But he stumbled over Andy's bike and fell onto the trash can.

"No!" Andy shrieked, looking on helplessly as the metal can toppled over, with Evan sprawled on top of it. The can hit the driveway with a loud *clang*.

The lid popped off and rolled away.

The green gunk poured out.

It oozed away from the can, then stopped and appeared to stand up. Quivering, making loud sucking sounds, it righted itself, pulling itself up tall.

As the two kids stared in silent horror, the quivering green mass appeared to come to life, like a newly born creature pulling itself up, stretching, looking around.

Then, with a loud sucking sound, it arched toward Evan, who was still sprawled on the toppled can.

"Get up, Evan!" Andy cried. "Get up! It's going to roll right over you!"

# 23

"Noooooo!"

Evan uttered an animal cry, a sound he had never made before — and rolled away as the quivering green ball bounced toward him.

"Run, Evan!" Andy screamed. She grabbed his hand and pulled him to his feet. "It's alive!" she cried. "Run!"

The Monster Blood heaved itself against the garage wall. It seemed to stick there for a brief second. Then it peeled off, and came bouncing toward them with surprising speed.

"Help! Help!"

"Somebody — please — *help*!"

Screaming at the top of their lungs, Evan and Andy took off. Scrambling as fast as he could, his legs weak and rubbery from fear, Evan followed Andy down the driveway toward the front yard.

"Help! Oh, please! Help us!"

Evan's voice was hoarse from screaming. His heart thudded in his chest. His temples throbbed.

He turned and saw that the Monster Blood was right behind them, picking up speed as it bounced across the yard, making disgusting squishing noises with each bounce.

*Plop. Plop. Plop.*

A robin, pulling at a worm in the grass, didn't look up in time. The trembling green mass rolled over it.

"Oh!" Evan moaned, turning back to see the bird sucked into the green ball. Its wings flapping frantically, the bird uttered a final cry, then disappeared inside.

*Plop. Plop. Plop.*

The Monster Blood changed direction, still bouncing and quivering, and leaving white stains on the grass like enormous, round footsteps.

"It's alive!" Andy screamed, her hands pressed against her cheeks. "Oh, my God — it's *alive!*"

"What can we do? What can we do?" Evan didn't recognize his own terrified voice.

"It's catching up!" Andy screamed, pulling him by the hand. "Run!"

Gasping loudly, they made their way to the front of the house.

"Hey — what's happening?" a voice called.

"Huh?"

Startled by the voice, Evan stopped short. He looked to the sidewalk to see the Beymer twins, matching grins on their beefy faces.

"My favorite punching bag," one of them said

to Evan. He raised his fist menacingly.

They took a few steps toward Evan and Andy. Then their grins faded and their mouths dropped open in horror as the gigantic green mass appeared, heading down the drive, rolling as fast as a bicycle.

"Look out!" Evan screamed.

"Run!" Andy cried.

But the two brothers were too startled to move.

Their eyes bulging with fear, they threw their hands up as if trying to shield themselves.

*Plop. Plop. Plop.*

The enormous ball of Monster Blood picked up speed as it bounced forward. Evan shut his eyes as it hit the twins with a deafening *smack*.

"Ow!"

"No!"

Both brothers cried out, flailing their arms, struggling to pull themselves free.

"Help us! Please — help us!"

Their bodies twisted and writhed as they struggled.

But they were stuck tight. The green gunk oozed over them, covering them completely.

Then it pulled them inside with a loud sucking *pop.*

Andy shielded her eyes. "Sick," she muttered. "Oooh. Sick."

Evan gasped in helpless horror as the Beymer brothers finally stopped struggling.

Their arms went limp. Their faces disappeared into the quivering gunk.

The sucking sounds grew louder as the two boys were pulled deeper and deeper inside. Then the Monster Blood bounced high, turned, and started back up the drive.

Andy and Evan froze, unsure of which way to head.

"Split up!" Evan cried. "It can't go after us both!"

Andy returned his frightened stare. She opened her mouth, but no sound came out.

"Split up! Split up!" Evan repeated shrilly.

"But — " Andy started.

Before she could say anything, the front door of the house burst open, and Kathryn stepped out onto the stoop.

"Hey — what are you kids doing? What's *that*?" she cried, gripping the screen door, her eyes filling with horror.

Picking up speed, the giant ball bounded toward the stoop.

Kathryn tossed up her hands in fright. She stood frozen for a long moment, as if trying to make sense of what she was seeing. Then, leaving the front door wide open, she spun around and fled into the house.

*Plop. Plop.*

The Monster Blood hesitated at the front stoop.

It bounced in place once, twice, three times, as if considering what to do next.

Evan and Andy gaped in horror from across the lawn, trying to catch their breath.

A wave of nausea swept over Evan as he saw the Beymer twins, still visible deep within the quivering glob, faceless prisoners bouncing inside it.

Then suddenly, the Monster Blood bounced high and hurtled up the stairs of the stoop.

"No!" Evan screamed as it squeezed through the open doorway and disappeared into the house.

From the middle of the yard, Andy and Evan heard Kathryn's bloodcurdling scream.

"It's got Aunt Kathryn," Evan said weakly.

# 24

Evan reached the house first. He had run so fast, his lungs felt as if they were about to burst.

"What are you going to do?" Andy called, following close behind.

"I don't know," Evan replied. He grabbed on to the screen door and propelled himself into the house.

"Aunt Kathryn!" Evan screamed, bursting into the living room.

The enormous glob filled the center of the small room. The Beymer twins were outlined in its side as it bounced and quivered, oozing over the carpet, leaving its sticky footprints in its path.

It took Evan a few seconds to see his aunt. The bouncing hunk of Monster Blood had backed her against the fireplace.

"Aunt Kathryn — run!" Evan cried.

But even he could see that she had nowhere to run.

"Get out of here, kids!" Kathryn cried, her voice

shrill and trembling, suddenly sounding very old.

"But, Aunt Kathryn — "

"Get out of here — now!" the old woman insisted, her black hair wild about her head, her eyes, those blue, penetrating eyes, staring hard at the green glob as if willing it away.

Evan turned to Andy, uncertain of what to do.

Andy's hands tugged at the sides of her hair, her eyes wide with growing fear as the seething green glob made its way steadily closer to Evan's aunt.

"Get out!" Kathryn repeated shrilly. "Save your lives! I made this thing! Now I must die for it!"

Evan gasped.

Had he heard correctly?

What had his aunt just said?

The words repeated in his mind, clear now, so clear — and so frightening.

*"I made this thing. Now I must die for it."*

# 25

"No!"

Gaping in horror, as the sickening glob of Monster Blood pushed toward his aunt, Evan felt the room tilt and begin to spin. He gripped the back of Kathryn's armchair as pictures flooded his mind.

He saw the strange bone pendant Kathryn always wore around her neck.

The mysterious books that lined the walls of his bedroom.

Sarabeth, the black cat with the glowing yellow eyes.

The black shawl Kathryn always wrapped around her shoulders in the evening.

*"I made this thing. Now I must die for it."*

Evan saw it all now, and it began to come clear to him.

Evan pictured the day he and Andy brought home the can of Monster Blood from the toy store. Kathryn had insisted on seeing it.

On studying it.

On touching it.

He remembered the way she rolled the can around in her hands, examining it so carefully. Moving her lips silently as she read the label.

What had she been doing? What had she been saying?

A thought flashed into Evan's mind.

Had she been casting a spell on the can?

A spell to make the Monster Blood grow? A spell to terrify Evan?

But why? She didn't even know Evan.

Why did she want to frighten him? To . . . *kill* him?

"Be careful," she had called to him after handing the blue can back. "Be careful."

It was a real warning.

A warning against her spell.

"You did this!" Evan shouted in a voice he didn't recognize. The words burst out of him. He had no control over them.

"You did this! You cast a spell!" he repeated, pointing an accusing finger at his aunt.

He saw her blue eyes shimmer as they read his lips. Then her eyes filled with tears, tears that overflowed onto her pale cheeks.

"No!" she cried. "No!"

"You did something to the can! You did this, Aunt Kathryn!"

"No!" she cried, shouting over the sickening

115

grunts and *plop*s of the mountainous ball that nearly hid her from view.

"No!" Kathryn cried, her back pressed tightly against the mantelpiece. "I didn't do it! *She* did!"

And she pointed an accusing finger at Andy.

# 26

Andy?

Was Aunt Kathryn accusing *Andy*?

Evan spun around to confront Andy.

But Andy turned, too.

And Evan realized immediately that his aunt wasn't pointing at Andy. She was pointing past Andy to Sarabeth.

Standing in the doorway to the living room, the black cat hissed and arched her back, her yellow eyes flaring at Kathryn.

"She did it! She's the one!" Kathryn declared, pointing frantically.

The enormous glob of green Monster Blood bounced back, retreated a step, as if stung by Kathryn's words. Shadows shifted inside the glob as it quivered, catching the light filtering in through the living room window.

Evan stared at the cat, then turned his eyes to Andy. She shrugged, her face frozen in horror and bewilderment.

Aunt Kathryn is crazy, Evan thought sadly.

She's totally lost it.

She isn't making any sense.

None of this makes sense.

"She's the one!" Kathryn repeated.

The cat hissed in response.

The glob bounced in place, carrying the unmoving Beymer brothers inside.

"Oh — look!" Evan cried to Andy as the black cat suddenly raised up on its hind legs.

Andy gasped and squeezed Evan's arm. Her hand was as cold as ice.

Still hissing, the cat grew like a shadow against the wall. It raised its claws, swiping the air. Its eyes closed, and it became consumed in darkness.

No one moved.

The only sounds Evan could hear were the bubbling of the green glob and the pounding of his own heart.

All eyes were on the cat as it rose up, stretched, and grew. And as it grew, it changed its shape.

Became human.

With shadowy arms and legs in the eerie darkness.

And then the shadow stepped away from the darkness.

And Sarabeth was now a young woman with fiery red hair and pale skin and yellow eyes, the same yellow cat eyes that had haunted Evan since he'd arrived. The young woman was dressed in a

118

swirling black gown down to her ankles.

She stood blocking the doorway, staring accusingly at Kathryn.

"You see? She's the one," Kathryn said, quietly now. And the next words were intended only for Sarabeth: "Your spell over me is broken. I will do no more work for you."

Sarabeth tossed her red hair behind a black-cloaked shoulder and laughed. "I'll decide what you will do, Kathryn."

"No," Kathryn insisted. "For twenty years, you have used me, Sarabeth. For twenty years you have imprisoned me here, held me in your spell. But now I will use this Monster Blood to escape."

Sarabeth laughed again. "There is no escape, fool. All of you must die now. *All* of you."

## 27

"All of you must die," Sarabeth repeated. Her smile revealed that she enjoyed saying those words.

Kathryn turned to Evan, her eyes reflecting her fear. "Twenty years ago, I thought she was my friend. I was all alone here. I thought I could trust her. But she cast a spell on me. And then another. Her dark magic made me deaf. She refused to let me lip-read or learn to sign. That was one way she kept me her prisoner."

"But, Aunt Kathryn — " Evan started.

She raised a finger to her lips to silence him.

"Sarabeth forced me to cast the spell on the can of Monster Blood. She had warned me that I was allowed no guests, you see. I was her slave. Her personal servant for all these years. She wanted me all to herself, to do her evil bidding.

"When you arrived," Kathryn continued, her back still pressed against the fireplace mantel, "she first decided to scare you away. But that was impossible. You had nowhere to go. Then she became desperate to get you out of the way. She was terrified that you would learn her secret, that you would somehow free me of her spell. So Sarabeth decided that you had to die."

Kathryn's eyes fell. She sighed. "I'm so sorry, Evan. I had no choice, no will of my own." She turned her eyes to Sarabeth. "But no more. No more. No more. As I plunge myself into this ghastly creation, Sarabeth, I will end your spell. I will end your hold over me."

"The children will still die," Sarabeth said quietly, coldly.

"What?" Kathryn's eyes filled with fury. "I will be gone, Sarabeth. You can let the children go. You have no reason to do them harm."

"They know too much," Sarabeth replied softly, crossing her slender arms in front of her, her yellow eyes aglow.

"We've got to get out of here," Evan whispered to Andy, staring at the seething green glob.

"But how?" Andy whispered back. "Sarabeth is blocking the doorway."

Evan's eyes darted around the small room, searching for an escape route.

Nothing.

Sarabeth raised one hand and drew it toward her slowly, as if summoning the green glob.

It quivered once, twice, then moved obediently in the direction of her hand.

"No! Sarabeth — stop!" Kathryn pleaded.

Ignoring Kathryn, Sarabeth gestured with her hand again.

The green gunk bubbled and rolled forward.

"Kill the children," Sarabeth commanded.

The enormous glob picked up speed as it rolled across the carpet toward Evan and Andy.

"Let's rush the door," Evan suggested to Andy, as they backed up away from the rolling Monster Blood.

"She'll never let us past," Andy cried.

"Kill the children!" Sarabeth repeated, raising both hands high above her head.

"Maybe one of us can get by her!" Evan cried.

"It's too late!" Andy shrieked.

The bouncing, pulsating, green glob was just a few feet away.

"We — we're going to be sucked in!" Evan screamed.

"Kill the children!" Sarabeth screamed triumphantly.

# 28

The glob rolled forward.

Evan sighed, feeling all hope sink. Frozen in place, he felt as if he weighed a thousand pounds.

Andy grabbed his hand.

They both closed their eyes and held their breath, and waited for the impact.

To their surprise, the Monster Blood emitted a deafening roar.

"Huh?"

Evan opened his eyes. Andy, he saw, was staring at the doorway, beyond Sarabeth.

The Monster Blood hadn't roared.

"Trigger!" Evan cried.

The huge dog bounded into the doorway, its deafening bark echoing off the low ceiling.

Sarabeth tried to get out of the dog's way. But she was too late.

Thrilled to see Evan, Trigger enthusiastically leapt at Sarabeth — and pushed her from behind.

Under the weight of the gigantic paws, Sara-

123

beth staggered forward . . . forward . . . forward — raising her hands as she collided with the Monster Blood.

There was a wet *smack* as Sarabeth hit the surface of the green glob.

Then loud, disgusting sucking noises.

Her hands hit first. They disappeared quickly. And then Sarabeth was in up to her elbows.

And then the glob seemed to give a hard tug, and her body hit the surface. Then her face was pulled in, covered over.

Sarabeth never uttered a sound as she was pulled inside.

Whimpering with joy, completely unaware of what he had done, the dog loped into the room and headed for Evan.

"Down, boy! Down!" Evan cried, as Trigger happily leapt at him.

And as the dog jumped, he began to shrink.

"Trigger!" Evan called in astonishment, reaching out to hold the dog.

Trigger didn't seem to notice that he was changing. He licked Evan's face as Evan held on tightly.

In seconds, Trigger was back to normal cocker spaniel size.

"Look — the glob is shrinking, too!" Andy cried, squeezing Evan's shoulder.

Evan turned to see that the green glob was rapidly growing smaller.

As it shrunk, the Beymer brothers fell to the floor.

They didn't move. They lay facedown in a crumpled heap. Their open eyes stared lifelessly. They didn't appear to be breathing.

Then one blinked. The other blinked.

Their mouths opened and closed.

"Ohhh." One of them uttered a long, low groan.

Then, pulling themselves up slowly, they both looked around the room, dazed.

The trapped robin had also fallen to the floor. Chirping furiously, it flapped its wings wildly and fluttered about the room in a panic — until it found the open living room window and sailed out.

Andy held on to Evan as they stared at the Monster Blood, expecting Sarabeth to reappear, too.

But Sarabeth was gone.

Vanished.

The Monster Blood, shrunk to its original size, lay lifeless, inert, a dull green spot on the carpet, no bigger than a tennis ball.

The Beymer brothers stood up uncertainly, their eyes still reflecting terror and confusion. They stretched as if testing their arms and legs, seeing if their muscles still worked. Then they scrambled out of the house, slamming the screen door behind them.

"It's over," Kathryn said softly, moving forward to put an arm around Evan and Andy.

"Sarabeth is gone," Evan said, holding Trigger tightly in his arms, still staring at the tiny wedge of Monster Blood on the floor.

"And I can hear!" Kathryn said jubilantly, hugging them both. "Sarabeth *and* her spells are gone for good."

But as she said this, the screen door swung open and a shadowy figure stepped into the living room doorway.

# 29

"Mom!" Evan cried.

He set down Trigger and hurried to greet her, throwing his arms around her in a tight hug.

"What on earth is going on here?" Mrs. Ross asked. "Why did those two boys come bursting out like that? They looked scared to *death!*"

"It — it's a little hard to explain," Evan told her. "I'm so glad to see you!"

Trigger was glad, too. When he finally had finished jumping up and down and whimpering, Kathryn led Evan's mom to the kitchen. "I'll make some tea," she said. "I have a rather long story to tell you."

"I hope it isn't *too* long," Mrs. Ross said, glancing back questioningly at Evan. "We have a four o'clock plane to catch."

"Mom, I think you'll find this story interesting," Evan said, flashing Andy an amused look.

The two women disappeared into the kitchen.

Andy and Evan dropped down wearily onto the couch.

"I guess you're going forever," Andy said. "I mean, to Atlanta and everything — "

"I'd like to . . . uh . . . write to you," Evan said, suddenly feeling awkward.

"Yeah. Good," Andy replied, brightening. "And my dad has a phone credit card. Maybe I could get the number and . . . you know . . . call you."

"Yeah. Great," Evan said.

"Could I ask one small favor?" Andy asked.

"Yeah. Sure," Evan replied, curious.

"Well, it's going to sound strange," Andy said reluctantly. "But can I . . . uh . . . can I have the little bit of Monster Blood that's left? You know. Sort of as a memento or something?"

"Sure. Okay with me," Evan said.

They both turned their eyes to where it had come to rest on the carpet.

"Hey — " Andy cried in surprise.

It was gone.

# Goosebumps®

MONSTER BLOOD II

# 1

Evan Ross backed into the corner of the den as he stared at his dog Trigger.

The tan cocker spaniel lowered his head and stared back at Evan with wet, brown eyes. The old dog's tail began to wag excitedly.

"Trigger — " Evan cried angrily. "Did you eat Monster Blood again?"

The dog's tail began wagging faster. Trigger let out a low bark that rumbled like thunder.

Evan's back pressed against the dark-paneled den wall.

Trigger took a few heavy steps toward him, panting hard. His huge pink tongue, as big as a salami, hung out of his enormous mouth.

"Did you?" Evan demanded. "Did you eat more Monster Blood?"

The answer to Evan's question was obvious.

Trigger had been normal cocker spaniel size that morning. Now the dog stared down at Evan, as big as a pony.

Trigger's furry paws, the size of elephant hooves, thudded on the den carpet. His enormous tail pounded louder than a bass drum against the side of a leather couch.

Evan covered his ears as Trigger let out an excited, high-pitched bark that shook the den walls. "Stay! Stay!" Evan shouted.

The enormous dog panted hard, his tail wagging furiously.

Oh, no! Evan thought in horror. He wants to play!

"Sit!" Evan screamed. "Sit!"

But Trigger didn't know how to sit. For ten years — *seventy dog years!* — Evan had tried to teach Trigger to sit on command.

But Trigger just didn't get it.

"Where did you find the Monster Blood?" Evan demanded. "We all saw it disappear into thin air. Gone. It was just gone. You know that stuff makes you grow. And grow and grow and grow. Where did you find it?"

Trigger tilted his big head at an angle, as if trying to understand Evan's words. Then, wagging his huge tail excitedly, he started to run to Evan.

No! Evan thought. He's going to jump on me! He's going to jump! If he jumps, he'll *crush* me!

An enormous glob of drool escaped Trigger's open mouth and hit the carpet with a loud *smack*.

"Sit!" Evan cried, his voice choked with panic. "Sit, boy! Sit!"

Trigger hesitated, staring down at Evan. To Evan's horror, the dog was growing even bigger. Trigger was now as tall as a horse!

Where did he find the container of Monster Blood? Evan wondered, his back pressed against the wall. Where?

The dog's brown eyes gaped at Evan like shimmering, dark pools. Trigger uttered another deafening bark that shook the whole house.

"Yuck!" Evan cried, squeezing his nose with two fingers. The dog's breath rushed at him like a strong wind. And it smelled as sour as a dead mouse.

"Back! Get back, Trigger!" Evan pleaded.

But Trigger had never learned that command, either.

Without warning, the giant dog leaped at Evan.

"Down! Down!" Evan shrieked.

Trigger's mouth gaped open. The dog's huge tongue licked the side of Evan's face. The tongue felt scratchy and hot. Evan's carrot-colored hair was matted down with sticky dog saliva.

"No — please!" Evan screamed. "I'm only twelve! I'm too young to die!"

He started to scream again. But Trigger's big teeth clamped around his waist, cutting off his breath.

"Trigger — put me down! Put me down!" Evan choked out.

The dog's wagging tail sent a lamp crashing to the floor.

The teeth held Evan gently but firmly. He felt himself being lifted off the floor.

"Put me down! Put me down!"

Why wouldn't the stupid dog listen?

Evan thrashed his arms and legs frantically, trying to squirm free. But Trigger held on tightly.

The dog's enormous paws pounded on the carpet. He carried Evan through the hall and across the kitchen. Then he lowered his head and butted the kitchen screen door open.

The door slammed hard behind them. Trigger began trotting over the grass.

"Bad dog! Bad dog!" Evan cried. His voice came out in a tiny squeak.

Had Trigger grown even bigger?

Evan was at least three feet off the ground now!

"Put me down! Down!" he cried.

Evan watched the green grass of the back yard bounce beneath him. Trigger was panting as he walked. The panting sounds made Evan's whole body vibrate. He realized his jeans and T-shirt were soaked from dog saliva.

Trigger doesn't mean to hurt me, Evan told himself. He's just being playful. Thank goodness he's such an old dog. His teeth aren't very sharp.

The dog stopped at the edge of the flower garden in the back of the yard. He lowered Evan nearly to the ground, but didn't let go.

His paws began to churn up the soft dirt.

"Let me down!" Evan shrieked. "Trigger — listen to me!"

Breathing hard, his hot, sour breath pouring over Evan, the big dog continued to dig.

A wave of horror swept over Evan as he realized what Trigger was doing. "No!" Evan shrieked. "Don't bury me, Trigger!"

The dog dug faster, its front paws churning furiously. The soft dirt flew past Evan's face.

"I'm not a bone!" Evan cried frantically. "Trigger — I'm not a bone! Don't bury me, Trigger! Please — don't bury me!"

# 2

"Don't bury me. *Please* don't bury me!" Evan murmured.

He heard laughter.

He raised his head and glanced around — and realized that he wasn't home in his back yard. He was sitting in his assigned seat in the third row near the window in Mr. Murphy's science class.

And Mr. Murphy was standing right at Evan's side, his enormous, round body blocking the sunlight from the window. "Earth calling Evan! Earth calling Evan!" Mr. Murphy called, cupping his chubby pink hands over his mouth to make a megaphone.

The kids all laughed.

Evan could feel his face growing hot. "S-sorry," he stammered.

"You seem to have been somewhere in Daydream Land," Mr. Murphy said, his tiny black eyes twinkling merrily.

"Yes," Evan replied solemnly. "I was dreaming

about Monster Blood. I — I can't stop thinking about it."

Ever since his frightening adventure the past summer with the green, sticky stuff, Evan had been dreaming and daydreaming about it.

"Evan, please," Mr. Murphy said softly. He shook his round, pink head and made a "tsk-tsk" sound.

"Monster Blood is real!" Evan blurted out angrily.

The kids laughed again.

Mr. Murphy's expression grew stern. His tiny eyes locked onto Evan's. "Evan, I am a science teacher. You don't expect a science teacher to believe that you found a can of sticky green gunk in a toy store that makes things grow and grow."

"Y-yes, I do," Evan insisted.

"Maybe a science-*fiction* teacher would believe it," Mr. Murphy replied, grinning at his own joke. "Not a *science* teacher."

"Well, you're dumb!" Evan cried.

He didn't mean to say it. He knew immediately that he had just made a major mistake.

He heard gasps all around the big classroom.

Mr. Murphy's pink face darkened until it looked like a red balloon. But he didn't lose his temper. He clasped his chubby hands over the big stomach of his green sportshirt, and Evan could see him silently counting to ten.

"Evan, you're a new student here, isn't that

137

right?" he asked finally. His face slowly returned to its normal pink color.

"Yes," Evan replied, his voice just above a whisper. "My family just moved to Atlanta this fall."

"Well, perhaps you're not familiar with the way things work here. Perhaps at your old school the teachers liked it when you called them dumb. Perhaps you called your teachers ugly names all day long. Perhaps — "

"No, sir," Evan interrupted, lowering his head. "It just slipped out."

Laughter rang through the classroom. Mr. Murphy glared sternly at Evan, his face twisted in an angry frown.

Give me a break, Evan thought unhappily. Glancing quickly around the room, Evan saw a sea of grinning faces.

I think I'm in trouble again, Evan thought glumly. Why can't I keep my big mouth shut?

Mr. Murphy glanced up at the wall clock. "School is nearly over," he said. "Why don't you do us all a little favor, Evan, to make up for the time you made us waste today?"

Uh oh, Evan thought darkly. Here it comes.

"When the bell rings, go put your books away in your locker," Mr. Murphy instructed. "Then come back here and clean Cuddles's cage."

Evan groaned.

His eyes darted to the hamster cage against the

138

wall. Cuddles was scratching around in the wood shavings on the cage floor.

Not the hamster! Evan thought unhappily.

Evan hated Cuddles. And Mr. Murphy knew it. This was the third time Mr. Murphy had made Evan stay after school and clean out the gross, disgusting cage.

"Perhaps while you clean the hamster cage," Mr. Murphy said, returning to his desk, "you can think about how to do better in science class, Evan."

Evan jumped to his feet. "I won't do it!" he cried.

He heard shocked gasps all around him.

"I hate Cuddles!" Evan screamed. "I *hate* that stupid, fat hamster!"

As everyone stared in amazed horror, Evan ran over to the cage, pulled open the door, and grabbed Cuddles up in one hand.

Then, with an easy, graceful motion, he flung the hamster across the room — and out the open window.

# 3

Evan knew he was having another daydream.

He didn't jump up screaming and throw the hamster out the window.

He only thought about it. *Everyone* thinks about doing crazy, wild things once in a while.

But Evan would never do anything that crazy.

Instead, he said, "Okay, Mr. Murphy." Then he sat quietly in his seat, staring out the window at the puffy white clouds in the bright blue sky.

He could see his own reflection staring back at him in the glass. His curly, carrot-colored hair looked darker in the reflection. So did the freckles that dotted his cheeks.

His expression was mournful. He hated being made fun of in front of the entire class.

Why am I always getting myself into trouble? he wondered. Why can't Mr. Murphy ever give me a break? Didn't the teacher realize how hard it was to be the new kid in school? How am I supposed to make new friends if Murphy is always making me look like a total jerk in class?

Bad enough that no one believed him about the Monster Blood.

Evan had eagerly told the kids in his new school about it. How he had stayed with his great-aunt the past summer. How he and a girl he met named Andy had found the blue container of Monster Blood in a creepy, old toy store.

And how the green, yucky Monster Blood had started to grow and grow. How it had bubbled out of its container, outgrown a bucket, outgrown a *bath tub*! And just kept growing and growing as if it were alive!

And Evan had told kids how Trigger had eaten just a little of the Monster Blood — and had grown nearly as big as a house!

It was such a frightening, amazing story. Evan was sure his new friends would find it really cool.

But, instead, they just thought he was weird.

No one believed him. They laughed at him and told him he had a sick imagination.

Evan became known around his new school as the kid who made up stupid stories.

If only I could prove to them that the story is true, Evan often thought sadly. If only I could show them the Monster Blood.

But the mysterious green gunk had vanished from sight before Evan left his great-aunt's house. Not a trace of it had been left. Not a trace.

The bell rang. Everyone jumped up and headed for the door, talking and laughing.

Evan knew that a lot of his classmates were laughing at *him*. Ignoring them, Evan picked up his backpack and started to the door.

"Hurry back, Evan," Mr. Murphy called from behind his desk. "Cuddles is waiting!"

Evan growled under his breath and stepped out into the crowded hallway. If Murphy loves that stupid hamster so much, why doesn't *he* ever clean out the cage? he wondered bitterly.

A group of kids laughed loudly as Evan passed by. Were they laughing at him? Evan couldn't tell.

He started jogging to his locker — when something hit his leg just above the ankle. His feet flew out from under him, and he toppled face down onto the hard tile floor.

"Hey — !" Evan cried angrily.

He stared up at a big, tough-looking kid from his class named Conan Barber. All the kids called him Conan the Barbarian. For good reason.

Conan was twelve, but he looked about twenty years older! He was taller and wider and stronger and meaner than any kid in the school.

He wasn't a bad-looking guy, Evan grudgingly admitted. He had wavy, blond hair, blue eyes, and a handsome face. He was very athletic-looking, and played all the sports at school.

He was an okay guy, Evan thought wistfully.

Except that he had one very bad habit. Conan loved to live up to his nickname.

He *loved* being Conan the Barbarian.

He loved strutting around, pounding kids who weren't his size — which included *everyone*!

Evan had not hit it off with Conan.

He met Conan on the playground a few weeks after moving to Atlanta. Eager to make a good impression, Evan told him the whole Monster Blood story.

Conan didn't like the story. He stared back at Evan with his cold, blue eyes for a long, long time. Then his expression hardened, and he murmured through clenched teeth: "We don't like wise guys down here in Atlanta."

He gave Evan a pretty good pounding that day.

Evan had tried to stay away from Conan ever since. But it wasn't easy.

Now he gazed up at Conan from his position on the floor. "Hey — why'd you trip me?" Evan demanded shrilly.

Conan grinned down at him and shrugged. "It was an accident."

Evan tried to decide whether it was safer to stand up or to stay down on the floor. If I stand up, he'll punch me, he thought. If I stay down here, he'll step on me.

Tough choice.

He didn't get to make it. Conan reached down and, with one hand, pulled Evan to his feet.

"Give me a break, Conan!" Evan pleaded. "Why can't you leave me alone?"

Conan shrugged again. It was one of his favorite replies. His blue eyes twinkled merrily. "You're right, Evan," he said, his grin fading. "I shouldn't have tripped you."

"Yeah," Evan agreed, straightening his T-shirt.

"So you can pay me back," Conan offered.

"Huh?" Evan gaped at him.

Conan stuck out his massive chest. "Go ahead. Hit me in the stomach. I'll let you."

"Whoa. No way," Evan replied, trying to back up. He stumbled into a group of kids.

"Go ahead," Conan urged, following after him. "Hit me in the stomach. As hard as you can. It's only fair."

Evan studied his expression. "You really mean it?"

Conan nodded, tight-lipped. He stuck out his chest. "As hard as you can. Go ahead. I won't hit back. I promise."

Evan hesitated. Should he go ahead and do it?

I may never get a chance like this again, he thought.

A lot of kids were watching, Evan realized.

If I hit him really hard, if I hurt him, if I make him cry out — then maybe kids around here will have a little respect for me.

I'll be Evan the Giant Killer. The guy who pounded Conan the Barbarian.

He balled his hand into a tight fist and raised it.

"Is *that* your fist?" Conan cried, laughing.

Evan nodded.

"Oooh — this is going to hurt!" Conan cried sarcastically. He made his knees tremble.

Everyone laughed.

I may surprise him, Evan thought angrily.

"Go ahead. As hard as you can," Conan urged. He sucked in a deep breath and held it.

Evan pulled his arm back and swung his fist as hard as he could.

The fist made a solid *thud* as it hit Conan's stomach.

It felt like hitting a concrete wall.

Evan's hand throbbed with pain.

"Hey — !" a man's voice called angrily.

Startled, Evan spun around — to see Mr. Murphy glaring at him.

"No fighting!" Mr. Murphy yelled at Evan.

The teacher came bouncing up to them and stepped between the two boys. Huffing for breath, he turned to Conan. "Why did Evan hit you?" he demanded.

Conan shrugged. His blue eyes went wide and innocent. "I don't know, Mr. Murphy," he replied in a tiny, forlorn voice. "Evan just walked up and hit me as hard as he could."

Conan rubbed his stomach and uttered a short whimper. "Ow. He really hurt me."

Mr. Murphy narrowed his beady black eyes at Evan. His chubby face turned bright red again. "Evan, I saw the whole thing. I really don't understand you," he said softly.

"But Mr. Murphy — " Evan started.

The teacher raised a hand to silence him. "If you were angry about what happened in class," Mr. Murphy said, "you shouldn't take it out on other kids."

Conan rubbed his stomach tenderly. "I hope Evan didn't *break* anything!" he murmured.

"Do you want to see the nurse?" Mr. Murphy asked.

Conan shook his head. Evan could see he was having trouble keeping a straight face. "I'll be okay," he said, and staggered away.

What a phony! Evan thought bitterly.

Did Conan know the whole time that Murphy was standing there? Probably.

"Go take care of Cuddles," Mr. Murphy told Evan, frowning. "And try to shape up, Evan. I'm going to be watching you."

Evan muttered a reply and trudged back into the classroom. Sunlight streamed in through the wall of windows. A strong breeze made the window shade flap over the open window near the teacher's desk.

Feeling angry and upset, his stomach churning, Evan made his way through the empty room to the hamster cage. Cuddles wrinkled his nose in greeting. The hamster knew the routine by now.

Evan gazed into the metal cage at the brown-and-white creature. Why do people think hamsters are cute? he wondered.

Because they wrinkle their noses? Because they run around and around on wheels like total jerks? Because of their cute little buck teeth?

Cuddles stared up at him with his little black eyes.

He has Mr. Murphy's eyes, Evan thought, chuckling to himself. Maybe that's why Murphy likes him so much.

"Okay, okay. So you're kind of cute," Evan told the hamster. "But I know your secret. You're just a big fat rat in disguise!"

Cuddles wrinkled his nose again in reply.

With a loud sigh, Evan went to work. Holding his breath because he hated the smell, he pulled out the bottom tray.

"You're a messy little guy," he told the hamster. "When are you going to learn to clean up your own room?"

Still holding his breath, he dumped out the old newspaper shavings and replaced them with fresh shavings from the box in the supply closet.

He returned the bottom tray to its place as Cuddles watched with great interest. Then he poured fresh water into the water bottle.

"How about some sunflower seeds?" Evan asked. He began to feel a little more cheerful, knowing his job was almost finished.

He removed the seed cup from the cage and made his way across the room to the supply closet to get fresh sunflower seeds.

"Okay, Cuddles," he called, "these look yummy!"

He started to carry the seeds back to the cage. Halfway across the room, Evan stopped and uttered a startled gasp.

The cage door hung wide open.

The hamster was gone.

# 5

A choking sound escaped Evan's lips as he stared at the empty cage.

His eyes darted frantically around the room. "Cuddles? Cuddles?" he called in a frightened voice.

Why am I yelling? he asked himself, spinning around in a total panic. The dumb hamster doesn't know its name!

He heard footsteps out in the hall.

Mr. Murphy?

No, please — no! Evan pleaded silently.

Don't let it be Mr. Murphy. Don't let him return until I have Cuddles safely back in his cage.

Cuddles was Mr. Murphy's most precious possession. He had told this to the class time and again.

Evan knew that if anything happened to Cuddles, Mr. Murphy would be on Evan's case for the rest of the year. No — for the rest of his *life*!

Evan froze in the center of the room, listening hard.

The footsteps passed by the room.

Evan started breathing again.

"Cuddles? Where are you, Cuddles?" he called in a trembling voice. "I have some delicious sunflower seeds for you."

He spotted the furry, brown-and-white creature on the chalk tray under the front chalkboard.

"There you are! I see you!" Evan whispered, tiptoeing toward it.

Cuddles was busily chewing on something. A small piece of white chalk.

Evan tiptoed closer. "I have seeds for you, Cuddles," he whispered. "Much tastier than chalk."

Cuddles held the stick of chalk in his front paws, turning it as he chewed.

Evan crept closer. Closer.

"Look. Seeds." He held the plastic seed cup toward the hamster.

Cuddles didn't look up.

Evan crept up closer. Closer.

Close enough to dive forward —

—and *miss*!

The hamster dropped the chalk and scampered down the chalk tray.

Evan made another frantic grab — and came up with nothing but air.

Letting out a frustrated groan, Evan saw the hamster dive to the floor and scamper behind Mr.

Murphy's desk. The hamster's feet skidded and slid on the linoleum floor, its toenails clicking loudly.

"You can't get away! You're too fat!" Evan cried. He dropped to his knees and peered under the desk.

He could see Cuddles staring back at him from the darkness. The animal was breathing rapidly, its sides swelling with each breath.

"Don't be scared," Evan whispered soothingly. "I'm going to put you back in your nice, safe cage."

He crawled quickly to the desk.

The hamster stared back at him, breathing hard. It didn't move — until Evan reached for him. Then Cuddles scampered away, his tiny paws sliding on the floor.

Evan jumped angrily to his feet. "Cuddles — what's your problem?" he demanded loudly. "This isn't a stupid game!"

It wasn't a game at all, Evan knew.

If he didn't get the hamster back in the cage, Mr. Murphy would flunk him for sure. Or suspend him from school. Or get his family kicked out of Atlanta!

Calm down, Evan urged himself. Don't panic.

He took a deep breath and held it.

Then he saw the hamster on the window ledge just inside the open window.

Okay, Evan — go ahead and panic! he told himself.

This was definitely panic time.

He tried to call to the hamster. But his voice came out a choked whisper.

Swallowing hard, Evan edged slowly toward the window ledge.

"Come here, Cuddles," he whispered. "Please, Cuddles — come here."

Closer, closer.

Almost close enough to reach the hamster.

Almost close enough.

"Don't move, Cuddles. Don't move."

He reached out his hand slowly. Slowly.

Cuddles glanced back at him with his soft black eyes.

Then the hamster jumped out the window.

# 6

Evan hung back for only a second.

Then he jumped out the window after the hamster.

Luckily, the science classroom was on the ground floor. Evan landed face down in a low evergreen hedge. Struggling and squirming, it took him a while to climb to his feet.

He took several steps over the grass, then turned and stared back along the bottom of the long hedge. "Cuddles — are you under there?"

Evan squatted down to get a better view. The hedge stretched the entire length of the school building. Cuddles could hide under there forever.

And if I don't find him, Evan told himself bitterly, I'd better hide under there forever, too!

To the right, Evan could hear voices from the playground. Happy, shouting voices. Carefree voices.

Still squatting, he turned toward the happy

voices — and saw a fat brown ball wobbling over the grass toward the playground.

No. Not a ball. "Cuddles!"

That fat hamster isn't getting away this time! Evan decided, jumping up and starting to chase after the creature. I'll catch him if I have to *sit* on him!

A picture flashed into Evan's mind of Cuddles, flat as a pancake after Evan had sat upon him. A little, round, furry hamster rug.

Despite his panic, the thought of Cuddles as a rug brought a smile to Evan's perspiring face.

As he ran, he kept his eyes on Cuddles. The hamster was wobbling rapidly over the grass toward the playground.

"Oh, no!" Evan cried out in horror as Cuddles darted in front of two girls speeding across the grass on bikes.

Laughing together, they didn't even see the hamster.

Cuddles is about to be road kill! Evan thought, shrinking back. He shut his eyes and waited for the *squish*.

But the bikes rolled smoothly on. And when they had passed, Evan spotted Cuddles continuing his journey to the playground unharmed.

"Cuddles — come back here!" he shouted furiously.

The hamster appeared to speed up. He tumbled

onto the baseball diamond, all four paws scurrying over the dirt of the third-base line.

Several kids stopped their game to stare.

"Stop him! Grab the hamster!" Evan shouted desperately.

But the kids only laughed.

"Know how to catch him?" a joker named Robbie Greene called to Evan. "Make a sound like a sunflower seed!"

"That's an old joke!" a girl called to Robbie.

"Thanks for your help!" Evan shouted sarcastically. He ran over the pitching mound and had crossed second base when he realized he had lost sight of Cuddles.

He stopped and spun around, his heart thudding wildly in his chest. He searched the grass of the infield. "Where — where is he?" he stammered. "Do you see him?"

But the kids had returned to their softball game.

I can't lose him now! Evan told himself, choked with panic. I *can't!*

Sweat poured down Evan's forehead. He mopped it with one hand, brushing back his curly, red hair. His T-shirt clung wetly to his back. His mouth felt dry as cotton.

Jogging into the outfield, he searched the grass. "Cuddles?"

No sign of him.

A round, brownish lump in the grass turned out to be someone's baseball glove.

"Cuddles?"

A kickball game was underway on the opposite diamond. Kids were shouting and cheering. Evan saw Bree Douglas, a girl from his class, slide hard into second base just before the ball.

"Has — has anyone seen Cuddles?" Evan gasped, trotting onto the diamond.

Kids turned to gawk at him.

"Out here?" Bree called, brushing off the knees of her jeans. "Evan, did you take the hamster out for a walk?"

Everyone laughed. Scornful laughter.

"He — he got away," Evan replied, panting.

"Is *this* what you're looking for?" a familiar voice called.

Evan turned to see Conan Barber, a pleased smile on his handsome face, his blue eyes gleaming.

Gripping it by its furry back, Conan held the hamster up in one hand. Cuddles's four legs scurried in midair.

"You — you caught him!" Evan cried gratefully. He let out a long sigh of relief. "He jumped out the window."

Evan reached out both hands for the hamster, but Conan jerked Cuddles out of his reach. "Prove it's yours," Conan said, grinning.

"Huh?"

"Can you identify it?" Conan demanded, his eyes burning into Evan's, challenging Evan. "Prove this hamster is yours."

Evan swallowed hard and glanced around.

Kids from the kickball game were huddling near. They were all grinning, delighted with Conan's mean joke.

Evan sighed wearily and reached again for the hamster.

But Conan was at least a foot taller than Evan. He lifted the hamster high above Evan's head, out of Evan's reach.

"Prove it's yours," he repeated, flashing the others a grin.

"Give me a break, Conan," Evan pleaded. "I've been chasing this stupid hamster for hours. I just want to get him back in his cage before Mr. Murphy — "

"Do you have a license for him?" Conan demanded, still holding the squirming hamster above Evan's head. "Show me the license."

Evan jumped and stretched both hands up, trying to grab Cuddles away.

But Conan was too fast for him. He dodged away. Evan grabbed air.

Some kids laughed.

"Give him the hamster, Conan," Bree called. She hadn't moved from second base.

Conan's cold blue eyes sparkled excitedly. "I'll tell you how you can get the hamster back," he told Evan.

"Huh?" Evan glared at him. He was getting really tired of Conan's game.

"Here's how to get old Cuddles back," Conan continued, holding the hamster tightly against his chest in one hand and petting its back with the other. "Sing a song for it."

"Hey — no way!" Evan snapped. "Give it to me, Conan!"

Evan could feel his face growing even hotter. His knees started to tremble. He hoped no one could see it.

"Sing 'Row, Row, Row Your Boat,' and I'll give you Cuddles. Promise," Conan said, smirking.

Some kids laughed. They moved closer, eager to see what Evan would do.

Evan shook his head. "No way."

"Come on," Conan urged softly, stroking the hamster's brown fur. " 'Row, Row, Row Your Boat.' Just a few choruses. You know how it goes, don't you?"

More cruel laughter from the others.

Conan's grin grew wider. "Come on, Evan. You like to sing, don't you?"

"No, I *hate* singing," Evan muttered, his eyes on Cuddles.

"Hey, don't be modest," Conan insisted. "I'll

bet you're a great singer. Are you a soprano or an alto?"

Loud laughter.

Evan's hands tightened into hard fists at his sides. He wanted to punch Conan, and punch him and punch him. He wanted to wipe the grin off Conan's handsome face with his fists.

But he remembered what it had felt like to punch Conan. It had felt like hitting the side of a truck.

He took a deep breath. "If I sing the stupid song, will you really give me back the hamster?"

Conan didn't reply.

Evan suddenly realized that Conan wasn't looking at him anymore. No one was. They had all raised their eyes over Evan's shoulder.

Confused, Evan spun around — to face Mr. Murphy.

"What is going on here?" the teacher demanded, his tiny black eyes moving from Evan to Conan, then back to Evan.

Before Evan could reply, Conan held up the hamster. "Here's Cuddles, Mr. Murphy," Conan said. "Evan let him get away. But I rescued Cuddles just as he was going to get run over."

Mr. Murphy let out a horrified gasp. "Run over?" he cried. "Cuddles? Run over?"

The teacher reached out his chubby pink hands and took the hamster from Conan. He held the hamster against his bulging shirt and petted it, making soothing sounds to it.

"Thank you, Conan," Mr. Murphy said after calming Cuddles. He glared at Evan. "I'm very disappointed in you, Evan."

Evan started to defend himself. But Mr. Murphy raised a hand to silence him. "We'll talk about it tomorrow. Right now I must get poor Cuddles back into his cage."

Evan slumped to the ground. He watched Mr. Murphy carry the hamster back to the school building. Mr. Murphy waddles just like the hamster, Evan realized.

Normally, that thought would have cheered him up.

But Evan was far too unhappy to be cheered up by anything.

Conan had embarrassed him in front of all the others. And the big, grinning hulk had managed to get Evan in trouble with Mr. Murphy *twice* in one afternoon!

The kickball game had started up again. Evan climbed slowly to his feet and began trudging to the school building to get his backpack.

He couldn't decide who he hated more — Cuddles or Conan.

He had a sudden picture of Cuddles stuffed inside a muffin tin, being baked in an oven.

Even that lovely thought didn't cheer Evan up.

He pulled his backpack out of the locker and

slung it over his shoulder. Then he slammed the locker shut, the sound clanging down the empty hallway.

He pushed open the front door and headed for home, walking slowly, lost in his unhappy thoughts.

What a horrible day, he told himself. At least nothing *worse* could happen to me today.

He had just crossed the street and was making his way on the sidewalk in front of a tall hedge — when someone leaped out at him, grabbed his shoulders hard from behind, and pulled him roughly to the ground.

Evan let out a frightened cry and gazed into his attacker's face. *"You!"* he cried.

# 7

"Here's a little advice, Evan," Andy said, grinning down at him. "Don't go out for the wrestling team."

"Andy!" Evan cried, staring up at her in surprise. "What are *you* doing here?"

She reached out both hands and helped tug him to his feet. Then she tossed back her short, brown hair with a flick of her head. Her brown eyes flashed excitedly.

"Didn't you read any of my letters?" she demanded.

Evan had met Andy the past summer, when he'd stayed with his great-aunt for a few weeks. He and Andy had become good friends.

She was with him when he bought the container of Monster Blood. She shared the whole frightening Monster Blood adventure with him.

Evan liked Andy because she was funny, and fearless, and kind of crazy. He never could predict what she would do next!

162

She didn't even dress like other girls Evan knew. Andy loved bright colors. Right now she was wearing a sleeveless magenta T-shirt over bright yellow shorts, which matched her yellow sneakers.

"I *told* you in my last letter that my parents were sent overseas for a year," Andy said, giving Evan a playful shove. "I *told* you they were sending me to Atlanta to live with my aunt and uncle. I *told* you I'd be living just three blocks away from you!"

"I know. I know," Evan replied, rolling his eyes. "I just didn't expect to see you jump out of the hedge at me."

"Why not?" Andy demanded, her dark eyes exploring his.

Evan didn't know how to answer that question.

"Glad to see me?" Andy asked.

"No," he joked.

She pulled up a thick blade of grass and stuck it in the corner of her mouth. They began walking toward Evan's house.

"I'm starting at your school on Monday," she told him, chewing on the blade of grass.

"Thrills and chills," he replied, snickering.

She shoved him off the sidewalk. "I thought people were supposed to be polite in the South."

"I'm new here," Evan replied.

"How's Trigger?" she asked, kicking a pebble across the sidewalk.

"Good," Evan told her.

"Like to talk a lot?" she asked sarcastically.

"I'm in a bad mood," he confessed. "It hasn't been the greatest day."

"It *couldn't* be as bad as the day the Monster Blood went berserk!" Andy exclaimed.

Evan groaned. "Don't mention Monster Blood to me. Please!"

She studied him. Her expression turned serious. "What's wrong, Evan? You look really upset," she said. "Don't you like it here?"

He shook his head. "Not much."

As they walked, he told her about all the trouble he was having in his new school. He told her about Mr. Murphy and Cuddles, and how the teacher was always on his case.

And he told her about Conan the Barbarian, and how Conan was always picking on him, always getting him into trouble, always playing tricks on him and making him look bad.

"And no one will believe me about the Monster Blood," Evan added.

They were standing at the bottom of his driveway. They glanced up at Evan's new house, a two-story red brick house with a sloping red tile roof. The late afternoon sun dipped behind a large puff of cloud, and a broad shadow rolled across the lawn.

Andy's mouth dropped open. The blade of grass fell out. "You *told* kids about the Monster Blood?" she asked in surprise.

164

Evan nodded. "Yeah, why not? It's a cool story, isn't it?"

"And you expected kids to *believe* you?" Andy cried, slapping her forehead. "Didn't they just think you were *weird*?"

"Yeah," Evan replied bitterly. "They all think I'm weird."

Andy laughed. "Well, you *are* weird!"

"Thanks a bunch, Annnndrea!" Evan muttered. He knew she hated to be called by her real name.

"Don't call me Andrea," she replied sharply. She raised a fist. "I'll pound you."

"Annnnnndrea," he repeated. He ducked away as she swung her fist. "You punch like a girl!" he exclaimed.

"You'll *bleed* like a boy!" she threatened, laughing.

He stopped. He suddenly had an idea. "Hey — you can tell everyone I'm not weird!"

"Huh? Why would I do that?" Andy demanded.

"No. Really," Evan said excitedly. "You can tell everyone at school that the Monster Blood was real. That you were there. That you saw it."

Andy's expression suddenly changed. Her dark eyes lit up, and a sly grin crossed her face. "I can do better than that," she said mysteriously.

Evan grabbed her shoulder. "Huh? What do you mean? What do you mean you can do better?"

"You'll see," she replied, teasing him. "I brought something with me."

165

"What? What is it? What do you mean?" Evan demanded.

"Meet me tomorrow after school," she told him. "At that little park over there."

She pointed to the next block. A narrow park, only a few blocks long, ran along the bank of a shallow creek.

"But what *is* it?" Evan cried.

She laughed. "I *love* torturing you!" she declared. "But it's a little too easy."

Then she turned and headed down the street, running at full speed.

"Andy — wait!" Evan called. "What have you got? What did you bring?"

She didn't even turn around.

# 8

Evan dreamed about Monster Blood that night.

He dreamed about it nearly every night.

Tonight he dreamed that his dad had eaten a glob of it. Now Mr. Ross wanted to go to his office, but he had grown too big to fit through the door.

"You're in trouble now, Evan!" Mr. Ross bellowed, making the whole house shake. "Big trouble!"

*Big trouble.*

The words stuck in Evan's mind as he sat up in bed and tried to shake away the dream.

The curtains flapped silently in front of his open bedroom window. Pale yellow stars dotted the charcoal sky. Staring hard, Evan could see the Big Dipper. Or was it the Little Dipper? He never could remember.

Shutting his eyes and settling back on the pillow, Evan thought about Andy. He was glad she had come to stay in Atlanta for a while. She could be a real pain. But she was also a lot of fun.

What did she want to show him in the park after school?

Probably nothing, Evan guessed. It was probably just a dumb joke. Andy loved dumb jokes.

How can I get her to tell the kids at school about Monster Blood? he wondered. How can I get Andy to tell everyone that I didn't make it up, that it's true?

He was still thinking about this problem as he fell back into a restless sleep.

The next day at school wasn't much better than the last.

Somehow during free reading period, Conan had crept under the table and tied Evan's sneaker laces together. When Evan got up to go to the water fountain, he fell flat on his face. He scraped a knee, but no one cared. The kids laughed for hours.

"Evan's mommy tied his shoes funny this morning!" Conan told everyone. And they laughed even harder.

In science class, Mr. Murphy called Evan over to the hamster cage. "Look at poor Cuddles," the teacher said, shaking his round head solemnly.

Evan peered down into the metal cage. Cuddles was curled up in a corner under a pile of shavings. The hamster was trembling and breathing in short gasps.

"Poor Cuddles has been like that ever since yesterday," Mr. Murphy told Evan with an accusing frown. "Cuddles is sick because of your carelessness."

"I — I'm sorry," Evan stammered. He stared hard at the quivering hamster. You're faking — aren't you, Cuddles? Evan thought. You're faking just to get me in trouble!

The hamster twitched and stared up at him with mournful, black eyes.

When Evan sat back down in his seat, he felt cold water seep through the back of his jeans. With a startled cry, he jumped right back up. Someone — probably Conan — had poured a cup of water on his chair.

That had the class laughing for at least ten minutes. They stopped only when Mr. Murphy threatened to keep everyone after school.

"Sit down, Evan," the teacher ordered.

"But, Mr. Murphy — " Evan started.

"Sit down — now!" Mr. Murphy insisted.

Evan dropped back down into the wet chair. What choice did he have?

Andy was waiting for Evan by the trickling brown creek that rolled through the tiny park. The old sassafras trees bent and whispered in a hot breeze. A tall Georgia pine leaned over the water as if trying to reach across the creek.

Andy was wearing a bright blue T-shirt over lime-green short-shorts. She had been staring at her reflection in the muddy creek water. She spun around smiling as Evan called to her.

"Hey, how's it going?" he called. He stepped up beside her and dropped his backpack to the ground.

"How was school?" Andy asked.

"Same as always," Evan replied, sighing. Then his expression brightened. "What did you bring?" he asked eagerly.

"You'll see." She clasped a hand over his eyes. "Shut your eyes, Evan. And don't open them until I say."

He obediently shut his eyes. But when she pulled her hand away, he opened them a tiny crack, just enough to see. He watched her go behind the pine tree and pick up a small brown paper bag.

She carried the bag over to him. "You're peeking — aren't you!" she accused him.

"Maybe," he confessed, grinning.

She punched him playfully in the stomach. He cried out and his eyes shot open. "What's in the bag?"

Grinning, Andy handed the bag to him.

He pulled it open, peered inside — and his mouth dropped open in shock.

The familiar blue can, about the size of a can of soup.

"Andy — you — you — " Evan stammered, still staring wide-eyed into the bag.

He reached in and pulled out the plastic can.

He read the faded label: MONSTER BLOOD.

Then he read the words in tiny type below it: SURPRISING MIRACLE SUBSTANCE.

"I saved it," Andy said, beaming proudly.

Evan couldn't get over his shock. "You brought Monster Blood! I don't believe it! You brought Monster Blood!"

"No." She shook her head. "It's empty, Evan. The can is empty."

His face fell. He sighed in total disappointment.

"But you can show the can to everyone," Andy insisted. "That will prove you didn't make it up. It will prove that Monster Blood really exists."

Evan sighed again. "What good is an empty can?" he groaned.

He pulled off the top, peered inside — and screamed.

171

# 9

With a trembling hand, Evan tilted the can so that Andy could see inside.

"Oh, no!" she shrieked, pulling her hands to her cheeks.

The can was half full.

Inside, a green glob of gooey Monster Blood shimmered in the sunlight like lime jello.

"But it was *empty*!" Andy protested, staring into the can. "I *know* it was!"

Evan shook the can. The green glob inside quivered.

"There must have been a tiny speck in there," Evan guessed. "Down at the bottom of the can. And now it's growing and growing again."

"Great!" Andy declared. She slapped him on the back so hard, he nearly dropped the blue can.

"Great? What's so great?" he demanded shakily.

"Now you can show this to the kids at your school," she replied. "Now they'll *have* to believe you."

"I guess," Evan replied in a low voice.

"Oh! I have a better idea!" she exclaimed, her dark eyes lighting up mischievously.

"Uh-oh," Evan moaned.

"Slip a little glob of it in that guy Conan's lunch tomorrow. When he starts to grow as big as a hippo, everyone will see that the Monster Blood is real."

"No way!" Evan cried. He cupped the blue can in both hands, as if protecting it from Andy. "Conan is already big enough!" he told her, taking a step back. "I don't want him to grow another inch. Do you know what he could *do* to me if he became a giant?"

Andy laughed and shrugged. "It was just an idea."

"A *bad* idea," Evan said sharply. "A really bad idea."

"You're no fun," she teased. She leaped forward and tried to wrestle the can from his hands.

He spun around, turning his back to her, and hunched over, protecting the can.

"Give it to me!" she cried, laughing. She started tickling his sides. "Give it! Give it!"

"No!" he protested, breaking free. He ran to the safety of a tall evergreen shrub.

"It's mine!" Andy declared, coming after him, hands at her waist. "If you're not going to use it, hand it back."

Evan stood his ground. His expression turned

serious. "Andy, don't you remember?" he demanded shrilly. "Don't you remember how scary this stuff was? Don't you remember how dangerous it was? All the trouble it caused?"

"So?" she replied, her eyes on the blue can.

"We have to get rid of it," Evan told her firmly. "We can't let it out of the can. It will grow and grow and never stop."

"But I thought you wanted to show it to the kids to prove that it's real."

"No," Evan interrupted. "I changed my mind. This stuff is too dangerous. We *have* to get rid of it." He locked his eyes on hers, his features tight with fear. "Andy, I've had nightmares every night because of this stuff. I don't want any *new* nightmares."

"Okay, okay," she muttered. She kicked at an upraised tree root. Then she handed him the brown paper bag.

Evan clicked the top back on the can of Monster Blood. Then he shoved the can into the bag. "Now how do we get rid of it?" he wondered out loud.

"I know. Dump it in the creek," Andy suggested.

Evan shook his head. "No good. What if it gets out and pollutes the creek?"

"This creek is *already* polluted!" Andy exclaimed. "It's just a big mud puddle!"

"It isn't deep enough," Evan insisted. "Someone

will find the can and pull it out. We can't take a chance."

"Then how do we get rid of it?" Andy asked, twisting her face in concentration. "Hmmmm. We could eat it ourselves. *That* would get rid of it!"

"Very funny," Evan muttered, rolling his eyes.

"Just trying to be helpful," Andy said.

"You're about as helpful as a toothache!" Evan shot back.

"Ha-ha. Remind me to laugh at that sometime," she replied, sticking her tongue out at him.

"How can we get rid of it?" Evan repeated, gripping the bag in both hands. "How?"

"I know!" a boy's voice called, startling them both.

Conan Barber stepped out from behind a tall shrub.

"You can give it to me!" he declared. He reached out a big, powerful-looking hand to grab the bag.

# 10

Evan swung the paper bag behind his back.

Conan lumbered toward them over the tall grass. His eyes were narrowed menacingly at Evan.

How long has he been hiding there? Evan wondered. Did he hear us talk about the Monster Blood? Is that why he wants the bag?

"Hi, I'm Andy," Andy chirped brightly. She stepped in between the two boys and flashed Conan a smile.

"Andy is a boy's name," Conan said, making a disgusted face. He turned his hard stare on her, challenging her.

"And what kind of a name is Conan?" Andy shot back, returning his stare.

"You *know* me?" Conan asked, sounding surprised.

"You're famous," Andy replied dryly.

Conan suddenly remembered Evan. He stuck out his big paw. "I'll take the bag now."

"Why should I give it to you?" Evan demanded, trying to keep his voice calm and steady.

"Because it's mine," Conan lied. "I dropped it here."

"You dropped an empty bag here?" Evan asked.

Conan swatted a fly from his blond hair. "It isn't empty. I saw you put something in it. Hand it over. Now."

"Well . . . okay." Evan handed him the paper bag. Conan eagerly reached inside.

His hand came out empty.

He peered inside the bag. Empty.

He stared hard at Andy, then at Evan.

"I *told* you it was empty," Evan said.

"Guess I made a mistake," Conan muttered. "Hey, no hard feelings. Shake." Conan reached out his big right hand to Evan.

Evan reluctantly stuck out his hand.

Conan slid his hand over Evan's and began to tighten his grip. Harder. Harder.

Evan's fingers cracked so loudly, they sounded like a tree falling!

Conan squeezed Evan's hand harder and harder until Evan screamed in pain. When Conan finally let go, the hand looked like a slab of raw hamburger.

"Nice handshake you got there!" Conan exclaimed, grinning.

He snapped his finger against Andy's nose, then

headed off quickly toward the street, taking long strides, laughing to himself.

"Great guy," Andy muttered, rubbing her nose.

Evan blew on his hand, as if trying to put out a fire. "Maybe I can learn to be left-handed," he murmured.

"Hey — where's the Monster Blood?" Andy demanded.

"I — I dropped it," Evan replied, still examining his hand.

"Huh?" She kicked away a clump of weeds and stepped over to him.

"I thought I could shove the can into my back jeans pocket while Conan was talking to you," Evan explained. "But it slipped out of my hand. I dropped it."

He turned, bent over, and picked it up from the tall grass. "Good thing it didn't roll or anything. Conan would have seen it."

"He wouldn't know what to do with it if he had it," Andy said.

"What are *we* going to do with it?" Evan demanded. "It's already caused us trouble. We've got to hide it, or throw it away, or — or — "

He pulled open the lid. "Oh, wow! Look!" He held the can up to Andy's face. The green goo had grown nearly to the top of the can. "It's starting to grow a lot faster. I guess because we exposed it to the air."

Evan slammed the lid on tight.

"Let's bury it," Andy suggested. "Here. Right under this tree. We'll dig a deep hole and bury it."

Evan liked the idea. It was simple and quick.

They squatted down and began digging with their hands. The dirt beneath the tree was soft. The hole grew deep before they had worked up a sweat.

Evan dropped the blue can of Monster Blood into the hole. Then they quickly covered it with dirt, smoothing it out until it was impossible to tell a hole had been dug.

"This was a good plan," Andy said, climbing to her feet, playfully wiping the dirt off her hands on the back of Evan's T-shirt. "If we need it, we'll know where it is."

Evan's red hair was matted to his forehead with sweat. He had a wide smear of dirt across his freckled forehead. "Huh? Why would we need it?" he demanded.

Andy shrugged. "You never know."

"We won't need it," Evan told her firmly. "We won't."

He was very, very wrong.

# 11

"Hey, Dad, what's up?" Evan stepped into the garage.

Mr. Ross stopped hammering and turned around. He smiled at Evan. "Want to see my newest work?"

"Yeah. Sure," Evan replied. Every weekend, his father spent hour after hour in his garage workshop, banging away on large sheets of metal, making what he called his "works."

He chiseled and hammered and sawed, and put a lot of effort into his sculptures. But to Evan, they all looked like banged-up sheets of metal when they were finished.

Mr. Ross took a few steps back to admire his current project. He lowered his heavy mallet in one hand and pointed with the chisel he held in his other hand. "I used brass for this one," he told Evan. "I call it 'Autumn Leaf.' "

Evan studied it thoughtfully. "It looks like a leaf," he lied. It looks like Dad ruined a perfectly good piece of brass, he thought, trying to keep a straight face.

"It's not supposed to look like a leaf," Mr. Ross corrected Evan. "It's supposed to look like my *impression* of a leaf."

"Oh." Evan scratched his curly, red hair as he studied it some more. "Neat, Dad," he said. "I see what you mean."

Then something else caught his eye. "Hey — what's this?"

Evan carefully stepped over several jagged, bent shards of metal. He made his way to another metal sculpture and ran his hand over the smooth, shiny surface. It was an enormous aluminum cylinder that rested above a flat wooden base.

"Go ahead. Spin it," Mr. Ross instructed, smiling proudly.

Evan pushed the cylinder with both hands. It spun slowly over the wooden base.

"I call it 'The Wheel,' " his father told him.

Evan laughed. "That's cool, Dad. You invented the wheel!"

"Don't laugh!" Mr. Ross replied, grinning. "That sculpture was accepted at the annual arts competition at your school. I have to take it to the auditorium later this week."

Evan gave "The Wheel" another spin. "I'll bet no one else made a wheel that really spins," he told his father. "You can't lose with this, Dad," he teased.

"Sarcasm is the lowest form of humor," Mr. Ross muttered with a frown.

Evan said good-bye and made his way out of the garage, stepping carefully over the jagged pieces of brass and tin. As he headed to the house, he could hear the *clang clang clang* as his dad hammered away on his impression of a leaf.

In the halls after school on Monday, Evan hurried around a corner and bumped right into Andy. "I can't talk now," he told her breathlessly. "I'm late for basketball tryouts."

He glanced down the long hall. It was nearly empty. The gym door opened, and he could hear the *thump* of basketballs against the floor.

"How come you're late?" Andy demanded, blocking his path.

"Murphy kept me after class," Evan told her with a groan. "He put me on permanent hamster duty. I have to take care of Cuddles every afternoon for the rest of my life."

"Bad news," Andy murmured.

"No. That's the *good* news," Evan replied bitterly.

"What's the *bad* news?"

"The bad news is that Mr. Murphy is also the basketball coach!"

"Well, good luck," she said. "Hope you make the team."

Evan ran past her, his heart pounding.

Mr. Murphy is such a rat, he thought unhappily. He'll probably keep me off the team because I'm late to practice — even though it's *his* fault I'm late!

Evan took a deep breath. No. Stop thinking like that, he scolded himself.

Think positive. I've got to think positive.

Sure, I'm not as tall as the other guys. Maybe I'm not as big or as strong. But I'm a good basketball player. And I can make this team.

I can make this team. I know I can!

Having finished his pep talk to himself, Evan pulled open the double gym doors and stepped into the huge, brightly lit gym.

"Think fast!" a voice called.

Evan felt his face explode with pain.

Then everything went black.

# 12

When Evan opened his eyes, he found himself staring up at about twenty guys and Mr. Murphy.

He was stretched out flat on his back on the gym floor. His face still hurt. A lot.

He reached a hand up and touched his nose. To his dismay, it felt like a wilted leaf of lettuce.

"You okay, Evan?" Mr. Murphy asked quietly. As the teacher leaned over Evan, the whistle that was on a string around his neck bumped against Evan's chest.

"Did my face explode?" Evan asked weakly.

Some of the guys snickered. Mr. Murphy glowered at them angrily. Then he turned back to Evan. "Conan hit you in the face with the basketball," he reported.

"He's got bad reflexes, Coach," Evan heard Conan say from somewhere above him. "He should've caught the ball. I really thought he'd catch it. But he's got bad reflexes."

"I saw the whole thing," Conan's friend, a huge

hulk of a kid named Biggie Malick, chimed in. "It wasn't Conan's fault. Evan should've caught the ball. It was a perfect pass."

Perfect, Evan thought with a sigh. He touched his nose again. This time, it felt like a lump of mashed potatoes. At least it isn't broken, he thought glumly.

Evan's basketball tryout went downhill from there.

Mr. Murphy helped him to his feet. "You sure you want to try out?" he asked.

Thanks for the support, Evan thought bitterly.

"I think I can make the team," he said.

But Conan, Biggie, and the other guys had other ideas.

During the ball-handling tryout, Evan confidently began dribbling across the floor. Halfway to the basket, Biggie bumped him hard — and Conan stole the ball away.

They blocked Evan's shots. They stole his passes.

They bumped him every time he moved, sending him sprawling to the hardwood floor again and again.

A fast pass from Conan caught Evan in the mouth.

"Oops! Sorry!" Conan yelled.

Biggie laughed like a hyena.

"Defense! I want to see defense!" Mr. Murphy shouted from the sidelines.

Evan lowered himself into a defensive stance. As Conan dribbled the ball toward him, Evan prepared to defend the basket.

Conan drove closer. Closer.

Evan raised both hands to block Conan's shot.

But to Evan's surprise, Conan let the ball bounce away. In one swift motion, he grabbed Evan by the waist, leaped high in the air, and stuffed Evan into the basket.

"Three points!" Conan shouted in triumph.

Biggie and the other guys rushed to congratulate Conan, laughing and cheering.

Mr. Murphy had to get a stepladder to help Evan down.

His hand on Evan's shoulder, the teacher led him to the side. "You're just not tall enough, Evan," he said, rubbing his pink chins. "Don't take it personally. Maybe you'll grow. But for now, you're just not tall enough."

Evan didn't say a word. He lowered his head and sadly slumped out of the gym.

Conan came running up to him at the door. "Hey, Evan, no hard feelings," he said. He stuck out his big, sweaty hand. "Shake."

Evan held up his hand to show Andy.

"It looks like a wilted petunia," she said.

"I can't believe I fell for Conan's stupid handshake trick twice!" Evan wailed.

It was the next afternoon. Evan and Andy had

walked from school to the small park near their houses. Evan had complained about Mr. Murphy and Conan and the other basketball players the whole way.

The late afternoon sun beamed down on them as they walked. Andy stopped to watch two monarch butterflies, their black-and-gold wings fluttering majestically as they hovered over a patch of blue and yellow wildflowers along the creekbed.

Even the trickling brown creek looked pretty on this bright day. Tiny white gnats sparkled like diamonds in the sunlight over the shimmering water.

Evan kicked at a fallen tree branch. Everything looked dark to him today.

Dark and ugly.

"It just wasn't fair," he grumbled, kicking the branch again. "It wasn't a fair tryout. Mr. Murphy should have given me a better chance."

Andy tsk-tsked, her eyes on the sparkling creek.

"Someone should teach Mr. Murphy a lesson," Evan said. "I wish I could think of some way of paying him back. I really do."

Andy turned to him. A devilish grin crossed her face. "I have a plan," she said softly. "A really neat plan."

"What is it?" Evan demanded.

# 13

"What's your idea?" Evan demanded again.

Andy grinned at him. She was wearing a long, lime-green T-shirt over a Day-Glo orange T-shirt, pulled down over baggy blue shorts. The sunlight made all the colors so bright, Evan felt like shielding his eyes.

"You might not like it," Andy said coyly.

"Try me," Evan replied. "Come on. Don't keep me in suspense."

"Well . . ." Her eyes wandered over to the tree where they had buried the Monster Blood. "It has to do with the Monster Blood," she said reluctantly.

He swallowed hard. "That's okay. Go on."

"Well, it's a pretty simple plan. First, we dig up the Monster Blood," Andy said, watching his reaction.

"Yeah?"

"Then we take some to school," she continued.

"Yeah?"

"Then we feed it to Cuddles."

Evan's mouth dropped open.

"Just a little bit!" Andy quickly explained. "We feed Cuddles a tiny glob of it. Just enough to make him the size of a dog."

Evan laughed. It was a terrible idea, a truly evil idea — but he loved it!

He slapped Andy on the back. "You're bad, Andy!" he cried. "You're really bad!"

Andy grinned proudly. "I know."

Evan laughed again. "Can you see the look on Murphy's face when he comes in and sees his precious little hamster has grown as big as a cocker spaniel? What a riot!"

"So you'll do it?" Andy asked.

Evan's smile faded. "I guess," he replied thoughtfully. "If you promise we'll only use a tiny bit. And we'll bury the rest right away."

"Promise," Andy said. "Just enough to play our little joke on Mr. Murphy. Then we'll never use the stuff again."

"Okay," Evan agreed.

They shook hands solemnly.

Then they hurried to the tree. Evan searched the entire park, squinting against the bright sunlight. He wanted to make sure no one was spying on them this time.

When he was sure the park was empty, he and

Andy dropped to their knees under the tree and began scooping the dirt off the hole with their hands.

They had dug nearly two feet down when they realized the hole was empty.

"The Monster Blood!" Evan cried. "It — it's gone!"

# 14

"We must be digging under the wrong tree," Evan said, sweat pouring down his freckled forehead.

Andy pushed a wet strand of brown hair off her face with a dirt-covered finger. "No way." She shook her head. "This is the right tree. And the right hole."

"Then where is the Monster Blood?" Evan demanded shrilly.

They both came up with the answer to his question at the same time: "Conan!"

"He must have watched us bury it," Evan said, his eyes darting around the park as if he expected to see Conan jump out from behind a bush. "I *thought* he hurried away awfully fast that afternoon. He *knew* the paper bag wasn't empty."

Andy agreed. "He hid and watched us bury it. Then he waited till we were gone, and dug it up."

They both stared into the empty hole in horrified silence.

Andy broke the silence. "What is Conan going to do with it?" she asked, her voice just above a whisper.

"Probably eat it so he can grow bigger and pound me harder," Evan replied bitterly.

"But he doesn't know what Monster Blood does," Andy said. "He doesn't know how dangerous it is."

"Of course he does. I told him all about it," Evan replied. He slammed his hand against the tree trunk. "We have to get it back!"

Before science class the next afternoon, Evan found Conan in the hall. He and Biggie were standing next to Evan's locker. They were laughing loudly about something, slapping each other high-fives.

Conan wore a tight blue muscle shirt and baggy faded denim jeans with enormous holes at the knees. Biggie had wavy brown hair down to his shoulders. He wore a sleeveless white T-shirt and tight-fitting black denims.

They look like a couple of tag-team wrestlers! Evan thought as he stepped between them.

"Hey, look — it's Air Evan!" Conan joked. "King of the slam dunk!"

He and Biggie guffawed loudly. Conan gave

Evan a slap on the back that sent him sprawling into Biggie.

"Uh . . . Conan? Did you find something in the park?" Evan asked, struggling to regain his balance.

Conan narrowed his eyes at Evan and didn't reply.

"Did you find something that belongs to Andy and me?" Evan repeated.

"You mean like your *brains*?" Conan exclaimed. He and his tag-team partner roared with laughter over that gem.

"Why don't we dribble him to class?" Biggie asked Conan. "Coach Murphy would like to see us get in some extra practice."

Conan laughed gleefully at that idea.

"Ha-ha. Very funny," Evan said sarcastically. "Look, Conan — that stuff you took. It's really dangerous. You have to give it back."

Conan opened his eyes in wide-eyed innocence. "I really don't know what you're talking about, Evan. Did you lose something?"

"You *know* I lost something," Evan replied sharply. "And I want it back."

Conan flashed a sly grin at Biggie. Then he turned back to Evan, his expression hardening. "I don't know what you mean, Evan," he said. "Really. I don't know what you and that girl lost. But tell you what. I'm a nice guy. I'll help you look for it."

He grabbed Evan around the waist with both hands. Biggie pulled Evan's locker door open.

"I'll help you look for it in your locker," Conan said.

He shoved Evan inside the locker and slammed the door shut.

Evan started pounding on the metal door, shouting for help.

But the bell had rung. Evan knew the hall was empty. There was no one to hear his cries.

He decided to try fiddling with the latch. But it was too dark to see anything. And he was so jammed in, he couldn't raise his arms.

Finally, two girls happened to walk by, and they pulled open the locker door.

Evan came bursting out, red-faced, gasping for air.

The girls' laughter followed him all the way to Mr. Murphy's class. "You're late," the teacher said sternly, glancing up at the wall clock as Evan staggered in.

Evan tried to explain why. But all that escaped his lips was a whistling wheeze.

"I'm really tired of you disrupting my class, Evan," Mr. Murphy said, rubbing his nearly bald head. "I'm afraid I'll be seeing you after school again. You can give Cuddles's cage a double cleaning. And while you're at it, you can scrub the chalkboards and clean out all the test tubes, too."

*     *     *

"It's so dark," Evan whispered.

"It usually gets dark at night," Andy replied, rolling her eyes.

"The streetlight is out," Evan said, pointing. "And there's no moon tonight. That's why it's so dark."

"Hide!" Andy whispered.

They ducked behind the hedge as a car rolled slowly past. Evan shut his eyes as the white headlights moved over him. When the car turned the corner, they climbed to their feet.

It was a little after eight o'clock. They were standing in the street in front of Conan's house. Leaning against the low hedge, they stared across the sloping front lawn into the large picture window in the front of the house.

The lamp in the living room was lit, casting a dim rectangle of orange light that spilled onto the front yard. The old trees at the sides of the small brick house whispered in a hot breeze.

"Are we really doing this?" Evan asked, huddling close to Andy. "Are we really going to break into Conan's house?"

"We're not going to *break* in," Andy whispered. "We're going to *sneak* in."

"But what if the Monster Blood isn't there?" Evan asked, hoping she couldn't see his knees trembling.

"We *have* to look, don't we?" Andy shot back.

195

She turned to study his face. He saw that she was frightened, too. "The Monster Blood will be there," she told him. "It's *got* to be."

Bending low, she started to creep across the dark yard to the house.

Evan hung back. "You checked it out?" he called to her. "Everyone is really gone?"

"His parents left right after dinner," Andy told him. "Then I saw Conan go out about ten minutes ago."

"Where?" Evan demanded.

"How should I know?" she asked sharply, putting her hands on her waist. "He left. The house is empty." She came back and tugged Evan's arm. "Come on. Let's sneak into Conan's room, get the Monster Blood, and get out of here!"

"I can't believe we're doing this," Evan said, sighing. "We — we could be arrested!"

"It was *your* idea!" Andy reminded him.

"Oh. Yeah. Right." He took a deep breath and held it, hoping it would help calm him down. "If we don't find it right away, we get out of there — right?"

"Right," Andy agreed. "Now come on." She gave him a little shove toward the house.

They took a few steps over the dew-wet grass.

They both stopped when they heard the low barking.

Andy grabbed Evan's arm.

The barking grew louder. They could hear the

dog's heavy paws pounding the ground, approaching fast.

Two angry eyes. A loud warning bark. Another. The dog attacked at full speed.

"Run!" Evan cried. "Conan has a guard dog!"

"Too late to run!" Andy shrieked.

# 15

The dog barked again.

Evan cried out and threw up his hands as the dog leaped for his throat.

The dog wasn't as big as Evan had thought — but it was strong.

It licked his face, pressing its wet snout into his cheek.

It licked his chin. And then his lips.

"Yuck!" Evan cried, laughing. "Trigger — how did you get here?"

Evan pulled the cocker spaniel off him and lowered it to the ground. Its stubby tail wagging furiously, Trigger started jumping on Andy.

"Your dumb dog scared me to death," she moaned.

"Me, too," Evan admitted. "I didn't hear him following us, did you?"

Andy squatted down and gave Trigger a few quick pats. Then she glanced down the street.

"Let's get inside," she said. "Conan or his parents could be back any minute."

Trigger pranced along as they made their way over the grass to the front door. The house loomed much bigger and darker as they crept onto the stoop.

"Down, Trigger. Stay down," Evan whispered. "You can't come in with us."

Andy tried the front door. "Locked."

Evan groaned. "Now what?"

"We try the back door, of course," Andy replied. She had already jumped down off the stoop and was heading around the side of the house.

"You've done this before — haven't you?" Evan demanded, following her.

"Maybe," she replied, grinning at him in the dark.

A loud howl somewhere nearby made them both stop.

"What was that?" Evan cried.

"A werewolf," Andy told him calmly. "Or maybe a cat."

They both laughed. Nervous laughter.

The back door was locked, too. But the kitchen window was open a crack. Evan pushed it open wider, and they crept into the dark kitchen.

Holding his breath, Evan could hear every sound. Their sneakers scraped noisily against the linoleum. The refrigerator hummed. Water swirled in the dishwasher.

I can even hear the pounding of my heart, Evan thought. What am I doing? Have I really broken into Conan's house?

"This way," Andy whispered. "His room is probably upstairs."

Evan kept against the wall as he followed Andy to the front stairs. They passed the small living room, bathed in orange light. The floorboards creaked under their shoes. Evan stumbled over a pile of old newspapers stacked in the narrow hallway.

Up the wooden stairs. The banister squeaked under Evan's hand. A venetian blind rattled against an open window, startling him.

"Sure is dark," Andy muttered as they reached the top of the stairs.

Evan tried to reply, but his breath caught in his throat.

Holding onto the wall, he followed Andy to the first bedroom. She fumbled until she found a light switch, then clicked it on. The ceiling light revealed that they had found Conan's room.

They both stood in the doorway, waiting for their eyes to adjust to the light. Then they quickly glanced around.

The walls of the small, square room were filled with posters of sports stars. The biggest poster, above Conan's bed, showed Michael Jordan jumping about ten feet in the air as he slam-dunked a basketball. A bookshelf against one wall held very few books — but was loaded with sports trophies that Conan had won on various teams.

Suddenly, Andy started to laugh.

Evan turned to her, startled. "What's so funny?"

She pointed to Conan's bed. "Look — he still has a teddy bear!"

Evan turned his eyes to the bed, where a forlorn-looking, nearly flat, one-eyed teddy bear rested on the pillow. "Conan the Barbarian?" he cried, laughing. "He sleeps with a teddy bear?"

A loud creak made them cut their laughter short.

They listened hard, their eyes wide with fear. "Just the house," Evan whispered.

Andy shivered. "Enough fooling around. Let's find the Monster Blood and get out of here."

They moved into the center of the room. "Where do you think he hid it?" Evan asked, pulling open the closet door.

"He didn't," Andy replied.

"Huh?" Evan spun around.

Andy had the blue can of Monster Blood in her hand. Grinning, she held it up to show Evan.

Evan let out a surprised cry. "You found it? Where?"

"Right on this shelf," she replied, pointing. "He put it next to his tennis trophies."

Evan hurried over to her and took the blue can from her hand. As he held it up to examine it, the lid popped off.

The green Monster Blood began bubbling over the top of the can.

"It's growing fast!" Evan declared.

Andy stooped down and picked up the lid. She handed it to Evan. "Put it back on. Hurry."

Evan tried pushing the lid back on. It kept slipping off.

"Hurry up," Andy urged. "We've got to go."

"The Monster Blood — it's up over the top," Evan cried.

"Shove it down," Andy instructed.

Evan tried pushing the green gunk down into the can, pressing against it with the palm of his hand. Then he tried pushing it with three fingers.

He gasped as he felt the green goo tighten around his fingers and start to pull them down.

"It — it's got me!" Evan stammered.

Andy's mouth dropped open. "Huh?"

"It's got my fingers!" Evan cried shrilly. "It won't let go!"

As Andy hurried to help him, they both heard the front door slam.

"Someone's home!" Evan whispered, tugging to pull his fingers free. "We're caught!"

# 16

Andy froze in the center of the room, her eyes wide with horror.

Evan nearly dropped the can of Monster Blood. The sticky green substance tightened its grip on his fingers, making loud sucking sounds.

But Evan only cared about the sounds coming from downstairs.

"I'm home!" he heard Conan shout.

"We're home, too!" It was a woman's voice, probably Conan's mother.

"They're all home," Evan whispered.

"We're dead meat!" Andy murmured.

"I'm going upstairs," Conan called to his parents.

Evan let out a terrified cry as he heard Conan's heavy footsteps on the stairs. "Andy — wh-what do we do?" he stammered.

"The window!" she replied.

They both lunged toward the open window and

peered out. A narrow concrete ledge stretched just beneath the window.

Without hesitating, Andy raised a leg over the windowsill and climbed out onto the ledge. "Evan — hurry!" she whispered, gesturing frantically.

Evan was still desperately trying to pull his fingers from the bubbling green goo. Andy reached in through the window and grabbed him by the shoulder. "Evan — !"

He heard Conan's footsteps in the upstairs hall just outside the bedroom.

Using his free hand for support, Evan scrambled out the window and joined Andy on the narrow ledge.

"D-don't look down," Andy instructed in a trembling whisper.

Evan didn't obey. He glanced down. The ground seemed very far below.

They each stood on a side of the window — Andy to the left, Evan the right. They pressed their bodies against the brick wall — and listened.

They heard Conan step into the room.

Did he notice that the light had been turned on? No way to tell.

Loud rap music suddenly jarred the silence. Conan had turned on his boom box. He started chanting off-key along with the music.

Evan pressed as tightly against the side of the house as he could.

*Go back downstairs, Conan,* he pleaded silently. *Please — go back downstairs!*

How will Andy and I ever get away from here? he wondered, feeling all of his muscles tighten in panic.

Despite the hot night air, a cold chill ran down Evan's back. He shuddered so hard, he nearly toppled off the ledge.

The blue can stuck to his hand. The Monster Blood sucked at his fingers. But he couldn't worry about that now.

He could hear Conan moving around inside the room. Was he dancing to the loud music?

Evan glanced across the window at Andy. Her eyes were shut. Her face was clenched in a tight frown.

"Andy — !" Evan whispered. He knew that Conan couldn't hear a whisper over the booming music. "Andy — it'll be okay. As soon as he leaves, we'll jump inside and sneak down the stairs."

Andy nodded without opening her eyes. "Did I ever tell you I'm afraid of heights?" she whispered.

"No," Evan replied.

"Well, remind me to tell you!"

"We'll be okay," he murmured.

Clinging to the side of the house, Evan kept repeating those words to himself. "We'll be okay. We'll be okay. We'll be okay."

205

Then Trigger started to bark.

A low bark of surprise at first. And then a louder series of barks, insistent barks, excited barks.

Evan swallowed hard. He glanced down to the ground.

Trigger was peering up at him, jumping against the side of the house, as if trying to reach the ledge. The dog barked louder with each jump.

"Trigger — no!" Evan called down in a frantic whisper.

That only made the dog bark more furiously.

Did Conan hear it? Could he hear Trigger's ferocious barks over the music?

"Trigger — stop! Go home! Go home!"

Suddenly the music stopped.

Trigger's excited barks rose up even louder against the new silence.

Conan *must* hear them now, Evan realized.

The cocker spaniel threw himself wildly against the side of the house, trying to get up to Evan and Andy. Despite Evan's frantic signals to be quiet, the dumb dog barked his head off.

Evan's breath caught in his throat as he heard Conan making his way to the window.

A second later, Conan stuck his head out. "What's going on?" he shouted.

Evan's knees buckled. He started to fall.

# 17

Evan clung to the brick wall and stopped his fall.

He stared at Conan's blond hair poking out the window. Evan was close enough to reach out and touch it.

"Shut up down there!" Conan shouted.

That made Trigger bark even louder.

He's going to see us, Evan thought, trembling all over.

There's no way Conan won't see us.

"Conan — come downstairs!" Mrs. Barber's voice floated up from downstairs. "Conan — come down and have your cake and ice cream. You said you were dying for dessert!" she called.

Conan's head disappeared back into the bedroom. "There's some stupid dog barking down there," he called to his mother.

Clinging to the side of the house, struggling to keep his quivering knees from buckling again, Evan shut his eyes and listened.

He heard Conan's footsteps cross the room. The bedroom light went out.

Silence.

"He — left," Evan choked out.

Andy let out a long breath. "I can't believe he didn't see us out here."

Evan glanced down to the ground. Trigger had finally stopped barking. But he continued to stand and stare up at them, his front paws against the side of the house, his stubby tail spinning like a propeller.

"Dumb dog," Evan muttered.

"Let's go," Andy urged. She didn't wait for Evan. She practically did a swan dive into the house.

It took Evan a few moments to get his legs to work. Then he ducked his head and climbed through the window after Andy.

Holding his breath, he led the way on tiptoe to the bedroom door. He stopped and listened.

Silence. No one in the dark hallway.

He could hear the Barbers' voices downstairs in the kitchen.

He and Andy made their way to the top of the stairs. Then, holding tightly to the banister, they crept halfway down.

Evan stopped to listen again. Andy bumped right into him, nearly sending him sailing down the stairs. "Shhh!" she cried.

They could hear Conan talking to his parents

in the kitchen. He was complaining about the other guys on the basketball team. "They're all wimps," Evan heard Conan say.

"Well, that'll make you look even better," Mr. Barber replied.

Evan took another deep breath and held it. Then he made his way down to the bottom of the stairs.

Almost out, he thought, his entire body shaking. Almost out of here.

He reached for the front doorknob.

"Conan, go upstairs and get your math book," he heard Mr. Barber say. "I want to see the homework you had trouble with."

"Okay," Conan replied. His chair scraped against the floor.

Andy grabbed Evan's shoulder.

They stared in frozen horror at each other — one foot away from escape — and waited to be caught.

# 18

"Conan — don't go now. Get the book later," Mrs. Barber chimed in. Then they heard her scold Conan's father: "Let the boy have his cake and ice cream."

"Fine, fine," Mr. Barber replied. "He can show me the book later."

Conan's chair scraped back into place under the table.

Evan didn't wait another second.

He jerked open the front door, pushed open the screen door, and burst out of the house like a rocket.

He could hear Andy gasping as she ran behind him. And then he could hear Trigger's shrill yips as the dog followed, too.

Down the Barbers' front lawn, into the street. Their sneakers slapped the pavement as they ran full speed through the darkness.

They didn't stop until they reached Evan's driveway.

Evan leaned against his family's mailbox and struggled to catch his breath. He raised his hand to wipe the sweat off his forehead — and saw the blue can still stuck there.

"Help me," he pleaded. He reached out his hand to Andy.

She was breathing hard, too. Her eyes kept darting back down the street, as if she expected Conan to be chasing after them.

"Close one," she murmured. She turned to Evan. Her eyes glowed excitedly in the light from the streetlamp. "That was fun!"

Evan didn't agree. In his opinion, it was far too scary to be fun. And here he was, still stuck to the can of Monster Blood.

He pushed his hand toward Andy. "Pull it off," he told her. "I think you need both hands. I can't do it."

She grabbed the can in both hands. The green gunk bubbled over the sides, making loud sucking sounds.

Andy tugged. Then tugged harder. Then she took a deep breath, leaned back, and tugged with all her might.

The Monster Blood finally let go of its grip on Evan's fingers. The can slid off with a loud *pop*. Andy went tumbling back onto the pavement.

"Ow!" Evan held up his three fingers and tried to examine them under the streetlight. They were all wrinkled and pruney, the way they looked when he had been swimming for an hour or two.

"Yuck! That stuff is so gross!" he cried.

Andy climbed slowly to her feet. She still cradled the Monster Blood can in both hands. "At least we got it back," she murmured.

"Yeah. Now we can bury it again," Evan said, still examining his fingers.

"Huh? Bury it?" Andy pulled the can away, as if protecting it from Evan.

"You heard me," Evan said firmly. "It's just too dangerous to mess with, Andy. Take it home and bury it in your back yard, okay?"

Andy stared down at the can. She didn't reply.

"Bury it," Evan repeated. "Take it home and bury it. Promise?"

"Well . . ." Andy hesitated. Then she said, "Okay. Promise."

Evan woke up with a bad sore throat the next morning.

His mother worried that he might be coming down with the flu. So she kept him home from school. Evan spent the day reading comic books and watching MTV. His sore throat disappeared by midafternoon.

He returned to school the next day, feeling refreshed and ready to see everyone.

The good feeling lasted until he stepped into Mr. Murphy's science class near the end of the day. Evan had to walk past the hamster cage to get to his seat.

As he neared the cage, he peered in.

That's weird, he thought. Where's Cuddles?

When did Mr. Murphy get a rabbit?

A *rabbit*?!

He stopped and leaned closer to the cage.

Familiar black eyes stared up at him. A familiar pink nose twitched at him.

It was Cuddles, Evan realized.

Cuddles had grown as big as a rabbit!

# 19

Evan leaned over the hamster cage, staring at the giant-sized Cuddles, as the bell rang. He turned to see that the other kids had all taken their seats.

"Evan, I see you're examining your victim," Mr. Murphy said from the front of the room.

"I — uh — " Evan couldn't think of a reply. "Victim?"

Mr. Murphy angrily narrowed his beady black eyes at Evan. "You've been overfeeding Cuddles, Evan. Look how fat he has become."

*Almost as fat as you!* Evan wanted to say.

Evan knew that Cuddles's weight problem wasn't his fault.

And it had nothing to do with overeating.

Cuddles had grown to triple-hamster size because of Monster Blood.

"When I find Andy, I'll *strangle* her!" Evan muttered.

"What did you say, Evan?" Mr. Murphy demanded.

Evan could feel his face turning bright red. He hadn't meant to talk out loud.

"Uh . . . nothing," he replied, totally embarrassed. He slunk to his seat.

Andy has gone too far this time, he thought bitterly. She promised she'd bury the Monster Blood. She promised!

And now she's turned Cuddles into a fat freak! And Murphy thinks it's all my fault!

"Please stay after school," Mr. Murphy told Evan, "so we can discuss Cuddles's diet."

Evan heard some kids snickering. He knew they were laughing at him.

He saw Conan and Biggie at their seats in the back. Conan was twitching his nose, puffing out his cheeks, pretending to be a fat hamster. Biggie was laughing his head off.

Evan stared at the hamster all through class. Cuddles appeared to grow right before Evan's eyes. With each breath, the hamster seemed to puff up wider and taller.

Its black eyes were as big as marbles now. They stared back at Evan, as if accusing him.

When the hamster moved to its water tube, the entire cage rattled and shook.

*Please don't grow anymore!* Evan pleaded silently, staring at the shaking cage. *Please stop right now, Cuddles. Okay?*

The hamster breathed noisily. Wheezing gasps. Evan could hear Cuddles panting all the way across the room.

The cage shook again as Cuddles turned around. Evan watched in horror as the cage nearly toppled off its table.

I'll *kill* Andy! Evan thought bitterly. How could she *do* this to me?

When the bell rang, the other kids all gathered up their books and headed out the door. Evan stood up and walked over to Cuddles's cage.

Panting loudly, Cuddles stared up at him. He's too big to fit on his wheel, Evan realized. If he grows any more, he'll burst out of the cage!

How much Monster Blood did Andy feed him? Evan wondered. He had to find out.

He turned to Mr. Murphy, who was reading over some papers at his desk. "I've got to find someone," Evan called up to him. "I'll be right back."

"Don't take too long," the teacher replied without looking up.

Evan hurried from the room — and ran into Conan. "Hey, I was looking for you," Conan said, sidestepping to the right, then the left, and stretching out both arms to keep Evan from getting away.

"No time now," Evan said sharply. But Conan wouldn't let him pass. "I'm kind of in a hurry,"

Evan told him. "I don't have time to be stuffed into my locker right now."

A big grin crossed Conan's handsome face. "Hey, I'm sorry about that," he said, his blue eyes twinkling.

"Huh? You're sorry?" Evan's mouth dropped open in shock.

"Yeah. No hard feelings," Conan said, lowering his eyes. "Shake."

Evan stuck out his hand. Then remembered Conan's crushing handshake. He tried to pull back his hand.

Too late.

Conan gripped it tightly and began to squeeze. As he squeezed Evan's hand, his grin grew wider and wider.

Down the hall, Evan saw Andy heading out the door. He tried to call to her. But all that came out of his mouth was a squeak of pain.

Andy disappeared out the front door of the school.

The bones in Evan's hand cracked and crunched.

When Conan finally let go, the hand looked like a sad lump of soft red clay.

"Wow! That's some handshake you've got!" Conan cried, laughing. He pretended his hand hurt. He shook it hard and blew on it. "You killed me that time! You been working out or something?"

Conan headed off to basketball practice, laughing and shaking his hand.

He really cracks himself up, Evan thought. An angry cry burst from his throat. He slammed his good hand into a locker. He was so furious, he thought he could feel steam pouring out his ears.

"Evan — you're keeping me waiting!" Mr. Murphy called in a singsong from the classroom doorway.

"Coming," Evan muttered miserably, and slunk back into the room.

He tried calling Andy for hours that night. But there was no one home.

In his sleep, he dreamed that Trigger ate a big glob of Monster Blood and grew to giant size. Evan tried to stop him. But the enormous dog took off after the mailman.

It wasn't much of a chase. Trigger caught the mailman easily. The mailman was the size of a hamster.

Evan woke up drenched with sweat. He glanced at his bedtable clock. Only six in the morning. He normally didn't get up until seven.

He climbed out of bed, anyway, feeling shaky and scared.

He decided he had to get to school before everyone else. He *had* to see if Cuddles had grown any bigger.

"Evan — where are you going?" his mother

218

called sleepily as Evan headed out the front door.

"Uh — school," Evan replied. He had hoped to sneak out before she woke up.

"So early?" She padded into the room, struggling with the belt to her blue cotton robe.

"Well . . . I have a science project I need to work on," Evan told her. It was *almost* the truth.

"A science project?" She eyed him suspiciously.

"Yeah. It's . . . big!" Evan replied, thinking quickly. "It's really big! So I couldn't bring it home."

"You're going without any breakfast?" Mrs. Ross demanded, yawning.

"I'll grab something at school," he said. "Later, Mom." He disappeared out the door before she could ask any more questions.

A red sun was just climbing over the trees in a gray sky. The air still carried the chill of the night. The lawns Evan passed shimmered wetly with morning dew.

He jogged the whole way, his backpack flopping heavily on his shoulder. There were no other kids on the playground or on the walk heading into the building.

He crept into the school and made his way down the silent, empty hall. His sneakers echoed loudly as he trotted toward the science classroom.

*Maybe Cuddles didn't grow overnight,* Evan told himself.

*Maybe he didn't grow at all. Maybe he shrank. Maybe he shrank back to his old size.*

It was possible.

It was possible that Andy had fed the hamster only a teeny tiny speck of Monster Blood. Just enough for Cuddles to swell up to the size of a fat rabbit — then shrink right back down to cute, cuddly hamster size.

It *was* possible — wasn't it?

Yes! Yes! Evan crossed his fingers on both hands. He wished he could cross his toes.

By the time he reached the classroom, he was breathless. His heart thudded loudly in his chest.

He hesitated at the door.

*Please, Cuddles — be small. Be small!*

Then Evan took a deep breath, held it — and stepped inside.

# 20

Evan stepped into the room, staring at the cage against the far wall. At first, he didn't see Cuddles.

Had Cuddles shrunk? Had he?

Sometimes prayers are answered, Evan told himself. Sometimes good things happen.

Evan took a few hesitant steps closer. Then a few more steps.

Every muscle in his body had tensed. He was so frightened, it was actually hard to walk.

He could feel the blood throbbing at his temples. He mopped the cold beads of sweat off his forehead.

He still couldn't see Cuddles. Where was he? Where?

Gray morning light filtered in through the windows. The floor creaked under Evan's sneakers.

Evan took another hesitant step toward the cage.

Another step.

Then he cried out in horror.

Evan hadn't seen Cuddles at first — because Cuddles was too *big*!

Cuddles filled the entire cage.

Evan held back, gaping in disbelief.

The hamster groaned noisily with every loud breath. It let out several disgusting grunts as its body pressed against the wire cage.

Its big, furry head pushed up against the top of the cage. Evan could see one enormous black eye, the size of a jar lid, staring out at him.

"No!" Evan cried out loud, feeling his knees begin to tremble. "This is impossible!"

The hamster uttered a few more low grunts.

The cage shook on its table.

The big black eye glared out at Evan.

And then as Evan stared in horrified disbelief, the hamster reached up its two pink paws. The toes slipped around the wires of the cage.

Cuddles let out an ugly groan.

Evan saw its spongy pink nose twitch. He saw a flash of big white teeth.

Another groan.

The two front paws pushed against the cage wires.

The wires bent away.

Cuddles grunted again, wheezing loudly, excitedly.

He pushed the cage wires aside.

Then he started to squeeze his big, fur-covered body through the opening.

*What do I do?* Evan frantically asked himself. *What do I do now?*

*Cuddles is escaping!*

# 21

"So what did you do?" Andy asked.

They were sitting together in the tall grass of the tiny park, watching the brown creek trickle past. The late afternoon sun felt warm on their backs. Crickets chirped in the trees behind them.

Three boys rolled past on bikes on the other side of the creek, heading home from school. One of them waved to Evan. He didn't wave back.

Andy wore a bright red sleeveless T-shirt over white denim jeans. She had slipped off her yellow sneakers and was digging her bare feet into the soft ground.

"So what did you do?" she repeated.

Evan picked up a hard clump of dirt and tossed it into the creek. Then he leaned back, his hands planted firmly behind him on the ground.

"I got a dog leash," he told Andy. "In the supply closet."

Andy's eyes widened in surprise. "Murphy keeps a dog leash? What for?"

Evan shrugged. "He has all kinds of junk back there."

"So you put the leash on Cuddles?"

"Yeah," Evan told her. "He was just the right size. As big as a dog. Maybe a little bigger."

"As big as Trigger?" Andy demanded.

Evan nodded. "Then I tied the other end to the leg of Murphy's desk — and I ran out of there as fast as I could."

Andy laughed. But she cut it short when she caught Evan's angry glare. "What happened when you went to science class?" she asked, turning back to the creek.

"I didn't," Evan muttered.

"Huh?"

"I didn't go," Evan said softly. "I was afraid to go. I didn't want Murphy to start blaming me in front of everyone."

"So you cut class?" Andy asked, startled.

Evan nodded.

"So what did you do?" Andy asked. She pulled up a handful of the tall grass and let it sift through her fingers.

"I sneaked out and came here," Evan replied, frowning.

"Everyone was talking about Cuddles all day," Andy reported. Her dark eyes flashed. She couldn't keep an amused grin off her face. "Everyone had to go in and see him. The stupid hamster practically caused a riot!"

"It isn't funny," Evan murmured.

"It's *kind* of funny!" Andy insisted. "Mr. Murphy was bragging that Cuddles could beat up any other hamster in the country. He said he was going to try to get Cuddles on TV!"

"Huh?" Evan jumped to his feet. "You mean Mr. Murphy wasn't upset?"

"I heard that he was at first," Andy replied thoughtfully. "But then I guess he got used to Cuddles being so big. And he was acting kind of proud. You know. Like he had the biggest pumpkin at the fair or something. A blue-ribbon winner!" Andy snickered.

Evan kicked at the grass. "I know he's going to blame me. I know it!"

"Everyone was feeding Cuddles carrots all day," Andy said, not seeming to hear Evan's unhappy wails. "The hamster ate the carrots whole. One big chomp. Then it made this really gross swallowing sound. It was a riot."

"I can't believe this!" Evan groaned. He lowered his eyes angrily to Andy. "Why did you do it? Why?"

Andy gazed up at him innocently. "I wanted to give you a laugh," she replied.

"Huh? A laugh?" he shrieked.

"You were looking pretty down. I thought it might cheer you up."

Evan let out an angry cry.

"I guess it didn't cheer you up," Andy muttered.

She pulled up another handful of grass and let the blades fall over the legs of her white jeans.

Evan stomped over to the edge of the creek. He kicked a rock into the water.

"Come on, Evan," Andy called. "You have to admit it's a *little* funny."

He spun around to face her. "It's not," he insisted. "Not funny at all. What if Cuddles just keeps growing and growing? Then what?"

"We could put a saddle on his back and give everyone hamster rides!" She giggled.

Evan scowled and kicked another rock into the creek. "You *know* how dangerous that Monster Blood is," he scolded. "What are we going to do? How are we going to get Cuddles back to hamster size?"

Andy shrugged. She pulled up another handful of grass.

The sun sank lower behind the trees. A shadow rolled over them. Two little kids chased a white-and-red soccer ball on the other side of the creek. Their mother shouted to them not to get wet.

"Where's the Monster Blood can?" Evan demanded, standing over Andy. "Maybe it tells the antidote on the can. Maybe it tells how to reverse the whole thing."

Andy shook her head. "Evan, you know it doesn't say anything on the can. No instructions. No ingredients. Nothing." She climbed to her feet and brushed off the legs of her jeans. "I've got to get home. My aunt doesn't know where I am. She's probably having a cow."

Evan followed her toward the street, shaking his head. "How big?" he muttered.

She glanced back at him. "What did you say?"

"How big will Cuddles be tomorrow?" Evan asked in a trembling voice. "How big?"

# 22

"Andy — will you hurry up?"

Evan had agreed to meet Andy at her aunt's house the next morning so they could go to school early. But Andy had found a spot on her jeans and had gone back up to her room to change.

And now they were no longer early.

"Sorry," she said, hurtling down the stairs two steps at a time. She had changed her entire outfit. Now she had on a red-and-black-striped vest over a yellow T-shirt, pulled down over pale blue shorts.

"Didn't you leave out a color?" Evan demanded sarcastically, grabbing Andy's backpack for her and hurrying to the front door.

She made a face at him. "I like bright colors. It suits my personality."

"Your personality is *late!*" he declared.

She followed him out the door and down the front lawn to the sidewalk. "At least I *have* a personality!" she cried. "What's your hurry, anyway?"

Evan didn't answer. He adjusted his backpack on his shoulder, then began running toward school.

"Hey — wait up!" Andy called, running after him.

"How much Monster Blood did you give Cuddles, anyway?" Evan demanded without slowing his pace. "The whole can?"

"No way!" Andy called breathlessly. "Just a spoonful. He seemed to like it."

"I guess he liked being as big as a dog, too," Evan said, turning the corner. The tall, redbrick school building came into view.

"Maybe he's back to normal today," Andy said.

But as they came near the building, it was easy to tell that things were *not* normal.

Evan heard a loud crash from the side of the building. It sounded like glass shattering.

Then he heard excited shouts. Loud kids' voices filled with alarm.

"What's going *on*?" Andy cried.

They dove up the stairs and burst into the building. Running full speed, they turned the corner and made their way to the science classroom.

Evan reached it a few steps ahead of Andy. Hearing excited shouts and cries, he lurched into the room — and then stopped with a startled cry.

"No! Oh, please — no!"

"Stand back! Everyone stand back!" a red-faced Mr. Murphy was screaming.

Cuddles uttered a loud grunt and flailed his giant legs wildly in the air.

"He — he's ten feet tall!" Evan heard Andy scream at his side.

"Al-almost!" Evan stammered.

The grunting, groaning hamster towered over Mr. Murphy. Its pink paws batted the air. Its monstrous mouth opened wide, revealing two enormous, sharp white teeth.

"Back! Everyone back!" Mr. Murphy shrieked.

The terrified kids in the classroom pressed back against the walls.

Mr. Murphy picked up a wooden chair in one hand, the torn dog leash in the other. Holding the chair by the back, he came at the grunting monster like a lion tamer.

"Down, Cuddles! Get down! Sit! Sit!"

He poked the wooden chair up at the giant hamster and snapped the dog leash like a whip.

Cuddles's watery black eyes, as big as soccer balls, glared down at the red-faced teacher. The hamster didn't seem terribly impressed with Mr. Murphy's lion-tamer act.

"Down, Cuddles! Get down!" The teacher's chins quivered, and his big belly bounced up and down beneath his tight gray knit polo shirt.

Cuddles pulled back his huge lips and bared his white teeth. He let out a growl that made the light fixtures shake.

Terrified cries rang out through the room. Evan glanced back to see a horrified crowd of teachers and students jammed in the doorway.

"Down, Cuddles!"

Mr. Murphy shoved the wooden chair up at the raging hamster. He cracked the dog-leash whip near the hamster's throbbing, fur-covered belly.

The huge black eyes stared down angrily at Mr. Murphy. The pink hamster paws clawed in the air.

Andy grabbed Evan's shoulder and held on tight. "This is terrible!" she cried. "Terrible!"

Evan started to reply — but frightened shrieks drowned out his words.

Cuddles grabbed the chair with both paws.

"Drop! Drop!" Mr. Murphy screamed. He struggled to hold on to the chair.

Cuddles pulled the chair. Mr. Murphy desperately held tight. He let the leash fall so he could hold on to the chair with both hands.

The teacher and Cuddles had a short tug-of-war.

Cuddles won easily. The hamster pulled the chair up, nearly jerking Mr. Murphy's arms out of their sockets.

With a loud groan, the teacher toppled heavily to the floor.

Kids screamed.

Two teachers rushed forward to help the gasping Mr. Murphy to his feet.

Evan stared up as the hamster raised the wooden chair to its mouth. The enormous white teeth opened quickly. The pink nose twitched. The watery black eyes blinked.

Then Cuddles chewed the wooden chair to pieces.

Splinters rained down on the floor.

The chomping teeth sounded like a lumberjack's ax biting into a tree.

Evan froze in horror along with everyone else in the room.

Andy was squeezing his shoulder so hard, it hurt. "This is *our* fault," she murmured.

"*Our* fault?" Evan cried. "*Our* fault?"

She ignored his sarcasm. He saw the fear in her eyes as she stared up at the hamster. Cuddles had turned the chair into toothpicks!

"We've got to do something, Evan," she whispered, huddled close to him.

"But what?" Evan replied in a trembling voice. "What can we do?"

Then, suddenly, he had an idea.

# 23

"Come with me!" Evan cried, tugging Andy's arm.

She hesitated, staring up at the giant hamster. "Where?"

"I have an idea," Evan told her. "But we have to hurry!"

Cuddles lumbered over to Mr. Murphy's desk. The hamster's heavy footsteps made the floor sag.

"Here, fella! Here!" Mr. Murphy was tossing handfuls of sunflower seeds up to Cuddles. Cuddles glared down at him. The seeds were too small to bother with.

"Hurry!" Evan pleaded. He pulled Andy through the frightened crowd of kids and teachers at the door. Then he began running full speed toward the auditorium.

"We can't just run away! We have to *do* something!" Andy cried.

"We're not running away," Evan called back to

her, turning a corner. "My father's sculpture —
it's in the auditorium."

"Huh?" Andy's eyes narrowed in confusion.
"Evan — have you totally *lost* it? Why do you
want to look at your father's sculpture now?"

He burst through the auditorium doors and ran
past the dark rows of seats toward the stage.
Several pieces of sculpture had been set up
there.

"Evan — I don't get it!" Andy cried, right behind him.

"Look," Evan said breathlessly. He pointed to
his father's work near the back of the stage. "My
dad's sculpture. It's just like a hamster wheel —
see?"

Her mouth dropped open as she stared at it.

"It's a big metal wheel and it spins," Evan explained as they pulled themselves up onto the
stage. "Come on. Help me drag it back to Murphy's room. It's big enough for Cuddles."

"Whoa!" Andy cried. "You want to bring Cuddles a wheel? What for?"

"To distract him," Evan replied, grabbing one
side of the big sculpture. "If we can get Cuddles
running on this wheel, it will give us time to figure
out where to keep him. And it will stop him from
chewing the whole school to pieces."

Andy grabbed hold of the other side, one hand
on the wheel, one hand on the platform. "Maybe

Cuddles will run so hard, he'll lose weight. Maybe he'll shrink back to his normal size," she said.

Luckily, the platform was on wheels. They rolled the sculpture toward the stage door at the side. "I just want to distract him," Evan said, tugging hard. "I just want to give us time to think, to make a plan."

"Wow! This is heavy!" Andy cried. They rolled it into the hall. "Heavy enough for Cuddles, I guess."

"I hope," Evan replied solemnly.

By the time they rolled the sculpture to the classroom, the crowd of frightened kids and teachers had grown even bigger. "Make way! Make way!" they both shouted, pushing their way through the crowd.

They set the wheel down in the center of the floor and gazed over at Cuddles. The hamster had two teachers cornered, their backs pressed against the chalkboard. It was gnashing its huge teeth at them, slapping its pink paws together as if eager to fight them.

Evan gasped when he saw Mr. Murphy's desk, crushed flat on the floor.

"I — I called the police!" Mr. Murphy cried, his face beaded with large drops of sweat. "I begged them to come. But when I said it was a giant hamster, they didn't believe me! They thought it was a practical joke!"

"Stand back, everyone!" Evan cried shrilly.

"Stand back — please! Let Cuddles see the wheel!"

The giant hamster turned suddenly. The two teachers scrambled away from the wall. Kids and teachers screamed and hurried toward the door.

"Maybe he'll run on the wheel for a while," Andy explained to Mr. Murphy. "Then we can figure out what to do with him!"

"He — he sees it!" Mr. Murphy cried breathlessly, all of his chins quivering at once.

Cuddles stared down at the wheel. His stub of a tail thudded loudly against the chalkboard. He dropped heavily to all fours and took a lumbering step toward the wheel.

"He sees it. He's going to it," Evan murmured softly.

A hush fell over the room as everyone stared at the hamster.

Will Cuddles climb inside? Evan wondered, holding his breath.

Will he run on the wheel?

Will my plan work?

# 24

The hamster sniffed the wheel. Its pink nose twitched. It uttered a low grunt.

Then it raised itself back onto its hind legs. The hamster's massive shadow fell over the room.

With another disgusting grunt, it picked the sculpture up in its front paws and raised it to its face.

"No!" Evan cried. "Cuddles — no!"

The metal clanged as Cuddles bit into the wheel. Evan saw deep tooth marks in the aluminum. Cuddles bit down again. Then, seeing that he couldn't chew the wheel up, he pulled it apart, holding the sculpture in his paws and twisting it furiously with his teeth.

Then he tossed the mangled wheel away. It slammed into a window, shattering it into a thousand pieces.

"Back to the drawing board," Andy muttered to Evan.

Evan shook his head glumly. That plan was a bust, he told himself. Now what?

He didn't have time to think about it.

He heard shrill cries and shrieks of terror.

"Put him down! Cuddles — put him down!" Mr. Murphy was screaming.

Evan turned and saw that the giant hamster had picked up a kid.

Conan!

Cuddles held Conan in both paws and was raising him toward his gaping mouth.

"Drop! Drop!" Mr. Murphy was shouting.

Conan thrashed his arms and legs. "Help me! Ohhh, hellllp me!" he shrieked. He started to cry. Gasping sobs. Tears rolled down his red cheeks.

"Helllllp! Mommmmmy! Mommmmmmy! Hellllp me!"

Normally Evan would have enjoyed watching Conan cry like a baby. But this was too serious. Cuddles could chew Conan in half! Evan realized.

He grabbed Andy. "Where's the Monster Blood?"

"Huh? In my locker. I hid it under a bunch of stuff in my locker. Why?"

"I need it," Evan said. "Come on. I have another idea."

"I hope it's better than the last one," Andy muttered.

They hurried to the door, then glanced back.

Cuddles was playing with Conan, tossing him from paw to paw, licking him with his huge, pink tongue. Conan was wailing his head off.

Evan led the way to Andy's locker. "I'm going to eat some Monster Blood," he told her, thinking out loud. "I'll eat a lot. I'll grow bigger than Cuddles."

"I get it," Andy said, running beside him. "You'll turn yourself into a giant. You'll make yourself as big as Cuddles."

"No," Evan replied. "Bigger. Much bigger. I'll make myself so big that Cuddles will look hamster size. Then I'll stuff him in the supply closet and lock the door."

"It's a stupid plan," Andy said.

"I know," Evan agreed.

"But it's worth a try," Andy added.

Evan swallowed hard and didn't reply. He was staring across the hall at Andy's locker.

"Oh, no!" Andy cried out when she saw what Evan was gaping at.

The locker door bulged as if about to burst open. And green goo poured out from the sides and the bottom.

"The Monster Blood — it outgrew my locker!" Andy cried.

Evan ran up to it and grabbed the door handle. He started to tug. "Is it locked?"

"No," Andy replied, hanging back.

Evan tugged. He tugged harder. With a loud

groan, he tugged with both hands. "It won't open!" he cried.

"Let me try it," Andy said.

But before she could step forward, the locker door burst open with a loud *whooooosh*.

Sticky, green gunk splashed over Evan.

He didn't have a chance to cry out.

It poured over him like a tall, cresting ocean wave.

An ocean wave of Monster Blood.

It's *burying* me! Evan realized.

The huge, sticky glob splashed out of the locker, plopped over him, smothering him, choking him.

It's sucking me in! I can't move!

I can't move!

# 25

Evan shut his eyes as the heavy, green gunk rolled over his head. He shot his arms out, trying to push it away.

As it swept over him, he fell to his knees. Kicking and thrashing, it forced him down to the floor.

I'm stuck inside, he thought. Stuck inside . . .

He felt hands grab his ankles.

The hands tugged hard.

He began to slide. Over the floor. Over the thick layer of Monster Blood.

"I've got you!" he heard Andy cry. "I've got you out!"

He opened his eyes. He saw her pulling him, tugging him out of the thick green gunk by the ankles.

It clung to his clothes and his skin. But he was out.

"Thanks," he murmured weakly. He climbed shakily to his feet.

He could hear Conan screaming and crying back

in the classroom. There was still time to save him, Evan realized.

He pulled a hunk of Monster Blood off the quivering green mound — and jammed it into his mouth.

"I'm going to be sick," Andy groaned, holding her stomach.

Evan swallowed and reached for another mouthful. "It doesn't taste bad," he told her. "A little lemony."

"Don't eat too much!" she cried, half-covering her eyes as she watched him swallow another mouthful.

"I have to grow big enough so that Cuddles is hamster size compared to me," Evan said. He grabbed another hunk.

He could already feel himself start to grow. His head was already over the tops of the lockers.

Back in the classroom, Conan let out another terrified wail.

"Let's go!" Evan boomed. His voice thundered deeply in his new, larger body. He could feel himself growing taller. Taller.

He had to lower his head to get through the classroom door.

Kids and teachers moved out of his way, crying out their surprise and alarm.

He crossed the room, passed Mr. Murphy, and stepped up to the giant hamster. "I'm as big as Cuddles!" Evan called down to Andy.

He reached out and lifted Conan from Cuddles's paws. Cuddles reached out to take Conan back. But Evan lowered him gently to the floor.

"Hellllp me! Helllp me!" Conan ran bawling from the room.

Evan turned to face the hamster. They stared at each other eye to eye.

Cuddles's huge pink nose twitched. He sniffed Evan, inhaling so hard that Evan was nearly sucked forward.

Evan took a step back.

*Keep growing!* he urged himself. *I've got to keep growing!*

Cuddles eyed him warily, still sniffing. His watery black eyes stared hard as if trying to figure out if Evan was friend or foe.

"Don't you remember me, Cuddles?" Evan said softly. "Remember, I'm the one who fed you after school every day?"

*Keep growing!* he silently urged himself.

*Why aren't I growing any taller?*

Down below, he could see Andy, Mr. Murphy, and the others huddled against the far wall, staring up at the two giants in hushed terror.

*Keep growing! Keep growing!*

There was no way he could pick Cuddles up now, Evan realized. They were exactly the same height. And Cuddles outweighed him by at least a ton!

*Keep growing!*

"What's wrong, Andy?" Evan called down to her in a trembling voice. "I ate tons of the stuff. Why did I stop growing?"

"I don't know!" she called up to him. Her voice sounded as tiny as a mouse's squeak.

He saw that she had the blue can in her hand. She was turning it over, reading the label. "I don't know, Evan!" she shouted. "I don't know why you're not growing!"

Then, as Evan turned back to face Cuddles, the hamster reached out and grabbed his waist with both front paws.

"Ow!" Evan cried as the hamster tried to lift him off the floor.

Gazing up, he saw the gaping hamster mouth open, the sharp white teeth emerge.

Evan squirmed desperately, pulling himself loose. Then he wrapped both arms around the hamster's middle.

They started to wrestle. Evan fought hard, but the hamster overpowered him. Cuddles rolled Evan onto his back on the floor.

Evan spun quickly away, climbed to his feet, and pulled the hamster down.

The two giants wrestled over the floor, surrounded by the shrill screams of teachers and kids.

*Grow bigger! Grow bigger — now!* Evan pleaded.

But it was too late, he saw.

The hamster lowered its hot, furry body over

him. Evan could feel the creature's booming heartbeat as it pressed him to the floor.

Then its teeth rose up over Evan's head.

The hamster's mouth opened wide.

The teeth swung down.

A wave of hot, sour hamster breath blew down over Evan.

He shut his eyes.

"Sorry," he murmured to Andy.

He held his breath and waited for the teeth to clamp down.

# 26

Evan heard a *pop*, like the sound of a cork flying off a bottle.

Still sprawled on his back on the floor, Evan opened his eyes.

"Huh?" Cuddles had disappeared. Vanished.

Evan stared up at the startled faces of kids and teachers against the wall. "Wh-where's Cuddles?" he stammered.

Andy stood frozen like a statue, her mouth open.

Evan slowly realized that she was nearly as big as he was. In fact, *everyone* was about his size.

He pulled himself up to a sitting position. "Hey — I'm back to my normal size!" he cried. He shook his head hard as if trying to shake away his close call with the giant hamster.

"There's Cuddles!" Andy cried, pointing.

Evan turned to see Cuddles huddled against the wall. "He's a little hamster again!" Evan exclaimed happily. He took three quick steps, bent down, and grabbed Cuddles between his hands. "Gotcha!"

Holding the hamster in front of him, he turned back to Andy and the others. "What happened? Why did we shrink back?"

Andy was studying the blue Monster Blood can. Suddenly she tossed back her dark hair, her brown eyes lit up, and she started to laugh. "It's the expiration date!" she cried happily. "The expiration date on the can — it's *today*! The Monster Blood stops working today! The magic has worn out!"

Evan let out a whoop of joy.

Mr. Murphy, a wide grin on his round face, hurried over and put his arm around Evan's shoulders. "Fine job, Evan! Fine job!" he exclaimed. "You saved the school. I'm proud of you!"

"Thanks, Mr. Murphy," Evan replied awkwardly.

"You'll never make a basketball player now that you're short again," Mr. Murphy said, smiling. "But that was quite a good match with Cuddles. Have you ever thought of trying out for the wrestling team?"

Andy came to Evan's house for dinner that night. He greeted her at the door, eager to tell her how all the kids had apologized for not believing him about the Monster Blood.

But before he could say anything, she held up a large brown envelope and grinned at him.

"What's that?" he asked, following her into the living room.

"It's a present my parents sent me from Europe," she replied, her grin growing wider. "You won't *believe* what it is."

She started to pull open the envelope. But the front doorbell rang.

Evan hurried to see who it was.

"Mr. Murphy!" he cried in surprise.

"Hi, Evan," the teacher said, his round body nearly filling the entire front stoop. "Hope I'm not interrupting your dinner."

"No," Evan replied. "Want to come in?"

"No thanks," Mr. Murphy replied. His expression turned solemn. "I came by because I thought you should have some sort of reward, Evan. You were a real hero at school today."

"Aw, not really," Evan said awkwardly. He could feel his face growing hot and knew he was blushing.

What kind of reward? Evan wondered, staring back at the teacher. A cash reward?

Mr. Murphy raised the hamster cage into Evan's view. "I've decided to reward you with Cuddles," the teacher said. "I know how fond of him you are."

"No, please!" Evan started to plead.

"It's a small token," Mr. Murphy said. "To show how grateful I am. How grateful we all are."

"Please — no — !"

But before Evan realized it, the hamster cage was in his hand, and Mr. Murphy was waddling back down the driveway to his car.

"He gave you Cuddles?" Andy asked as Evan returned to the living room carrying the cage. He set it down on the coffee table.

"It's my reward," Evan told her, rolling his eyes. "Do you believe it?"

"Well, you *won't* believe this!" Andy declared. "Look what my parents found in Europe!"

She reached into the envelope and pulled out a blue plastic can. "It's Monster Blood!"

"Oh, no!" Evan wailed.

"They wrote that they remembered how much fun I had with the old can," Andy said, holding up the blue container. "So when they saw this can in a toy store in Germany, they decided to send me a new one."

Evan's eyes went wide with fear. "You — you're not going to open it?" he demanded warily.

"Already did," Andy replied. "Just to take a look. But I'm not going to use it. Really. I promise."

Evan started to say something — but he was interrupted by his mother's call from the kitchen. "Dinnertime, you two! Wash your hands and come to the table!"

Andy set the can of Monster Blood down on the desk in the corner. They obediently hurried to wash their hands.

They had a lively dinner. There was *lots* to talk about. They laughed and joked about all that had happened at school. It was easy to laugh about it now that it was all over.

After dinner, Evan and Andy returned to the living room.

Andy was the first to see that the door to the hamster cage was wide open. The cage was empty.

Evan was the one who spotted Cuddles on the desk.

"Cuddles — what are you eating?" he cried. "What are you eating?"

# Goosebumps®

## MONSTER BLOOD III

"The Monster Blood! It's growing again!" Evan Ross stared at the quivering green blob in his driveway. It looked like an enormous wad of sticky green bubble gum, and was bigger than a beach ball. Bigger than *two* beach balls!

The green blob trembled and shook as if it were breathing hard. It made disgusting sucking sounds. Then it started to bounce.

Evan took a step back. How did the sticky goo get out of its can? he wondered. Who left it in the driveway? Who opened the can?

Evan knew that once Monster Blood starts to grow, it can't be stopped. It will grow and grow, and suck up everything in its path.

Evan knew this from painful experience.

He had seen a giant glob of Monster Blood swallow kids whole. And he had seen what had happened when his dog, Trigger, had eaten Monster Blood. The cocker spaniel had grown and grown and grown — until he was big enough to pick up Evan in his teeth and bury him in the backyard!

A small chunk of Monster Blood had turned Cuddles, the tiny hamster in Evan's class, into a raging, growling monster. The giant hamster — bigger than a gorilla — had roared through the school, destroying everything in its path!

This gunk is dangerous, Evan thought. It may be the most dangerous green slimy stuff on Earth!

So how did it get in Evan's driveway?

And what was he going to do about it?

The Monster Blood bounced and hiccupped. It made more disgusting sucking sounds.

As it bounced, it picked up sticks and gravel from the driveway. They stuck to its side for a moment, before being sucked into the center of the giant wet ball.

Evan took another step back as the ball slowly started to roll. "Oh, noooo." A low moan escaped his throat. "Please. Noooo."

The Monster Blood rolled over the driveway toward Evan, picking up speed as it moved. Evan had tossed one of his Rollerblades by the side of the house. The green goo swallowed up the skate with a loud *thwocccccck*.

Evan gulped as he saw the skate disappear into the bouncing green ball. "I — I'm next!" he stammered out loud.

No way! he told himself. I'm getting out of here.

He turned to run — and went sprawling over the other skate.

"Ow!" he cried out as he fell hard on his elbows and knees. Pain shot up his arms. He had landed on both funny bones.

Shaking away the tingling, he scrambled to his knees. He turned in time to see the seething goo roll over him.

He opened his mouth to scream. But the scream was trapped inside him as the heavy green gunk splatted over his face.

He thrashed both arms wildly. Kicked his feet.

But the sticky goo wrapped around him. Pulling him. Pulling him in.

I — I can't breathe! he realized.

And, then, everything turned green.

# 2

"Evan — stop daydreaming and eat your Jell-O," Mrs. Ross scolded.

Evan shook his head hard. The daydream had seemed so real. His mother's voice still sounded far away.

"Evan — hurry. Eat the Jell-O. You'll be late."

"Uh . . . Mom . . ." Evan said softly. "Could you do me a really big favor?"

"What favor?" his mother asked him patiently, pushing back her straight blond hair into a ponytail.

"Could we never have *green* Jell-O again? Could you just buy other colors? Not green?"

He stared at the shimmering, quivering green mound of Jell-O in the glass bowl in front of him on the kitchen counter.

"Evan, you're weird," Mrs. Ross replied, rolling her eyes. "Hurry up. Kermit is probably wondering where you are."

"Kermit is probably busy blowing up his house,"

Evan replied glumly. He pulled the spoon out of the Jell-O. It made a gross sucking sound.

"All the more reason for you to hurry over there," his mother said sharply. "You are responsible for him, Evan. You are in charge of your cousin until his mom gets home from work."

Evan shoved the green Jell-O away. "I can't eat this," he murmured. "It makes me think of Monster Blood."

Mrs. Ross made a disgusted face. "Don't mention that slimy stuff."

Evan climbed down from the stool. Mrs. Ross pushed a hand gently through his curly, carrot-colored hair. "It's nice of you to help out," she said softly. "Aunt Dee can't really afford a baby-sitter."

"Kermit doesn't need a baby-sitter. He needs a *keeper*!" Evan grumbled. "Or maybe a trainer. A guy with a whip and a chair. Like in the circus."

"Kermit looks up to you," Mrs. Ross insisted.

"Only because he's two feet tall!" Evan exclaimed. "I can't believe he's my cousin. He's such a nerd."

"Kermit isn't a nerd. Kermit is a genius!" Mrs. Ross declared. "He's only eight, and already he's a scientific genius."

"Some genius," Evan grumbled. "Mom, yesterday he melted my sneakers."

Mrs. Ross's pale blue eyes grew wide. "He *what*?"

"He made one of his concoctions. It was a bright yellow liquid. He said it would toughen up the sneakers so they would never wear out."

"And you let him pour the stuff on your sneakers?" Evan's mother demanded.

"I didn't have a choice," Evan replied unhappily. "I have to do everything Kermit wants. If I don't, he tells Aunt Dee I was mean to him."

Mrs. Ross shook her head. "I wondered why you came home barefoot yesterday."

"My sneakers are still stuck to Kermit's basement floor," Evan told her. "They melted right off my feet."

"Well, be careful over there, okay?"

"Yeah. Sure," Evan replied. He pulled his Atlanta Braves cap over his head, waved to his mother, and headed out the back door.

It was a warm spring day. Two black-and-yellow monarch butterflies fluttered over the flower garden. The bright new leaves on the trees shimmered in the sunlight.

Evan stopped at the bottom of the driveway and lowered the baseball cap to shield his eyes from the sun. He squinted down the street, hoping to see his friend Andy.

No sign of her.

Disappointed, he kicked a large pebble along the curb and started to make his way toward Kermit's house. Aunt Dee, Kermit's mom, paid Evan three dollars an hour to watch Kermit after school every afternoon. Three *hundred* dollars an hour would be a lot more fair! he thought angrily.

But Evan was glad to earn the money. He was saving for a new Walkman. Trigger had mistaken his old Walkman for a dog bone.

But Evan was earning every penny. Kermit was impossible. That was the only word for him. Impossible.

He didn't want to play video games. He didn't want to watch TV. He refused to go outside and play ball or toss a Frisbee around. He didn't even want to sneak down to the little grocery on the corner and load up on candy bars and potato chips.

All he wanted to do was stay downstairs in his dark, damp basement lab and mix beakers of chemicals together. "My experiments," he called them. "I have to do my experiments."

Maybe he *is* a genius, Evan thought bitterly. But that doesn't make him any fun. He's just *impossible*.

Evan definitely wasn't enjoying his after-school baby-sitting job watching Kermit. In fact, he had several daydreams in which Kermit tried one of his own mixtures and melted to the basement floor, just like Evan's sneakers.

Some afternoons, Andy came along, and that made the job a little easier. Andy thought Kermit was really weird, too. But at least when she was there, Evan had someone to talk to, someone who didn't want to talk about mixing aluminum pyrite with sodium chlorobenzadrate.

What is Kermit's problem, anyway? Evan wondered as he crossed the street and made his way through backyards toward Kermit's house. Why does he think *mixing* is so much fun? Why is he always mixing this with that and that with this?

I can't even mix chocolate milk!

Kermit's house came into view two yards down. It was a two-story white house with a sloping black roof.

Evan picked up his pace. He was about fifteen minutes late. He hoped that Kermit hadn't already gotten into some kind of trouble.

He had just pushed his way though the prickly, low hedges that fenced in Kermit's yard when a familiar gruff voice made him freeze.

"Evan — were you looking at my yard?"

"Huh?" Evan recognized the voice at once. It belonged to Kermit's next-door neighbor, a kid from Evan's school.

His name was Conan Barber. But the kids at school all called him Conan the Barbarian. That's because he had to be the biggest, meanest kid in Atlanta. Maybe in the universe.

Conan sat on top of the tall white fence that separated the yards. His cold blue eyes glared down at Evan. "Were you looking at my yard?" Conan demanded.

"No way!" Evan's voice came out in a squeak.

"You were looking at my yard. That's trespassing," Conan accused. He leaped down from the high fence. He was big and very athletic. His hobby was leaping over kids he had just pounded into the ground.

Conan wore a gray muscle shirt and baggy, faded jeans cutoffs. He also wore a very mean expression.

"Whoa. Wait a minute, Conan!" Evan protested. "I was looking at Kermit's yard. I *never* look at your yard. Never!"

Conan stepped up to Evan. He stuck out his chest and bumped Evan hard, so hard he stumbled backwards.

That was Conan's other hobby. Bumping kids with his chest. His chest didn't feel like a chest. It felt like a truck.

"Why *don't* you look at my yard?" Conan demanded. "Is there something wrong with my yard? Is my yard too ugly? Is that why you never look at it?"

Evan swallowed hard. It began to dawn on him that maybe Conan was itching for a fight.

Before he could answer Conan, he heard a scratchy voice reply for him. *"It's a free country, Conan!"*

"Oh, noooo," Evan groaned, shutting his eyes.

Evan's cousin, Kermit, stepped out from behind Evan. He was tiny and skinny. A very pale kid with a pile of white-blond hair, and round black eyes behind big red plastic-framed glasses. Evan always thought his cousin looked like a white mouse wearing glasses.

Kermit wore enormous red shorts that came down nearly to his ankles, and a red-and-black Braves T-shirt. The short sleeves hung down past the elbows of his skinny arms.

"What did you say?" Conan demanded, glaring down menacingly at Kermit.

"It's a free country!" Kermit repeated shrilly. "Evan can look at any yard he wants to!"

Conan let out an angry growl. As he lumbered forward to pound Evan's face into mashed potatoes, Evan turned to Kermit. "Thanks a lot," he told his cousin. "Thanks for all your help."

"Which way do you want your nose to slant?" Conan asked Evan. "To the right or to the left?"

# 3

"Don't do it!" Kermit shrieked in his scratchy mouse voice.

Conan raised a huge fist. With his other hand, he grabbed the front of Evan's T-shirt. He glared down at Kermit. "Why not?" he growled.

"Because I have *this*!" Kermit declared.

"Huh?" Conan let go of Evan's shirt. He stared at the glass beaker Kermit had raised in both hands. The beaker was half-full with a dark blue liquid.

Conan let out a sigh and swept a beefy hand back through his wavy blond hair. His blue eyes narrowed at Kermit. "What's that? Your baby formula?"

"Ha-ha," Kermit replied sarcastically.

If Kermit doesn't shut up, we're *both* going to get pounded! Evan realized. What is the little creep trying to do?

He tugged at Kermit's sleeve, trying to pull him

away from Conan. But Kermit ignored him. He raised the beaker close to Conan's face.

"It's an Invisibility Mixture," Kermit said. "If I pour it on you, you'll disappear."

We should *both* disappear! Evan thought frantically. He let his eyes dart around the backyard. Maybe I can make it through that hedge before Conan grabs me, he thought. If I can get around the next house and down to the street, I might escape.

But would it be right to leave little Kermit at Conan's mercy?

Evan sighed. He couldn't abandon his cousin like that. Even though Kermit was definitely asking for it.

"You're going to make me invisible with that stuff?" Conan asked Kermit with a sneer.

Kermit nodded. "If I pour a few drops on you, you'll disappear. Really. I mixed it myself. It works. It's a mixture of Teflon dioxinate and magnesium parasulfidine."

"Yeah. Right," Conan muttered. He peered at the liquid in the beaker. "What makes it blue?"

"Food coloring," Kermit replied. Then he lowered his squeaky voice, trying to sound tough. "You'd better go home now, Conan. I don't want to have to use this stuff."

Oh, wow! Evan thought, pulling the bill of his Braves cap down over his face. I can't bear to watch this. This is sad. Really sad. Kermit is such a jerk.

"Go ahead. Try it," Evan heard Conan say.

Evan raised the cap so he could see. "Uh . . . Kermit . . . maybe we should go in the house now," he whispered.

"Go ahead. Make me invisible," Conan challenged.

"You really want me to?" Kermit demanded.

"Yeah," Conan replied. "I want to be invisible. Go ahead, Kermit. Pour it on me. Make me disappear. I dare you."

Kermit raised the beaker over the gray muscle shirt that covered Conan's broad chest.

"Kermit — no!" Evan pleaded. "Don't! Please *don't!*"

Evan made a frantic grab for the beaker.

Too late.

Kermit turned the beaker over and let the thick blue liquid pour onto the front of Conan's shirt.

# 4

Out of the corner of his eye, Evan saw a monarch butterfly fluttering over the low hedges. I wish I were a butterfly, he thought. I wish I could flap my wings and float away.

As far away from here as I can get!

The blue liquid oozed down the front of Conan's muscle shirt. All three boys stared at it in silence.

"Well? I'm not disappearing," Conan murmured, narrowing his eyes suspiciously at Kermit.

Then his shirt started to shrink.

"Hey — !" Conan cried angrily. He struggled to pull off the shrinking shirt. It got tinier and tinier. "It — it's *choking* me!" Conan shrieked.

"Wow!" Kermit squeaked, his black eyes glowing excitedly behind his glasses. "This is cool!"

Evan gazed in amazement as the muscle shirt shrank down to a tiny shred of cloth. And then it vanished completely.

Now Conan stood in front of them bare-chested.

A heavy silence fell over the backyard. All three of them stared at Conan's broad, bare chest for a few moments.

Conan broke the silence. "That was my best muscle shirt," he told Evan through gritted teeth.

"Uh-oh," Evan uttered.

"I like your nose that way," Andy told Evan. "It kind of tilts in both directions at once."

"I think it will go back to the way it was," Evan replied, patting his nose tenderly. "At least it stopped hurting so much." He sighed. "All the other cuts and bruises will go away, too. In time."

It was two days later. Evan sat across from Andy in the lunchroom at school. He stared down sadly at the tuna fish sandwich his mom had packed for him. He hadn't taken a bite. His mouth wasn't working exactly right yet. It kept going sideways instead of up and down.

Andy wiped a chunk of egg salad off her cheek. She had short brown hair and big brown eyes that stared across the table at Evan.

Andy didn't dress like most of the other kids in their sixth-grade class. She liked bright colors. A lot of bright colors.

Today she wore a yellow vest over a magenta T-shirt and orange Day-Glo shorts.

When Andy moved to Atlanta in the beginning of the school year, some kids made fun of her colorful clothes. But they didn't anymore. Now everyone agreed that Andy had style. And a few kids were even copying her look.

"So what happened after Conan the Barbarian pounded your body into coleslaw?" Andy asked. She pulled a handful of potato chips from her bag and shoved them one by one into her mouth.

Evan took a few bites from a section of his tuna fish sandwich. It took him a long time to swallow. "Conan made me promise I'd never look in his yard again," he told Andy. "I had to raise my right hand and swear. Then he went home."

Evan sighed. He touched his sore nose again. "After Conan left, Kermit helped me hobble into his house," Evan continued. "A little while later, Aunt Dee got home."

"Then what happened?" Andy asked, crinkling up the empty potato chip bag.

"She saw that I was messed up," Evan replied. "So she asked what happened."

Evan shook his head and scowled. "And before I could say anything, that little rat Kermit piped up and said, 'Evan picked a fight with Conan.' "

"Oh, wow," Andy murmured.

"And Aunt Dee said, 'Well, Evan, if you're just going to get into fights instead of taking care of Kermit, I'm going to have to talk to your mom about you. Maybe you're not mature enough for this job.' "

"Oh, wow," Andy repeated.

"And the whole thing was Kermit's fault!" Evan shouted, pounding his fist so hard on the table that his milk carton tipped over. Milk spilled over the tabletop, onto the front of his jeans.

Evan was so upset, he didn't even move out of the way. "And do you know the worst thing?" Evan demanded. "The *worst* thing?"

"What?" Andy asked.

"Kermit did it deliberately. He knew what that blue mixture would do. He knew it would shrink Conan's shirt. Kermit wanted me to get pounded by Conan. He did the whole thing to get me in trouble with Conan."

"How do you know?" Andy asked.

"The smile," Evan told her.

"Huh? What smile?"

"The smile on Kermit's face. You know that twisted little smile he has where his two front teeth stick out? That's the smile he had when he helped me back to the house."

Andy tsk-tsked.

Evan finished the section of tuna fish sandwich. "Is that all you're going to say?" he snapped.

"What can I say?" Andy replied. "Your cousin, Kermit, is a weird little dude. I think you should teach him a lesson. Pay him back."

"Huh?" Evan gaped at her. "How do I do that?"

Andy shrugged. "I don't know. Maybe you could . . . uh . . ." Her dark eyes suddenly flashed with excitement. "I know! Doesn't he have

271

a snack after school every day? You could slip some Monster Blood into his food."

Evan gulped and jumped to his feet. "Hey — no way! No way, Andy!" he shouted.

Several kids turned to stare at Evan, startled by his loud cries.

"Don't even think it!" Evan shouted, ignoring the stares. "No Monster Blood. Ever! I never want to hear those words again!"

"Okay, okay!" Andy cried. She raised both hands, as if to shield herself from him.

"By the way," Evan said, a little calmer, "where is the Monster Blood? Where did you hide it? You didn't take any of it out — did you?"

"Well . . ." Andy replied, lowering her eyes. A devilish grin spread across her face. "I put a little bit of it in the tuna fish sandwich you just ate."

# 5

Evan let out a cry so loud, it made two kids fall off their chairs. Two other kids dropped their lunch trays.

His eyes bulged and his voice rose higher than the gym teacher's whistle. "You — you — you — !" he sputtered, grabbing his throat.

Andy laughed. She pointed at his chair. "Evan, sit down. I was only joking."

"Huh?"

"You heard me," Andy said. "It was a joke. The Monster Blood is home, safe and sound."

Evan let out a long sigh. He sank back into the chair. He didn't care that he was sitting in the milk he had spilled.

"Annndrea," he said unhappily, stretching out the word. "Annnndrea, that wasn't funny."

"Sure it was," Andy insisted. "And don't call me Andrea. You know I hate that name."

"Andrea. Andrea. Andrea," Evan repeated, paying her back for her mean joke. He narrowed his eyes at her sternly. "That new can of Monster Blood your parents sent you from Europe — it really is hidden away?"

Andy nodded. "On the top shelf of a closet in the basement. Way in the back," she told him. "The can is shut tight. No way the stuff can get out."

He stared hard at her, studying her face.

"Don't *look* at me like that!" she cried. She balled up the sandwich tinfoil and tossed it at him. "I'm telling the truth. The Monster Blood is totally hidden away. You don't have to worry about it."

Evan relaxed. He pulled the Fruit Roll-Up from his lunch bag and started to unwrap it. "You owe me now," he said softly.

"Excuse me?"

"You owe me for playing that stupid joke," Evan said.

"Oh, yeah? What do I have to do?" Andy demanded.

"Come with me after school. To Kermit's," Evan said.

Andy made a disgusted face.

"Please," Evan added.

"Okay," she said. "Kermit isn't that bad when I'm around."

Evan held up the sticky Fruit Roll-Up. "Want this? I *begged* my mom not to buy the green ones!"

*   *   *

After school, Evan and Andy walked together to Kermit's house. It was a gray day, threatening rain. The air felt heavy and wet, as humid as summer.

Evan led the way across the street. He started to cut through the backyards — but stopped. "Let's go the front way," he instructed. "Conan might be hanging out in back. Waiting for us."

"Don't say *us*," Andy muttered. She shifted her backpack to the other shoulder. She scratched her arm. "Ow. Look at this."

Evan lowered his eyes to the large red bump on Andy's right arm. "What is that? A mosquito bite?"

Andy scratched it some more. "I guess so. It itches like crazy."

"You're not supposed to scratch it," Evan told her.

"Thanks, Doc," she replied sarcastically. She scratched it even harder to annoy him.

A few sprinkles of rain came down as they made their way up Kermit's driveway. Evan opened the front door and stepped into the living room.

"Kermit — are you here?"

No reply.

A sour smell attacked Evan's nostrils. He pressed his fingers over his nose. "Yuck. Do you smell that?"

275

Andy nodded, her face twisted in disgust. "I think it's coming from the basement."

"For sure," Evan muttered. "Kermit must already be in his lab."

"Kermit? Hey — Kermit, what are you doing down there?" Evan called out.

Holding their noses, they made their way quickly down the stairs. The basement was divided into two rooms. To the right stood the laundry room and furnace; to the left the rec room with Kermit's lab set up along the back wall.

Evan hurried across the tiled floor into the lab. He spotted Kermit behind his lab table, several beakers of colored liquids in front of him. "Kermit — what's that disgusting smell?" he demanded.

As Evan and Andy ran up to the lab table, Kermit poured a yellow liquid into a green liquid. "Uh-oh!" he cried, staring down at the bubbling mixture.

Behind his glasses, his eyes grew wide with horror.

"Run!" Kermit screamed. "Hurry! Get out! It's going to BLOW!"

# 6

The liquid swirled and bubbled.

Kermit ducked under the lab table.

With a cry of horror, Evan spun round. Grabbed Andy's hand. Started to pull her to the stairs.

But he had only taken a step when he stumbled over Dogface, Kermit's huge sheepdog.

"Oof!" Evan felt the wind knocked out of him as he fell over the dog and landed facedown on the tile floor. He gasped. Struggled to choke in a mouthful of air.

The room tilted and swayed.

"It's going to BLOW!" Kermit's shrill warning rang in Evan's ears.

He finally managed to take a deep breath. Raised himself to one knee. Turned back to the lab table.

And saw Andy standing calmly in the center of the rec room, her hands at her waist.

"Andy — it's going to BLOW!" Evan choked out.

She rolled her eyes. "Evan, really," she muttered, shaking her head. "Did you really fall for that?"

"Huh?" Evan gazed past her to the long glass table.

Kermit had climbed back to his feet. He was leaning with both elbows on the table. And he had the grin on his face. *That* grin.

The twisted grin with the two front teeth sticking out. The grin Evan hated more than any grin in the world.

"Yeah, Evan," Kermit repeated, mimicking Andy, "did you really fall for that?" He burst into his squealing-high laugh that sounded like a pig stuck in a fence.

Evan pulled himself up, muttering under his breath. Dogface hiccupped. The dog's tongue tumbled out, and he began to pant loudly.

Evan turned to Andy. "I didn't really fall for it," he claimed. "I knew it was another one of Kermit's dumb jokes. I was just seeing if *you* believed it."

"For sure." Andy rolled her eyes again. She was doing a lot of eye-rolling this afternoon, Evan realized.

Evan and Andy stepped up to the table. It was littered with bottles and glass tubes, beakers and jars — all filled with colored liquids.

On the wall behind the table stood a high bookshelf. The shelves were also jammed with bottles and jars of liquids and chemicals. Kermit's mixtures.

"I was only a few minutes late getting here," Evan told Kermit. "From now on, don't do anything. Just wait for me." He sniffed the air. "What's that really gross smell?"

Kermit grinned back at him. "I didn't notice it until *you* came in!" he joked.

Evan didn't laugh. "Give me a break," he muttered.

Andy scratched her mosquito bite. "Yeah. No more jokes today, Kermit."

The big sheepdog hiccupped again.

"I'm mixing up something to cure Dogface's hiccups," Kermit announced.

"Oh, no!" Evan replied sharply. "No way! I can't let you give the dog one of your mixtures to drink."

"It's a very simple hiccup cure," Kermit said, pouring a blue liquid into a green liquid. "It's just maglesium harposyrate and ribotussal polythorbital. With a little sugar for sweetness."

"No way," Evan insisted. "You're not giving Dogface anything to drink but water. It's too dangerous."

Kermit ignored him and continued to mix chemicals from one glass beaker into another. He glanced up at Andy. "What's wrong with your arm?"

"It's a really big mosquito bite," Andy told him. "It itches like crazy."

"Let me see it," Kermit urged.

Andy eyed him suspiciously. "Why?"

Kermit grabbed Andy's hand and tugged her closer. "Let me see it," he insisted.

"It's just a mosquito bite," Andy said.

"I have some of that blue shrinking mixture left," Kermit announced. "The stuff I shrank Conan's shirt with."

"Don't remind me," Evan groaned.

"It'll shrink your mosquito bite," Kermit told Andy. He picked up the beaker.

"You're going to pour that stuff on my arm?" Andy cried. "I don't think so!"

She tried to step away.

But Kermit grabbed her arm. And poured.

The blue liquid spread over the mosquito bite.

"No! Oh, no!" Andy shrieked.

# 7

"My arm!" Andy shrieked. "What did you *do* to me?"

Evan lurched to the lab table, nearly stumbling over the dog again. He grabbed Andy's arm and examined it. "It — it —" he stammered.

"It's gone!" Andy cried. "The mosquito bite — it's gone!"

Evan stared at Andy's arm. Perfectly smooth, except for a few drips of the blue liquid.

"Kermit — you're a *genius*!" Andy cried. "That mixture of yours shrank the mosquito bite away!"

"Told you," Kermit replied, grinning happily.

"You can make a fortune!" Andy exclaimed. "Don't you realize what you've done? You've invented the greatest cure for mosquito bites ever!"

Kermit held up the beaker. He tilted it one way, then the other. "Not much left," he said softly.

"But you can mix up some more — right?" Andy demanded.

Kermit frowned. "I'm not sure," he said softly.

"I think I can mix up a new batch. But I'm not sure. I didn't write down what I put in it."

He scratched his white-blond hair and stared at the empty glass beaker, twitching his nose like a mouse, thinking hard.

Dogface let out another loud hiccup. The hiccup was followed by a howl. Evan saw that the poor dog was getting very unhappy about the hiccups. Dogface was a big dog — and so he had big hiccups that shook his sheepdog body like an earthquake.

"I'd better get to work on the hiccup cure," Kermit announced. He pulled some jars of chemicals off the shelf and started to open them.

"Whoa. Wait a minute," Evan told him. "I told you, Kermit — I can't let you feed anything to the dog. Aunt Dee will *kill* me if —"

"Oh, let him try!" Andy interrupted. She rubbed her smooth arm. "Kermit is a genius, Evan. You have to let a genius work."

Evan glared at her. "Whose side are you on?" he demanded in a loud whisper.

Andy didn't answer. She unzipped her orange-and-blue backpack and pulled out some papers. "I think I'll do my math homework while Kermit mixes up his hiccup cure."

Kermit's eyes lit up excitedly behind his glasses. "Math? Do you have math problems?"

Andy nodded. "It's a take-home equations exam. Very hard."

Kermit set down the test tubes and beakers. He hurried out from behind the lab table. "Can I do the problems for you, Andy?" he asked eagerly. "You know I love to do math problems."

Andy flashed Evan a quick wink. Evan frowned back at her. He shook his head.

So *that's* why Andy is being so nice to Kermit! Evan told himself. It was all a trick. A trick to get Kermit to do the math test for her.

Kermit could never resist math problems. His parents had to buy him stacks and stacks of math workbooks. He could spend an entire afternoon doing all the problems in the workbooks — *for fun*!

Dogface hiccupped.

Kermit grabbed the math test from Andy's hand. "Please let me do the equations," he begged. "Pretty please?"

"Well . . . okay," Andy agreed. She flashed Evan another wink.

Evan scowled back at her. Andy is going to get in trouble for this, he thought. Andy is a *terrible* math student. It's her worst subject. Mrs. McGrady is going to get very suspicious when Andy gets every problem right.

But Evan didn't say anything. What was the point?

Kermit was already scribbling answers on the page, solving the equations as fast as he could read them. His eyes were dancing wildly. He was breathing hard. And he had a happy grin on his face.

"All done," he announced.

Wow, he's fast! Evan thought. He finished that math test in the time it would take me to write my name at the top of the page!

Kermit handed the pencil and math pages back to Andy. "Thanks a lot," she said. "I really need a good grade in math this term."

"Cheater," Evan whispered in her ear.

"I just did it for Kermit," Andy whispered back. "He loves doing math problems. So why shouldn't I give him a break?"

"Cheater," Evan repeated.

Dogface hiccupped. Then he let out a pained howl.

Kermit returned to his lab table. He poured a yellow liquid into a red liquid. It started to smoke. Then it turned bright orange.

Andy tucked the math test into her backpack.

Kermit poured the orange liquid into a large glass beaker. He picked up a tiny bottle, turned it upside down, and emptied silvery crystals into the beaker.

Evan stepped up beside Kermit. "You can't feed that to Dogface," Evan insisted. "I really mean it. I won't let you give it to him."

Kermit ignored him. He stirred the mixture until it turned white. Then he added another powder that made it turn orange again.

"You have to listen to me, Kermit," Evan said. "I'm in charge, right?"

Kermit continued to ignore him.

Dogface hiccupped. His white furry body quivered and shook.

"Let Kermit work," Andy told Evan. "He's a genius."

"Maybe he's a genius," Evan replied. "But I'm in charge. Until Kermit's mom gets home, I'm the boss."

Kermit poured the mixture into a red dog dish.

"I'm the boss," said Evan. "And the boss says no."

Kermit lowered the dog dish to the floor.

"The boss says you can't feed that to Dogface," Evan said.

"Here, boy! Here, boy!" Kermit called.

"No way!" Evan cried. "No way the dog is drinking that!"

Evan made a dive for the bowl. He planned to grab it away.

But he dove too hard — and went sliding under the lab table.

Dogface lowered his head to the dog dish and began lapping up the orange mixture.

Evan spun around and stared eagerly at the dog. All three of them were waiting . . . waiting . . . waiting to see what would happen.

Dogface licked the bowl clean. Then he stared up at Kermit, as if to say, "Thank you."

Kermit petted the big dog's head. He smoothed the white, curly fur from in front of Dogface's eyes. The fur fell right back in place. Dogface licked Kermit's hand.

"See? The hiccups are gone," Kermit declared to Evan.

Evan stared at the dog. He waited a few seconds more. "You're right," he confessed. "The hiccups are gone."

"It was a simple mixture," Kermit bragged. "Just a little tetrahydropodol with some hydradroxilate crystals and an ounce of megahydracyl oxyneuroplat. Any child could do it."

"What a genius!" Andy exclaimed.

Evan started to say something. But Dogface interrupted with a sharp yip.

Then, without warning, the big sheepdog sprang forward. With another shrill yip, Dogface raised his enormous front paws — and leaped on to Kermit.

Kermit let out a startled cry and stumbled back against the wall. Bottles and jars shook on the shelves behind him.

Dogface began barking wildly, uttering shrill, excited yips. The dog jumped again, as if trying to leap into Kermit's arms.

"Down, boy! Down!" Kermit squealed.

The dog jumped again.

The shelves shook. Kermit sank to the floor.

"Down, boy! Down!" Kermit shrieked, covering his head with both arms. "Stop it, Dogface! Stop jumping!"

The excited dog used his head to push Kermit's arm away. Then he began licking Kermit's face frantically. Then he began nipping at his T-shirt.

"Stop! Yuck! Stop!" Kermit struggled to get away. But the big dog had Kermit pinned to the floor.

"What's going on?" Andy cried. "What's gotten into that dog?"

"Kermit's mixture!" Evan replied. He dove at the dog, grabbed Dogface with both hands, and tried to tug him off Kermit.

Dogface spun around. With another high-pitched yip, he bounded away, running at full speed across the basement.

"Stop him!" Kermit cried. "He's out of control! He'll break something!"

CRAAAASH.

A shelf of canning jars toppled to the floor.

Barking loudly, the dog bounded away from the shelf and began running in wide circles, his big paws clomping on the tile floor. Round and round, as if chasing his tail.

"Dogface — whoa!' Evan called, chasing after the sheepdog. He turned back to Andy. "Help me! We've got to stop him! He's acting crazy!"

Dogface disappeared into the laundry room. "Dogface — come back here!" Evan called.

He burst into the laundry room in time to see the dog crash into the ironing board. It toppled over, along with a stack of clothes that had been resting on it. The iron clattered over the hard floor.

Dogface yelped and climbed out from under the spilled clothes. Spotting Evan, the dog's stubby tail began wagging — and he leaped across the room.

"No!" Evan screeched as the huge dog knocked him over backwards to the ground. Dogface frantically licked Evan's face.

Behind him, Evan heard Andy laugh. "Too much energy! He's acting like a crazy puppy!" she declared.

"He's too big to think he's a puppy!" Evan wailed.

Dogface was sniffing furiously under the washing machine. He pounced on a large black ant.

Then he turned and came bounding over to Andy and Evan.

"Look out!" Evan cried.

But the big sheepdog lumbered past them, back into the other room. They followed him, watching him roll over a few times, kicking his big, furry paws in the air.

Then Dogface jumped to his feet — and came charging at Kermit.

"Whoa! Whoa, boy!" Kermit cried. He turned to Andy. "You're right. This is just the way Dogface acted when he was a puppy. The mixture gave him too much energy!"

The sheepdog crashed into an old couch against the wall. He climbed up onto the couch, sniffing the cushions, exploring. His stubby tail wagged furiously.

"Dogface, you're not a puppy!" Evan cried. "Please listen to me! You're too big to be a puppy! Dogface — please!"

"Look out!" Andy shrieked.

The dog jumped off the couch and went running full speed toward Kermit.

"No! Stop!" Kermit cried. He dove behind the lab table.

The dog tried to slow down. But his big legs were carrying him too fast.

Dogface crashed into the lab table. Bottles and beakers flew into the air, then crashed to the floor. The table toppled over on top of Kermit.

The shelves fell off the wall, and all of the jars and tubes and beakers tumbled to the floor, shattering, clattering, chemicals pouring out over the floor.

"What a mess!" Evan cried. "What a horrible mess!"

He turned — and let out a loud gasp.

Aunt Dee stood in the doorway. Her mouth was opened wide in surprise, and her eyes nearly bulged out of her head.

"What on Earth is going on down here?" she shrieked.

"Uh . . . well . . ." Evan started.

How could he begin to explain? And if he did find a way to explain, would Aunt Dee believe him?

Aunt Dee pressed her hands against her waist and tapped one foot on the floor. "What has happened here?" she demanded angrily.

"Uh . . . well . . ." Evan repeated.

Kermit spoke up first. He pointed an accusing finger at Evan. "Evan was teasing the dog!" he cried.

# 9

Kermit's mom glared angrily at Evan. "I'm paying you to take care of Kermit," she said sternly. "Not to play silly jokes on the dog and wreck my house."

"But — but — but —" Evan sputtered.

"Evan didn't do it!" Andy protested.

But her words were drowned out by Kermit, who let out a loud, phony wail — and burst into tears. "I tried to stop Evan!" Kermit sobbed. "I didn't want him to tease Dogface! But he wouldn't stop!"

Kermit rushed into his mother's arms. "It's okay," Aunt Dee said soothingly. "It's okay, Kermit. I'll make sure Evan never does it again."

She narrowed her eyes angrily at Evan as Kermit continued to sob, holding on to his mother like a baby.

Evan rolled his eyes at Andy. Andy replied with a shrug.

"Evan, you and Andy can start cleaning up this mess," Mrs. Majors ordered. "Kermit is a very sensitive boy. When you play jokes like this, it upsets him terribly."

Kermit sobbed even louder. His mom tenderly patted his head. "It's okay, Kermit. It's okay. Evan won't ever tease Dogface again," she whispered.

"But — but —" Evan sputtered.

How could Kermit put on such an act?

How could he deliberately get Evan into trouble? This mess wasn't Evan's fault. It was Kermit's!

"I really don't think —" Andy started.

But Aunt Dee raised a hand to silence her. "Just get this mess cleaned up — okay?"

She turned to Evan. "I'm not going to tell your mom about this, Evan," she said, still patting Kermit's head.

"Thanks," Evan muttered.

"I'm going to give you one more chance," she continued. "You don't really deserve it. If you weren't my nephew, I'd make you pay for all the damage. And I'd get someone else to take care of Kermit."

"Evan is mean," Kermit murmured, removing his glasses and wiping tears off his cheeks. "Evan is really mean."

What a little rat! Evan thought. But he remained silent, his eyes lowered to the floor.

"Kermit, let's get you cleaned up," Aunt Dee

said, leading him to the stairs. "Then we'll have to give the dog a bath."

She turned back to Evan and pointed a finger at him. "One more chance," she warned. "One more chance."

In the corner, Dogface let out a loud hiccup.

"See how you've upset the dog?" Kermit's mom called to Evan. "You've given poor Dogface the hiccups!"

"But — but —" Evan sputtered again.

As Evan struggled to find words to defend himself, Kermit and his mom disappeared up the stairs.

Two hours later, Andy and Evan wearily headed for home.

"What a mess," Evan moaned. "Look at me. I'm covered in chemicals."

"Two hours," Andy muttered. "Two hours to clean up the basement. And Dogface stood there watching us, hiccupping the whole time."

"Kermit is such a little creep," Evan said, kicking a stone across the sidewalk.

Andy shook her head bitterly. "Do you have any more cousins like him?"

"No," Evan replied. "Kermit is one of a kind."

"He's such a little liar," Andy said.

"Hey — you stuck up for him," Evan accused. "You said he was a genius, remember? You were so happy that he did your math problems for you, you thought he was wonderful."

Andy shifted her backpack onto her other shoulder. A smile crossed her face. "I forgot all about the math problems," she said. "Kermit may be a little creep — but he's also a genius. I'm going to get an A in math!" She let out a happy cheer.

"Winners never cheat, and cheaters never win," Evan muttered.

Andy gave him a playful shove. "Did you just make that up? It's very catchy."

"Give me a break," Evan growled. He turned and made his way up his driveway without saying good-bye.

Andy called him two nights later. "Your cousin Kermit is a total creep!" She shouted so loudly, Evan had to hold his phone away from his ear.

"Do you know what he did? Do you know what he did?" Andy shrieked.

"No. What?" Evan asked softly.

"He did all the math equations wrong," Andy cried.

"Excuse me?" Evan wasn't sure he heard correctly. "The genius got everything wrong?"

"On purpose!" Andy declared. "He got them wrong on purpose. He made up answers for all of them! He didn't even read the problems. He just wrote down stupid answers."

"But why?" Evan demanded.

"Why? Why? Because he's Kermit!" Andy screamed.

Evan swallowed hard. Poor Andy, he thought. Now she will fail in math.

"What a mean, rotten trick!" Andy shrieked into the phone. "Mrs. McGrady called me up to her desk and asked me to explain my answers. She asked me how I could possibly be so totally off on every single equation."

Andy sighed bitterly. "Of course I couldn't answer her. I just stood there with my mouth open. I think I drooled on her desk!"

"After we left his house, Kermit probably laughed his head off," Evan said.

"That brat has such a sick sense of humor," Andy wailed. "We have to pay him back, Evan. We really have to."

"Yeah. We do," Evan agreed.

"We have to get out the Monster Blood," Andy urged. "We have to use the Monster Blood to pay him back."

"Yeah. We do," Evan agreed.

# 10

Evan called Andy back later that night. "I changed my mind," he said. "I don't want to use the Monster Blood."

"What's your problem?" Andy demanded. "Kermit deserves it. You know he does."

"Monster Blood is too dangerous," Evan told her. "It turned Cuddles the hamster into a giant, roaring monster. I don't want to turn Kermit into a giant, roaring monster."

"Neither do I!" Andy exclaimed. "I don't want to *feed* it to him, Evan. I just want to slip a tiny bit into one of his mixtures. He thinks he's so smart and can do anything. I want to see Kermit's face when his mixture goes berserk!"

She laughed gleefully.

What an evil laugh, Evan thought.

"It'll be awesome!" Andy exclaimed.

"Forget about it," Evan insisted. "I have nightmares about Monster Blood almost every night.

I don't want to see that stuff again, Andy. I really don't. Leave it locked up — please!"

"But you *said* we could do it!" Andy pleaded.

"I made a mistake," Evan told her. "Don't take it out of the closet, Andy. Leave it safe and sound in its can — okay?"

Andy didn't reply.

"Okay?" Evan demanded. "Okay?"

"Okay," Andy finally agreed.


"We're going to play outside today, Kermit," Evan said firmly. "It's a beautiful day, and we're going to go out and not stay in the stupid basement. Get it?"

It was a sunny, warm Thursday afternoon. Golden sunlight filtered down through the dust-covered basement windows up near the ceiling.

Standing behind his lab table, arranging his jars and bottles of chemicals, Kermit muttered something to himself.

"No argument," Andy added. "We're going outside even if Evan and I have to drag you out."

"But I have a mixture I want to try," Kermit whined.

"You need some sunshine," Evan told him. "Look how pale you are. You look just like a white mouse."

Kermit was wearing a huge olive-colored T-shirt over baggy brown shorts. With his white-blond hair, beady eyes, and buck teeth, he looked more like a rat in human clothes.

He frowned, hurt by Evan's description.

"Okay. I'll go outside with you," he murmured unhappily.

"Yaay!" Andy whooped. It was the first time Kermit had ever agreed to leave his basement lab.

"But first I have to have a drink," Kermit said. He stepped out from behind the lab table and made his way toward the basement stairs. "You want an orange soda?"

"Yeah. Sure," Evan replied. He and Andy followed Kermit up the stairs to the kitchen.

"I can't believe he agreed to go out and play," Andy whispered. "Do you think he's sick or something?"

"Maybe he feels bad about the mean tricks he's pulled," Evan whispered.

The kitchen phone rang. Evan answered it. It was the wrong number.

He hung up the phone. He and Andy stepped up to the counter. Andy was wearing pink jeans, a yellow sleeveless T-shirt, and bright orange high-tops.

Kermit had already poured out three glasses of orange soda. The soda was the same color as Andy's high-tops, Evan noticed. They all drank the soda down quickly.

"I was really thirsty," Kermit said. Evan didn't pay any attention to the strange smile on Kermit's face. After all, Kermit *always* had a strange smile on his face.

"This orange soda is very sweet," Andy commented. She made a face. "Too sweet! It makes my teeth itch!"

Kermit laughed. "I think it's good," he said.

They set their glasses down in the sink and stepped out the back door. Evan found a red Frisbee on the back stoop. He flipped it to Andy.

Andy trotted across the backyard and flipped it back to Evan. "Let's play keep-away from Kermit!" she cried.

"Hey — no way!" Kermit protested. "Toss it to me!"

Andy sent the Frisbee flying over Kermit's head to Evan. Kermit made a wild grab for it, but it sailed out of his reach. It hit Evan's hands, but Evan dropped it.

Andy started to laugh.

"What's so funny?" Evan demanded.

Andy shrugged. "I don't know." She let out another giggle.

Evan flipped the Frisbee to Kermit. It bounced off Kermit's chest.

This kid is a real klutz, Evan thought. It's because he never plays sports. He never comes up out of his basement.

Andy uttered a high-pitched laugh.

Evan started to laugh, too.

Kermit picked up the Frisbee. He tried to toss

it to Andy, but the Frisbee sailed way over her head. It hit the side of the garage and bounced off.

Evan and Andy both laughed harder.

Evan trotted over to the garage. He sent a sidearm toss toward Andy. She missed, and the Frisbee flew into the low hedges at the side of the yard.

Andy didn't chase after it. She was laughing too hard.

Evan laughed even harder. Tears ran down his cheeks.

What's happening to me? he wondered, suddenly feeling frightened.

Why can't I stop laughing? What's going on?

Kermit grinned at both of them. *That* grin!

Evan laughed even harder. So hard, his stomach hurt.

Something is wrong, Evan realized. Something is terribly wrong.

"K-Kermit — why are we l-laughing?" he stammered.

Andy wiped tears from her eyes. She held her sides and laughed some more.

"Why are we laughing?" Evan demanded.

"I gave you my laughing mixture," Kermit told them. "I put it in the orange soda."

Evan tossed back his head and laughed. Andy giggled so hard, she choked. But she kept on laughing.

This isn't funny. This is scary, Evan thought. But he let out a shrill giggle.

"How — how long are we going to laugh like this, Kermit?" Evan managed to ask.

"Probably forever," Kermit replied, flashing his famous toothy grin.

# 11

Evan took a deep breath and tried to hold it. But the laughter burst out of him so hard, his chest ached.

Laughing giddily, Andy made a grab for Kermit.

Kermit ducked out of her reach and went scampering toward the fence at the back of the yard.

Evan shook his head hard, trying to shake off the effect of the laughter potion. But it didn't help. He laughed until tears rolled down his face.

Andy chased after Kermit, laughing shrilly.

Evan followed, gasping for breath. I can't breathe, he realized. I'm laughing so hard, I can't breathe.

"K-Kermit —!" Evan choked out. "You've got to s-stop it!" A high giggle burst out of his throat. "You've g-got to!"

"I don't know how," Kermit replied calmly.

Andy and Evan laughed in reply.

302

"It's awesome — isn't it!" Kermit declared happily. "The mixture works perfectly!"

Andy made a grab for Kermit's throat.

Again, Kermit ducked away.

Andy and Evan laughed a little harder.

Andy picked up the Frisbee and tried to heave it at Kermit. But she was laughing too hard to control it. The Frisbee sailed over the fence.

"Hey — get that back. That's mine!" Kermit demanded.

Evan and Andy laughed.

A familiar face popped up on the other side of the fence.

"Conan!" Kermit cried.

Conan peered first at Andy, then at Evan. "Are you looking at my yard?" he asked Evan.

Evan struggled to hold it in. But he let out a high, shrill laugh.

"Didn't I warn you last week about looking at my yard?" Conan demanded.

Evan laughed.

"Conan, give me back my Frisbee," Kermit whined.

Conan leaped over the fence. Evan saw that he had the Frisbee in his left hand. Conan quickly hid the Frisbee behind his back.

Andy and Evan laughed. Andy wiped tears from her eyes. Her whole body shook with laughter.

"Give me back my Frisbee," Kermit insisted.

Conan ignored him. "What's so funny?" he asked Andy and Evan. He balled his right hand into a fist.

Andy giggled.

If we keep laughing, he'll pound us! Evan realized. But he couldn't help himself. He let out a loud belly laugh.

"Hey — I want my Frisbee!" Kermit whined.

"I don't have your Frisbee," Conan lied, keeping his left hand behind his back.

Evan tossed his head back and laughed.

"Yes, you do. It's behind your back," Kermit said. "Give it back, Conan."

"Who's going to make me?" Conan demanded in a low, menacing voice.

Evan let out a high giggle. Andy laughed, too.

"They are!" Kermit replied to Conan. "They're going to make you!" He turned to Evan. "Make Conan give back my Frisbee."

Evan laughed in reply.

"What's so funny?" Conan asked again.

Andy shook her head. "Nothing. Nothing's funny," she choked. Then she burst out laughing.

"I don't like people laughing at me," Conan said.

*This is horrible!* Evan thought. One more laugh — and Conan could explode!

Evan let out a long hyena laugh.

"I really go ballistic when people laugh at me," Conan warned.

Evan and Andy laughed some more.

"I have to *hurt* people who laugh at me," Conan threatened.

Evan and Andy laughed in reply.

Conan turned to Kermit. "Why are they laughing like that?"

Kermit shrugged. "Beats me. I guess they think you're funny."

"Oh, is that right?" Conan shouted angrily, turning back to Evan and Andy. "You two think I'm *funny*?"

Evan and Andy held their sides and laughed.

"Give me my Frisbee!" Kermit shouted.

"Okay. Go chase it." Conan flung the Frisbee across the hedges. It sailed over two yards and disappeared in a clump of evergreen shrubs.

Kermit went running after it.

Conan scowled at Evan and Andy. "I'm going to count to three," he growled. "And if you don't stop laughing by the count of three, I'll *make* you stop!" He raised both fists to show them *how* he would make them stop.

"One . . ." Conan said.

Evan laughed. Andy pressed her hand over mouth, but couldn't stop a giggle from escaping.

"Two . . ." Conan counted, his face twisted in anger.

I've *got* to stop laughing! Evan told himself. I'm in serious trouble here. Serious.

He opened his mouth, and a booming "Hahahahaha!" burst out.

Andy had *both* hands pressed over her mouth. But it didn't stop the snickers and guffaws from pouring out her nose.

Kermit came jogging back into the backyard. "I can't find the Frisbee," he complained. "Somebody has to help me. I can't find it anywhere."

Conan turned to him. "You *sure* you don't know why they're laughing like that?" he asked.

Kermit shook his head. "They told me they think you're funny-looking," he told Conan. "I guess that's why they're laughing."

I don't believe this! Evan thought, so angry he wanted to explode. That little creep! How can he do this to us?

Conan turned back to Andy and Evan. "Last chance to stop," he said. He took a deep breath, stretching out his big, powerful chest. "Three!"

Andy laughed.

Evan laughed even harder.

"I warned you," Conan growled.

# 12

Andy phoned Evan that night to see how he was feeling. Evan had to hold the phone away from his ear. His head hurt too much to press a phone against it.

"I guess I'll survive," Evan groaned. "I'm getting used to looking in the mirror and seeing a pile of coleslaw where my head used to be."

Andy sighed. "Your cousin is such a creep," she said.

"How are *you* feeling?" Evan asked. "How long did it take you to climb down from the tree?"

"Not too many hours," Andy replied weakly.

Conan had said he never hit girls. So he picked Andy up and stuck her onto a high tree branch.

"At least Conan stopped us from laughing," Evan said. "My stomach still hurts from laughing so hard."

"Mine, too," Andy told him. "I'm never going to laugh again. Never. If someone tells me the funniest joke in the world, I'll just smile and say, 'Very funny.' "

"I can't believe Kermit did that to us," Evan moaned.

"I believe it," Andy replied dryly. "Kermit will do anything to get us into trouble. That's what he lives for — getting us into major trouble."

"Did you hear that little mouse laughing while Conan pounded me into the ground?" Evan asked.

"I was up in the tree, remember? I could *see* him laughing!" Andy declared.

There was a long silence at the other end. And then Andy spoke in a hushed voice, just above a whisper, "Evan — are you ready to use the Monster Blood on Kermit?"

"Yeah," Evan replied without having to think about it even for a second. "I'm ready."

# 13

After school the next afternoon, Evan and Andy found Kermit behind his lab table as usual. "Hi, Kermit," Evan called, tossing his backpack down and stepping up to the table.

Kermit didn't glance up. He was busy stirring ingredients in a large mixing bowl, using a large wooden spoon.

Evan peered into the bowl. It looked like pie dough in there. It was thick and gooey and yellowish.

Kermit hummed to himself as he stirred.

Andy was wearing a sleeveless, hot pink T-shirt over bright yellow shorts and matching yellow sneakers. She stepped up beside Evan and peeked into the bowl. "Making a pie?" she asked.

Kermit ignored her, too. He kept stirring and humming, stirring and humming.

Finally he stopped and glanced up at Evan. "I told my mom you lost my Frisbee," he said, sneering. "She says you have to get me a new one."

"Huh? Me?" Evan cried.

Andy walked around to Kermit's side of the table. She lowered her head to the bowl. "Smells lemony," she said. "What is it, Kermit? Is it some kind of dough?"

"It was your fault my Frisbee got lost," Kermit told Evan, ignoring Andy's questions. "Mom says you're a very bad baby-sitter."

Evan let out an angry cry. He balled his hands into fists. He struggled to keep himself from strangling Kermit.

It was a real struggle.

"Mom wanted to know who drank up all the orange soda," Kermit continued. "I told her you and Andy drank it."

"Kermit!" Evan shrieked. "You played a horrible trick on us yesterday! You put chemicals in our orange soda! You made us laugh and laugh and laugh — until it hurt. Then you got us in major trouble with Conan! Did you tell your mom that? Did you? *Did you?*"

Kermit put his hands over his ears. "Don't shout, Evan," he whined. "You know I have very sensitive ears."

Another angry growl escaped Evan's throat. He felt about to explode with rage.

"I told my mom that you shout at me all the time," Kermit continued. "Mom says you're just immature. She thinks you're very babyish. She

310

only lets you stay with me because you're my cousin."

Kermit picked up the wooden spoon and started to stir the doughy mixture again.

Evan spun away, trying to control his anger.

I'm glad Andy and I are going to do what we're going to do, he thought. I'm glad we're going to give Kermit a little scare. He's been asking for it. He really has. And now he's going to get it.

Evan walked over to his backpack. He unzipped it and pulled out a candy bar. "Mmmm. A Choc-O-Lik Bar," he murmured. He crossed back to the lab table, unwrapping the candy bar as he walked.

Standing in front of Kermit, Evan took a big bite of the chocolate bar. It made a loud *crunch* as his teeth sank into it. "Mmmmmm!" he proclaimed. "Choc-O-Lik Bars are cool."

The candy bar was part of the plot.

Evan knew that the Choc-O-Lik Bar was Kermit's favorite.

The candy bar was supposed to distract Kermit. While Kermit stared at the candy and pleaded with Evan to give him a bite, Andy would slip a tiny chunk of Monster Blood into Kermit's mixture.

Evan crunched the candy bar loudly, making lip-smacking sounds as he chewed.

Kermit glanced up. He stopped stirring the yellowish dough. "Is that really a Choc-O-Lik Bar?" he asked.

Evan nodded. "Yeah. Sure is."

"My favorite," Kermit said.

"I know," Evan replied. He took another crunchy bite.

Kermit stared at the candy bar.

Andy stood beside Kermit. Evan saw the blue container of Monster Blood in her hand. Just *seeing* the can made Evan shiver.

So many bad memories. So many nightmares.

The green gunk inside the can was so dangerous.

"Can I have a piece of the Choc-O-Lik Bar?" Kermit asked Evan.

Andy lifted off the top of the Monster Blood container.

"Maybe. Maybe not," Evan told Kermit.

Andy stuck two fingers in the container. She pulled out a gooey green hunk of Monster Blood.

"Please? Pretty please?" Kermit begged Evan.

Andy dropped the chunk of Monster Blood into Kermit's big bowl of dough. Then she quietly snapped the cap back on the container and slid it back into her bag.

Evan took another bite of the candy bar.

"You shouldn't eat a candy bar unless you have enough to share with everyone," Kermit scolded.

"You haven't been very nice to me," Evan told him. "So I'm not going to share."

Kermit started stirring the dough again. He stared angrily at Evan as he stirred. He didn't see the green Monster Blood being stirred up in the yellow dough.

Evan took another bite of the Choc-O-Lik Bar. Only a few bites left.

"I'm going to tell Mom you were mean to me," Kermit threatened. "I'm going to tell her you wouldn't share."

Evan shook his head. "See what I mean? You're not nice to me, Kermit. If you were nice to me, I'd share *all* my candy bars with you."

Andy winked at Evan. Then she peered into the bowl.

Kermit stirred and stirred.

Andy's expression became tense. She gripped the edge of the table with both hands. Evan saw her nibble her bottom lip.

Watching Kermit stir the Monster Blood, Evan suddenly had a heavy feeling in his stomach.

We've done it, he thought.

We've opened another can of Monster Blood.

He stared at the yellow dough in the bowl. It made a soft plopping sound as Kermit pushed the wooden spoon through it.

Now what? Evan wondered.

*Now* what's going to happen?

# 14

Kermit stirred the yellow dough. The big wooden spoon scraped the bowl. The doughy mixture plopped softly, tumbling and swirling as Kermit worked.

Andy kept nibbling her lower lip, her eyes locked on the bowl. Her brown hair fell over her face. But she made no move to push it back.

Evan watched from the other side of the table. His heart began doing flip-flops in his chest. He took another bite of the chocolate bar.

He chewed as quietly as possible. He didn't want to disturb Kermit. As he chewed, he stared at the bowl.

He and Andy were waiting. Waiting to see what the little hunk of Monster Blood would do to Kermit's mixture.

Waiting to see the look of horror on Kermit's face.

Waiting to pay him back for being such a little monster.

Kermit didn't seem to notice how quiet it had become in the basement. Dogface came lumbering in, panting loudly, his paws thudding on the tile floor.

No one turned to look at him.

The dog hiccupped, turned, and padded out of the room.

Evan bit off another chunk of the candy bar.

Kermit stirred, humming to himself. The spoon scraped the side of the bowl. The dough slapped against the edge.

And spilled over.

Kermit stopped stirring. "Weird," he muttered.

Evan's heart did a flip-flop up to his throat. "What's weird?" he asked.

"It grew," Kermit replied, scratching his white-blond hair. "Look."

Kermit pointed to the yellow dough with the wooden spoon. It plopped up over the top of the bowl.

"It — it's growing really fast!" Kermit declared.

Evan took a few steps closer. Andy leaned down to get a better look.

The dough rose up, shimmering and quivering.

"Wow!" Kermit cried. "It wasn't supposed to do this! It was supposed to turn sticky and black!"

Andy winked at Evan. Her brown eyes lit up excitedly. A smile spread across her face.

315

The yellow blob quivered up over the top of the bowl, as big as a beach ball.

How big was it going to get?

"Oh, wow! This is awesome!" Kermit declared.

The dough shimmered higher. Wider.

It rose up high over the bowl. It overflowed the sides.

Bigger. Bigger. It started to look like an enormous hot air balloon.

"It's taller than me!" Kermit declared. His voice had changed. He didn't sound excited now. He was beginning to sound frightened.

"We'd better stop it, I think," he murmured.

"How?" Andy asked. She stepped out from behind the lab table and joined Evan on the other side.

Andy grinned at Evan. She was enjoying the expression of fear on Kermit's face. Evan had to admit he enjoyed it, too.

The ball of yellow dough shimmered and shook, growing bigger every second. It bubbled up faster and faster, pressing Kermit back against the basement wall.

"Hey — help!" he sputtered.

Andy's grin grew wider. "He's terrified now," she whispered to Evan.

Evan nodded. He knew he was supposed to enjoy this. It was supposed to be sweet revenge.

But Evan was terrified, too.

How much bigger would the huge yellow blob

grow? Could they stop it? Or would it grow and grow and grow until it filled the entire basement?

"Evan — help me!" Kermit cried. "I'm trapped back here!"

The dough began to shake harder. It bobbed up against the basement ceiling.

Evan glanced down and realized he was still holding a chunk of candy bar in his hand. The chocolate had started to melt.

Evan started to pop the candy into his mouth — just as the giant dough ball exploded with a deafening roar.

# 15

"ULP!"

Evan swallowed hard as the doughy goop exploded. The force of the blast sent the candy chunk flying down his throat.

He started to cough and choke.

With a hard *splat*, globs of sticky dough hit him in the face. The yellow goo spread over his hair and covered his eyes.

"Hey!" Evan choked out. He frantically wiped the dough from his eyes, blinking hard.

He could taste it on his tongue. "Yuck!" He spit it out and rubbed the sticky stuff off his lips. Then he pulled thick wads of goo off his face.

"It's stuck to my hair!" Andy wailed.

"Help me! Help me!" Kermit's cries sounded as if they were coming from far away. Evan quickly saw why. Kermit was buried under a big heap of yellow goop.

Pulling dough from his hair, Evan hurried behind the lab table. He reached down with both hands and tugged Kermit up from under the dough.

"Wow. I'm kind of dizzy!" Kermit cried. He leaned heavily against the lab table. His hands slid in the yellow goo that covered the table.

"I'll never get it out of my hair!" Andy wailed, tugging at her hair with both hands. "Never!" She turned to Evan. "It wasn't supposed to explode. Just get big. I guess something in the dough made it blow up."

Wiping dough off the front of his T-shirt, Evan gazed around the basement. The yellow dough had splattered over everything. Now it dripped down the walls, making soft plopping sounds as it hit the floor.

"That was an awesome explosion!" Kermit declared. His eyeglasses were covered with yellow goop. He pulled them off and squinted around the room.

He turned to Andy. "Did you put something in the bowl?"

"Never mind," Andy replied, still pulling sticky yellow globs from her hair.

Kermit tugged her arm. "What was it? What did you put in my mixture?"

"Why do you want to know?" Andy demanded.

"So we can do that again!" Kermit declared gleefully. "It was so *awesome!*"

"No way we're doing it again!" Evan moaned.

Their revenge on Kermit hadn't exactly worked

319

out, Evan realized bitterly. Kermit should be in tears by now. Or he should be quivering in fear and terror.

Instead, his eyes were dancing with excitement and he was grinning from ear to ear.

We were total jerks! Evan thought sadly. Kermit is *loving* this!

Kermit pulled out a cloth and cleaned his glasses. "What a mess!" he declared, gazing around the room. "Evan, you're going to be in major trouble when Mom gets home."

Evan swallowed hard. He had forgotten about Kermit's mom.

She had given him one last chance to prove that he was a good baby-sitter.

Now she was going to come home to a basement splattered with sticky yellow goop from floor to ceiling. And Kermit was sure to tell her the whole thing was Evan's fault.

Aunt Dee will tell everyone in the world why she had to take the job away from me, Evan thought unhappily. And I'll never get another baby-sitting job as long as I live.

Bye-bye, Walkman, he thought grimly. No way he'd ever earn the money for one now.

"This is *your* fault!" he snapped at Andy, pointing an accusing finger at her. A spot of yellow dough stuck to his fingernail.

"*My* fault?" Andy shrieked. "*You're* the one who wanted to teach Kermit a lesson!"

"But *you're* the one who wanted to use the Monster Blood!" Evan cried.

"Look at my hair!" Andy wailed. "It's solid goop! It looks like I'm wearing a helmet! It's ruined! Ruined!" She uttered an angry growl.

Kermit giggled. He bent down and picked up a chunk of the sticky yellow dough. "Think fast!' he shouted — and heaved it at Evan.

The dough ball hit the front of Evan's T-shirt and stuck there. "Stop it, Kermit!" he shouted angrily.

"Let's have a dough fight!" Kermit suggested, grinning. He scooped up another handful of the stuff.

"No! No way! Stop it!" Evan cried. He pulled the dough ball off his T-shirt. "This is dangerous! We've got to clean this up!"

Kermit flung another big chunk of yellow goo at Evan.

Evan tried to dodge out of the way. But his sneakers slipped on a big, slimy puddle of goop, and he hit the floor hard. He landed on his side with a loud "OOF!"

Kermit let out a gleeful laugh. "That was awesome!" he declared. "What a shot!"

Andy hurried over and helped tug Evan to his feet. "Maybe we can vacuum it all up," she suggested. She turned to Kermit. "Where does your mom keep the vacuum cleaner?"

Kermit shrugged. "Beats me."

Evan leaned against the lab table. His hand rested in a puddle of dough, but he didn't care.

He suddenly felt strange.

His entire body started to tingle. His stomach felt queasy. He shut his eyes, trying to force the strange feeling away.

But the tingling grew stronger.

He heard a shrill whistling sound in his ears. His muscles started to ache. He could feel the blood throbbing at his temples.

"Maybe we can mop it up," Evan heard Andy say. But her voice sounded tiny and far away.

He turned to see her pick up a mop and bucket from against the basement wall.

That bucket is too tiny, Evan thought. Why does Andy want to use such a tiny mop?

The room tilted — to the right, then to the left.

Evan blinked hard, trying to straighten everything out.

His whole body buzzed, as if an electrical current were shooting through him. He shut his eyes and pressed both hands against his throbbing temples.

"Evan — aren't you going to help me?" Andy's voice sounded so faint, so far away. "Evan —?" he heard her call. "Evan —?"

When he opened his eyes, he saw that Andy and Kermit were staring up at him. Their expressions had changed. Their eyes bulged in fright and surprise. Their mouths were wide open.

"What's going on?" Evan demanded. His voice boomed through the basement, echoing off the concrete walls.

Andy and Kermit stared up at him. The tiny mop fell out of Andy's hand and clattered to the floor.

Such a tiny mop, Evan thought again, staring down at it. Such a tiny bucket.

And then he realized that Andy and Kermit were tiny, too.

"Oh!" A cry of surprise escaped Evan's throat.

Everyone is so small. Everything is so tiny.

It took Evan a long time to figure out what had happened.

But when it finally dawned on him, he let out a shriek of horror.

"Oh, no! No!" he moaned. "I'm *growing*! I'm growing bigger and bigger!"

# 16

Evan lowered his eyes to the floor. It seemed so far below.

"My — my legs —" he stammered.

Andy and Kermit still hadn't said a word. They stared up at him, their faces twisted in surprise.

Evan swallowed hard. "What's going on?" he cried. His voice boomed through the small room. "I must be eight feet tall!"

"You — you're a *giant*!" Kermit declared. He stepped forward and grabbed on to Evan's knee. "Me, too! Okay? Okay, Evan? Make me a giant, too!" he begged.

"Give me a break," Evan muttered. He picked up Kermit easily and set him down on top of the lab table.

Then Evan turned to Andy. "What am I going to do? This is terrible!"

"Not so loud!" Andy pleaded, covering her ears with her hands. "Please, Evan — try to whisper or something, okay?"

"What am I going to do?" Evan repeated, ignoring her plea.

Andy forced a smile. "Try out for basketball, I guess."

Evan balled his huge hands into huge fists. "I'm not in the mood for your sick sense of humor, Andy," he snapped.

His body started to tingle again. His muscles ached.

I'm growing even bigger, he realized.

Evan's throat suddenly felt very dry. He realized his knees were shaking. They made a loud banging sound as they hit together.

Don't panic! he instructed himself.

The first rule is — don't panic.

But why *shouldn't* he panic? His head was nearly pushing up against the basement ceiling.

Kermit stood up on top of the lab table. His white high-tops were splattered with yellow dough. They looked like little doll shoes to Evan.

"Make me a giant, too!" Kermit pleaded. "Why can't I be a giant?"

Evan stared down at his cousin. Kermit really *did* look like a little white mouse now.

Evan's body tingled harder. The room tilted and swayed again. "This is *your* fault, Andy!" he shouted.

Andy shrank back against the wall. "Huh? My fault?"

"You and your Monster Blood!" Evan thundered. "I — I swallowed some!"

Andy stared up at him. "How?"

"When Kermit's mixture exploded," Evan replied. "I was putting the candy bar in my mouth. The dough exploded. I started to choke. The dough hit me in the face. I remember I tasted it. It was on my lips. And — and —"

"And it had Monster Blood in it!" Andy finished his sentence for him. Her face filled with horror. "Oh, Evan. I'm sorry. I really am."

But then her face brightened. "The Monster Blood splashed on your clothes, too. That was lucky. They're growing with you."

Evan let out an exasperated sigh. "Lucky?" he cried. "You call this lucky? What if I keep growing and never stop?"

Kermit remained standing on the lab table. He stared up at Evan. "You mean if I eat some of the dough, I'll turn into a giant, too?" He bent down and scooped up a handful of dough.

"Don't you *dare*!" Evan screamed. He leaned over and flicked the dough out of Kermit's hand with two fingers. Then he hovered over Kermit, glaring at him menacingly. "I can squash you, Kermit. I really can," Evan warned.

"Okay, okay," Kermit muttered, his voice trembling. He slid off the table and stepped behind Andy.

Wow, Evan thought, I actually have Kermit

326

afraid of me! That's a first. Maybe growing so big isn't all bad!

His body tingled and vibrated. The whistling in his ears grew louder. He could feel himself grow some more.

He turned to see Dogface pad into the room. The big sheepdog looked like a tiny poodle.

The dog hiccupped. It sniffed at a yellow puddle of dough on the floor.

"No!" Evan cried. "Don't eat that! Dogface — no!"

He bent over and picked up the sheepdog.

Seeing a giant human lift him up easily off the floor, Dogface let out a yelp of terror. All four legs thrashed the air as the frightened dog struggled to break free.

But Evan cradled the sheepdog in one arm and held on to him tightly.

When he realized he couldn't escape from the giant, the dog's terrified yelps turned to quiet whimpers.

"Take Dogface out of here. Lock him outside," Evan ordered Kermit. He lowered the whimpering dog to the floor.

Kermit obediently led the dog away. Halfway to the stairs, he turned back to Evan. "Hey, you cured Dogface's hiccups!"

I guess I scared them out of him! Evan told himself.

Kermit led Dogface up the stairs. Evan turned

to Andy. "I *told* you to leave the Monster Blood in the closet!" he cried. "Now look at me!"

He had to duck his head. Otherwise it would brush against the ceiling.

"Who told you to *eat* the stuff?" Andy replied. "Why did you have to be eating that candy bar?"

"It was part of the plan — remember?" Evan snapped angrily. He uttered a bitter sigh. "Great plan we had!"

"I guess it didn't work out too well," Andy admitted.

"I guess it didn't," Evan muttered. "Now what will happen to me? What will Mom and Dad say?"

"What will you eat?" Andy added. "You'll probably have to eat sixteen meals a day! And where will you sleep? And how can you go to school? There aren't any desks big enough for you. And what will you wear? They'll have to make your T-shirts out of bedsheets!"

"You're not cheering me up," Evan murmured glumly.

He felt his body tingle. Again, he could feel his skin stretching, feel all of his muscles throb.

"Ow!" he cried out as the top of his head banged against the ceiling.

He had to lean over to rub his head.

"Evan — you're growing!" Andy exclaimed.

"I know. I know," Evan grumbled. The basement ceiling was at least nine feet high. Evan had to stoop to keep from banging the ceiling. That meant he was more than nine feet tall.

A shiver of fear shook his body. He glanced around the basement. "I have tc get out of here!" he cried.

Kermit returned to the room. He stopped and gawked at Evan. "You grew even more!" he cried. "I'll bet you weigh three hundred pounds!"

"I don't have time to weigh myself," Evan replied, rolling his eyes. "I have to get out of here. I'm so big, I can't stand up. I'm so big, I —"

He stopped. He felt himself grow a little more.

"I'm too big now!" he cried. "I'm trapped down here! There's no way I can get out!"

# 17

"Stay calm," Andy called up to him.

"Calm? How can I stay calm?" Evan shrieked. "I'm going to spend the rest of my life in this basement! I'm too big for the stairs!"

"Mom won't like that," Kermit said, shaking his head.

"Try the stairs!" Andy cried. "Maybe you can squeeze up if you hurry!"

Evan turned to the basement stairs. "I — I don't think I'll fit," he stammered. The stairway appeared very narrow. And Evan was now very wide.

"Come on," Andy urged. "We'll help you."

"You push and I'll pull," Kermit said, running to the stairs.

Evan lumbered toward the stairs. His sneakers thudded heavily on the tile floor. He stooped his shoulders to keep his head from crashing against the ceiling.

"Try not to grow any bigger!" Andy called, following closely behind him.

"Great advice!" Evan replied sarcastically. "Do you have any more advice like that?"

"Don't be nasty," Andy scolded. "I'm only trying to help you."

"You've already helped me more than enough," Evan grumbled.

He felt his body start to tingle. His muscles started to throb.

"No! Please — no!" He uttered a silent plea. I don't want to grow any more!

He sucked in a deep breath and held it. He shut his eyes tight and tried to concentrate — concentrate on not growing.

"I think I just saw you grow another few inches," Andy called to him. "You'd better hurry, Evan."

"How big is Evan going to get?" Kermit asked. He had climbed halfway up the stairs. "Is he going to get bigger than an elephant?"

"That's not helpful, Kermit," Evan muttered unhappily. "Please stop asking questions like that — okay?"

"If you get as big as an elephant, will you give me a ride?" Kermit demanded.

Evan glared angrily at his cousin. "Do you know what elephants do to mice?" he bellowed. Evan raised one foot and brought it down with a crunching *thud* to demonstrate to Kermit what elephants do to mice.

Kermit swallowed hard and didn't say anything more.

Evan walked over to the stairway. He glanced up the stairs. "I don't think I can make it," he told Andy. "I'm too big."

"Give it a try," she urged. "You've *got* to, Evan."

Evan stepped on to the first step. Leaning low, he raised himself to the next step.

"You're doing it!" Kermit cried happily. He stayed at the top of the stairs, watching Evan's progress eagerly.

Evan took another step. The wooden stairs creaked under his weight. He tried to lean on the banister. But it snapped beneath his hand.

He climbed two more steps.

He was a third of the way up when he became stuck.

His body was just too wide for the narrow stairway.

Kermit pulled both of Evan's hands. Andy pushed him from behind.

But they couldn't budge him.

"I — I can't move," Evan stammered. He felt panic choke his throat. "I'm jammed tight in here. There's no way I'll ever get out!"

Then he felt his body start to tingle. And he knew he was growing even more.

# 18

As Evan grew, he heard a cracking sound.

Soft at first. Then louder. Very close by.

He cried out as the wall to his left crumbled. His expanding body had broken the wall away.

As the wall cracked and fell, Evan took a deep breath and lurched up the stairs.

"Made it!" he cried as he squeezed through the doorway.

A few seconds later, he burst out through the kitchen door, into the sunlit backyard.

Dogface lay stretched out near the fence. The dog jumped to his feet as the gigantic Evan appeared. Frightened, Dogface gave a loud bark, his stubby tail wagging furiously, then turned and bolted from the yard.

Kermit and Andy followed Evan into the backyard, cheering and shouting, "You made it! You're free!"

Evan turned to face them. "But now what?" he

asked. "Now what do I do? I'm nearly as tall as the garage. How tall am I going to grow?"

Kermit stepped closer to Evan. "Look — I'm standing in your shade!" he declared.

Evan's shadow fell across the yard like the shadow of a tree trunk. "Kermit, give me a break," Evan muttered. "I have a little bit of a problem here, you know?"

"Maybe we should get you to a doctor," Andy suggested.

"A doctor?" Evan cried. "What could a doctor do for me?"

"Put you on a diet?" Andy joked.

Evan leaned over her, squinting down at her menacingly. "Andy, I'm warning you. One more bad joke, and —"

"Okay, okay." Andy raised her hands as if trying to shield herself from him. "Sorry. Just trying to keep it light."

"Evan isn't light. He's heavy!" Kermit chimed in. His idea of a joke.

Evan let out an unhappy growl. "I don't think a doctor can help me. I mean, I couldn't fit into a doctor's office."

"But maybe if we brought the can of Monster Blood along, the doctor could figure out an antidote," Andy suggested. "Some kind of cure."

Evan started to reply. But shrill voices on the other side of the tall wooden fence at the back of the yard made him stop.

"Cut it out, Conan!" a girl pleaded.

"Yeah. Leave us alone, Conan!" Evan heard a boy shout.

Evan lumbered over to the fence and peered into Conan's yard. He saw Conan Barber furiously swinging a baseball bat, swinging it hard, forcing a little boy and girl to back up against the fence.

"Let us go!" the little girl screamed. "Why are you so mean?"

Conan swung the bat, bringing it close to the boy and girl, making them cry out.

Evan leaned over the fence. His broad shadow fell over Conan. "Want to play ball with me, Conan?" Evan thundered.

The two little kids spun around. They stared up at the enormous Evan. It took them a long time to realize they were staring at a real, giant human.

Then they began to scream.

Conan's mouth dropped open and a strangled gurgling sound escaped his throat.

"Hey, Conan, how about a little batting practice?" Evan asked, his voice booming over the backyard. Evan reached over the fence and plucked the bat from Conan's hand.

The little boy and girl ran away screaming. They darted through the hedge at the side of Conan's yard and kept running until they vanished from view.

Evan took the bat and snapped it in two between his hands. It cracked apart like a toothpick.

Conan froze in place, staring up at Evan in disbelief. He pointed a trembling finger. "Evan — you — you — you —" he stammered.

Evan tossed the two pieces of the cracked bat at Conan's feet, forcing Conan to hop out of the way.

"You ate Monster Blood!" Conan accused. "That sticky green stuff. The stuff that Cuddles the hamster ate last year! You ate some — didn't you!"

Evan didn't want to be reminded of Cuddles the hamster. The little creature had turned into a huge, vicious beast after eating Monster Blood. Cuddles had returned to hamster size only because the Monster Blood was old and stale.

But the Monster Blood Evan had swallowed was new and fresh.

Now *I'm* a huge, vicious beast, Evan thought sadly.

"Are you crazy? Are you totally messed up? Why did you eat Monster Blood?" Conan demanded.

"It was an accident," Evan told him.

Conan continued to stare up at Evan, but his fearful expression faded. Conan suddenly started to laugh. "I'm glad it happened to you and not me!" he exclaimed.

"Huh? Why?" Evan demanded.

"Because I'm afraid of heights!" Conan replied. He laughed again. "I always thought you were a nerd, Evan!" Conan declared. "But now you're a BIG nerd!"

Evan let out an angry growl and lurched forward. He tried to climb over the fence. But he didn't step high enough. Conan's fence splintered beneath Evan's heavy sneaker.

"Hey —!" Conan cried in alarm.

He tried to turn and run, but Evan was too fast for him.

Evan grabbed Conan under the shoulders and lifted him off the ground as if he weighed nothing.

"Let go! Let go of me!" Conan screamed. He kicked his arms and legs like a baby.

"I never knew you were afraid of heights," Evan said. Holding Conan in both hands, he raised him high in the air.

"Let me go! Let me go!" Conan cried. "What are you going to do?"

"Let's see if you know how to fly!" Evan exclaimed.

"Noooooo!" Conan's shrill cry rose up over the yard. He kicked and thrashed as Evan raised him even higher. "Put me down! Put me down!"

"Okay," Evan agreed. "I'll put you down." He set Conan down on a high tree branch.

Conan clung to the trunk for dear life, trembling and crying. "Evan — don't leave me up here! Please! I told you, I'm afraid of heights! Evan — come back! Evan!"

A huge grin on his huge face, Evan turned away

337

from Conan. "That was a lot of fun!" he called down to his friends.

Conan continued to weep and wail up in the tree. Evan took a few steps toward the front yard. "That was excellent!" Evan said, still grinning. "Excellent!"

"Where are you going?" he heard Andy call up to him.

"Yeah! What are you going to do now?" Kermit asked eagerly.

"This is kind of cool!" Evan declared. Having his revenge on Conan had put him in a better mood. "Let's go see if we can have some more fun!"

"Yaaaay!" Kermit cried, racing to keep up with Evan.

Evan ducked his head to keep from banging it on a low tree branch. He took several big steps toward the street.

"Oh!" He stopped and cried out when he felt himself step on something. He heard a cracking, then a crunch beneath his enormous sneaker.

He turned to see Kermit raise both hands to his face. "Oh, no!" Kermit shrieked. "You squashed Andy! Evan — you squashed Andy!"

# 19

Evan gasped and jerked up his foot.

Kermit let out a high-pitched laugh. "Gotcha, Evan!"

Andy came running over from the driveway. "That wasn't funny!" she scolded Kermit. "That was a really dumb joke, Kermit. You scared Evan to death."

"I know!" Kermit laughed, very pleased with himself.

Evan let out a sigh of relief. He bent down to see what he had stepped on. Conan's skateboard. It lay crushed and splintered, flat on the grass.

He turned angrily to Kermit. "No more stupid jokes," he thundered. "Or I'll put you up in the tree with Conan."

"Okay. Okay," Kermit mumbled. "You think you're tough just because you're so big."

Evan held up a pointer finger. "Careful, Kermit," he warned. "I could knock you over with one finger."

"Conan is still yelling for help back there," Andy reported.

Evan smiled. "Let's see who's hanging out at the playground. Maybe we can surprise some other kids."

Evan crossed the street, taking long, heavy strides. He felt as if he were walking on stilts. This is kind of cool, he told himself. I'm the biggest person in the world!

He passed by the neighbors' basketball hoop, which stood on a pole at the curb. Hey — I'm at least six feet taller than the basket! he realized.

"Hey — wait up!" Andy called breathlessly. "Don't walk so fast!"

"I can't help it!" Evan called back.

A small blue car rolled by, then squealed to a stop. Evan could see a woman and two kids in the car. They were all staring out at him.

A little girl on a bike turned the corner. She started pedaling toward Evan. He saw the look of surprise on her face when she spotted him.

She braked her bike hard, nearly toppling over the handlebars. Then she wheeled around and sped out of sight.

Evan laughed.

Another car screeched to a halt.

As he started to cross another street, Evan turned to see who was in the car. He didn't watch where he was going.

A loud *crunch* made him stop.

340

With a gasp, he peered down — and saw that he had stepped on a car.

"Oh, no!" Evan cried. His sneaker had crushed in the top of the car — as if it were made of tinfoil.

Evan backed away in horror. Was someone inside?

He dropped to his knees to stare in the window. "Thank goodness!" he cried when he saw that the car was empty.

"Wow!" Kermit exclaimed, walking around and around the smashed-in car. "You must weigh at least a ton, Evan!"

Andy stepped up beside Evan, who remained on his knees. "Be careful," she warned. "You've got to watch every step."

Evan nodded in agreement. "At least I think I've stopped growing," he called down to her.

As they reached the playground, Evan saw several kids shouting and pointing excitedly at a tall maple tree on the corner.

What's going on? Evan wondered.

As he lumbered closer, he saw the problem. Their yellow kite had become stuck up in the tree.

"Hey — no problem!" Evan boomed.

The kids screamed and cried out in surprise as Evan stepped up to them. They all backed away, their faces tight with fear.

Evan reached up easily and tugged the kite loose from the tree limb. Then he leaned down and gently handed it to the nearest kid.

"Hey, thanks!" A grin spread across the kid's freckled face.

The other kids all cheered. Evan took a bow.

Andy laughed. "You need a red cape and a pair of blue tights," she shouted up to him. "It's Super Evan!"

"Super Evan!" the kids shouted as they ran off happily with their kite.

Evan leaned down to talk to Andy. "If I stay big like this, do you think I really could get a job as a superhero?"

"I don't think it pays very well," Kermit chimed in. "In the comic books, you *never* see those guys getting paid."

They crossed the street and headed toward the playground. Evan glanced at the redbrick school building on the corner. It's so small, he thought.

He suddenly realized that he stood at least two stories tall. If I walk over there, I can see into the second-floor classrooms, he thought.

How will I go to school? Evan wondered. I can't squeeze through the door. I won't fit in Mrs. McGrady's room anymore.

Feeling a wave of sadness roll over him, he turned away from the school building. He heard cheers and shouts. A softball game was underway on the practice diamond.

Evan recognized Billy Denver and Brian Johnson and some of the other kids. He always had to beg to play softball with them. They never wanted

Evan on their team because he wasn't a very good hitter.

He strolled over the grass to the practice diamond. Andy and Kermit ran behind him, struggling to keep up.

Brian was starting to pitch the ball. But he stopped short when he spotted Evan. The ball dropped from his hand and dribbled to the ground.

Players on both teams gasped and shouted.

Evan strode up to Brian on the pitcher's mound. Brian's eyes bulged in fear as Evan drew near. Brian raised his hands to shield himself. "Don't hurt me!" he pleaded.

"Hey — it's Evan!" Billy exclaimed. "Look, guys! It's Evan!"

Kids from both teams gathered around, murmuring excitedly, nervously.

Brian slowly lowered his hands and stared up at the giant Evan. "Wow! It really *is* you! Evan — how did you *do* that?"

"What happened to you?" another kid cried.

"He's been working out!" Andy told them.

The kids laughed. Very tense laughter.

Andy always has a joke for everything, Evan thought.

"Uh . . . want to play?" Brian asked. "You can be on my team."

"No. My team!" Billy insisted.

"No way! He's on my team!" Brian shouted. "We're one man short, remember?"

"Don't say *short* around Evan!" Andy joked.

Everyone laughed again.

Billy and Brian continued to fight over which team would get Evan. Evan stood back and enjoyed the argument. He picked up a wooden bat. It had always seemed so heavy before. Now it felt as light as a pencil.

Billy won the argument. "You can bat now, Evan," he said, grinning up at him.

"How can I pitch to him? He's a giant!" Brian complained.

"Pitch it really high," Evan suggested.

"Evan, do your mom and dad know you grew like this?" Billy asked, walking to home plate beside Evan.

Evan swallowed hard. He hadn't thought about his parents. They'd be getting home from work soon. They weren't going to be happy about this. How would he break the news to them? he wondered.

And then he thought: I won't *have* to break the news to them. They'll see for themselves what has happened!

He stepped up to the plate and swung the bat onto his shoulder. "Wish we had a bigger bat," he muttered. It was a little larger than a drinking straw.

"Get a hit!" Billy shouted from behind the backstop.

"Get a hit, Evan!" several other players called.

Brian's first pitch sailed past Evan's ankles.

"Higher!" Evan called out to him. "You'll have to throw it higher."

"I'm trying!" Brian grumbled. He pulled the softball back and tossed it again.

This time, the pitch flew past Evan's knees.

"It's hard to throw that high," Brian complained. "This isn't fair."

"Strike him out, Brian!" the first baseman cried. "You can do it. Evan always strikes out!"

It's true, Evan thought unhappily. I do usually strike out.

He gripped the little bat tighter, poising it over his shoulder. He suddenly wondered if being so big would make a difference.

Maybe he'd just strike out *bigger*!

Brian's next pitch sailed higher. Evan swung hard. The bat hit the softball with a deafening *thwack* — and cracked in two.

The ball sailed up, up, up. Off the playground. Over the school. And out of sight, somewhere in the next block.

Cheers and cries of amazement rang out over the diamond.

Evan watched the ball fly out of sight. Then he leaped joyfully in the air and began running the bases.

The longest home run in the history of the world!

It took only four steps between bases. He had

345

just rounded second base when he heard the sirens.

Evan turned his eyes to the street in time to see two fire trucks squeal around the corner. The trucks pulled right up onto the playground grass and came roaring toward the softball diamond, sirens blaring.

Evan stopped at third base.

The sirens cut off as the two fire engines skidded to a halt along the first base line.

Evan's mouth dropped open as Conan Barber leaped out of the first truck. Several black-uniformed firefighters dropped to the ground behind Conan.

"There he is!" Conan cried, pointing furiously at Evan. "That's him! Get him!"

# 20

Grim-faced firefighters began hoisting heavy fire-hoses off the trucks. Others moved toward Evan, hatchets clutched menacingly in their hands.

"That's him!" Conan shrieked. "He's the one who put me in the tree and wrecked my parents' fence!"

"Huh?" Still standing on third base, Evan froze in shock.

Was this really happening?

The playground rang out with shouts of surprise. But the voices were drowned out by more sirens.

Evan saw flashing red lights. And then two black-and-white police cars roared over the grass, screeching up behind the fire engines.

A man and woman came running behind the police cars. "That's the one!" they called breathlessly, pointing at Evan. "That's the one who crushed the car. We saw him do it!"

The firefighters were busily connecting the

347

hoses to hydrants at the curb. Blue-uniformed police swarmed on to the field. The kids on the two
softball teams huddled together on the pitcher's
mound. They all seemed dazed and frightened.

"He tried to kill me!" Conan was shouting to a
woman police officer. "That giant put me in a tree
and left me there!"

"He crushed a car!" a woman screamed.

Evan hadn't moved from third base. He gazed
past the fire engines to Andy and Kermit. They
stood near the backstop. Kermit had the dumb,
toothy grin on his face.

Andy had her hands cupped around her mouth.
She was shouting something to Evan. But he
couldn't hear her over the wail of sirens and the
excited shouts and cries of everyone in the
playground.

Some of the police and fire officers huddled together, talking rapidly. They kept glancing up at
Evan as they talked.

What are they going to do to me? Evan wondered, frozen in fear.

Should I run? Should I try to explain?

More people came hurrying across the playground. As soon as they spotted Evan, their
expressions turned to surprise and amazement.

They're all staring at me, Evan realized.
They're pointing at me as if I'm some kind of freak.

I *am* some kind of freak! he admitted to himself.

Firefighters formed a line, holding their hatchets waist-high. Others readied the firehoses, aiming them up at Evan's chest.

Evan heard more sirens. More police cars rolled on to the playground.

A young police officer with wavy red hair and a red mustache stepped up to Evan. "What — is — your — name?" he shouted, speaking each word slowly, as if maybe Evan didn't speak English.

"Uh . . . Evan. Evan Ross," Evan called down.

"Do you come from another planet?" the officer shouted.

"Huh?" Evan couldn't help himself. He burst out laughing.

He heard some of the softball players laughing, too.

"I live in Atlanta," he shouted down to the officer. "Around the corner. On Brookridge Drive."

Several officers and firefighters held their ears. Evan's voice came out louder than he had planned.

Evan took a step toward them.

The firefighters raised a firehose. Several others readied their hatchets.

"He's dangerous!" Evan heard Conan shout. "Watch out! He's really dangerous!"

That got everyone shouting and screaming.

The playground was filling with people. Neighborhood people. Kids and their parents. Cars stopped and people climbed out to see why the crowd had gathered.

More police cars bumped over the grass. Their wailing sirens added to the deafening noise, the shouts and cries, the frightened murmurs.

The noise. The staring eyes. The pointed fingers.

It all started to make Evan dizzy.

He felt his legs tremble. His forehead throbbed.

The police had formed a line. They started to circle Evan.

As they closed in, Evan felt himself explode. "I can't take any more!" he screamed, raising his fists. "Stop it! Stop it! All of you! Get away! Leave me alone! I mean it!"

Silence as the sirens cut off. The voices hushed.

And then Evan heard the red-haired police officer shout to the others: "He's turned violent. We have to bring him down!"

# 21

Evan didn't have time to be frightened.

The firehoses chugged and gurgled — then shot out thick streams of water.

Evan ducked low. Dove forward. Tried to get away from the roaring water.

The force of the water stream ripped the ground to his side.

Evan dodged to the other side.

Wow! That's powerful! he thought, horrified. The water is strong enough to knock me over!

Frightened shouts rose up over the roar of the water.

Evan plunged through the line of dark-uniformed police officers — and kept running. "Don't shoot!" he screamed. "Don't shoot me! I'm not from another planet! I'm just a boy!"

He didn't know if they could hear him or not.

He dodged past several startled onlookers. A long hook-and-ladder stood in his path.

He stopped. Glanced back.

Firefighters were turning the hoses. The powerful spray arced high. Water crashed to the ground just behind Evan, loud as thunder.

Kids and parents were running in all directions, frantic, frightened expressions locked on their faces.

Evan took a deep breath. Bent his knees. And leaped over the fire truck in his path.

He heard shouts of surprise behind him. He vaulted high over the truck. Landed hard on the other side. Stumbled. Caught his balance.

Then, ducking low, his arms stretched out in front of him, Evan ran.

His long legs carried him away quickly. As he reached the street, a low tree branch popped up as if from nowhere.

Evan dipped his head just in time.

Leaves scratched over his forehead, but he kept running.

Got to watch out for tree branches, he warned himself. Got to remember that I'm two stories tall.

Breathing hard, he plunged across the street. The late afternoon sun was lowering behind the trees. The shadows were longer now, and darker. Evan's shadow seemed a mile long as it stretched out in front of him.

He heard the rise and fall of shrill sirens behind him. Heard angry shouts. Heard the thud of footsteps, people running after him.

Where can I hide? he asked himself. Where will I be safe?

Home?

No. That's the first place the police will look.

Where? Where?

It was so hard to think clearly. They were close behind him, he knew. Chasing him. Eager to bring him down.

If only he could stop somewhere, close his eyes, shut them all out, and think. Then maybe he could come up with a plan.

But he knew he had to keep running.

His head throbbed. His chest ached.

His long legs were taking him quickly away from the playground. But he still felt awkward, with his sneakers so far below him and his head so high in the trees.

I'll hide out at Kermit's house, he thought.

Then he quickly decided that was a bad idea, too.

"I can't get *in* Kermit's house!" he cried out loud. "I'm too big!"

And then he had a truly frightening thought: "I can't fit in *any* house!"

Where will I sleep? he wondered. And then: Will they let me sleep?

Can't the police see I'm just a boy? Evan asked himself bitterly. He turned the corner and ran past his house. The lights were all off. The door closed. No car in the driveway.

His parents hadn't come home from work.

He kept running. Running across yards. Ducking low. Trying to hide behind shrubs and tall hedges.

Can't they see I'm a boy? Not a creature from another planet?

Why do they think I'm so dangerous?

It's all Conan's fault, Evan decided. Conan got the firefighters and police all crazy with his wild stories.

His wild, *true* stories.

And now where can I run? Where can I hide?

The answer came to him as he neared Kermit's house. Two doors down, a lot had been cleared. And an enormous stack of lumber had been piled at the back. Someone was about to build a house on the lot.

Breathing hard, sweat pouring down his broad forehead, Evan turned and ran across the lot. He ducked behind the tall pile of lumber. And stopped.

He dropped to his knees and leaned against the lumber stack, struggling to catch his breath. He wiped the sweat off his forehead with the sleeve of his T-shirt.

Maybe I'll hide here for a while, he thought. He lowered himself to a sitting position.

If I sit down and hunch my shoulders, the lumber pile hides me from the street. And it's shady and cool behind it. And I can keep an eye on Kermit's house from here.

Yes. This is a good hiding spot for now, Evan decided. Then, after dark, I'll sneak over to my house and try to explain to my parents what happened.

He leaned his back against the lumber pile and shut his eyes.

He had just started to relax a little when he heard a voice cry: "Got him!"

# 22

Evan's eyes shot open.

He tried to scramble to his feet.

But then he saw who had shouted.

"Kermit!" he cried angrily. "You scared me to death!"

Kermit flashed his annoying grin. "I *knew* you'd hide here, Evan," he said, smirking. "I'm so smart."

Kermit turned and called out, "He's back here! I was right!"

A few seconds later, Andy gingerly poked her head behind the stack of lumber. Her eyes studied Evan for a few seconds. Then a smile crossed her face.

"You're okay?" she asked softly. "I was so worried —"

"Yeah. I'm okay — for now," Evan replied bitterly.

"The whole town is after you!" Kermit exclaimed. "It's really awesome! It's like a movie!"

"I don't *want* to be in a movie!" Evan griped. "This movie is too scary."

"They've got guns and everything!" Kermit continued excitedly, ignoring Evan's complaint. "And did you see those firehoses? It's amazing! They all want to catch you!"

"They think you're an alien from outer space," Andy added, shaking her head.

"And who told them that? Conan?" Evan asked bitterly.

"Conan made them believe you're real dangerous," Kermit said, grinning that grin Evan hated so much.

"I *am* dangerous!" Evan declared. He growled menacingly at Kermit.

The growl shocked the grin off Kermit's face.

Evan turned to Andy. "What am I going to do? I can't run and hide for the rest of my life. They're going to catch me. If you two tracked me down, the police will track me down, too."

Evan let out a long, frightened sigh. "There's nowhere I can hide. I'm too big to hide! So what can I do? What?"

Andy scratched her arm. She knotted up her face, thinking hard. "Well . . ."

And suddenly Evan knew exactly what to do.

Watching Andy, Evan knew how to solve the whole problem.

# 23

Evan jumped to his feet. His heart began to pound. For the first time in hours, a big smile spread across his face.

"Evan — what's wrong?" Andy demanded. His sudden move had startled her.

"I know what we can do!" Evan declared. "Everything is going to be okay!"

"Get down!" Kermit cried. "I hear sirens. They'll see you."

In his excitement, Evan had forgotten that he was taller than the lumber pile. He dropped back to his knees. Even on his knees, he was a lot taller than Kermit and Andy.

The sirens blared louder. Closer.

Evan gazed around. The sun had fallen behind the trees. The sky was evening gray now. The air grew cooler.

"We've got to hurry," Evan told them. He put a hand on Kermit's slender shoulder. "Kermit, you've got to help me."

Behind his glasses, Kermit's little mouse eyes bulged with excitement. "Me? What can I do?"

"The blue mixture," Evan said, holding on to his cousin's shoulder. "Remember the blue mixture?"

"Wh-which one?" Kermit stammered.

"The one that shrank my mosquito bite!" Andy chimed in. She suddenly realized what Evan was thinking.

"That's right," Evan explained to Kermit. "Watching Andy scratch her arm reminded me. That blue mixture of yours shrank the mosquito bite instantly."

"Maybe it can shrink Evan, too!" Andy exclaimed excitedly.

Kermit nodded, thinking hard. "Yeah. Maybe it can."

"I'll rub it all over my body, and I'll shrink back to my normal size," Evan said happily.

"It'll work! I *know* it will!" Andy cried enthusiastically. She let out a cheer and jumped up and down. Then she tugged Kermit's arm. "Come on, Kermit. Hurry! Let's get to your basement. You still have the blue mixture, don't you?"

Kermit narrowed his eyes, trying to remember. "I think so," he told them. "A lot of stuff got wrecked, remember? But I think I have it."

"He has to have it!" Evan cried. "He *has* to!"

Evan climbed to his feet. "Come on. Hurry."

They heard sirens. Loud and near.

Kermit peered around the lumber pile toward the street. "A police car!" he whispered. "They're cruising this block."

"You'd better wait here," Andy warned Evan.

Evan shook his head. "No way. I'm coming with you. I want to get that blue mixture as fast as I can."

He ducked his head. "We can walk through the backyards. No one will see us."

"But, Evan —" Andy started to protest.

She stopped when Evan stepped away from the lumber pile and started loping quickly across the backyard toward Kermit's house.

Dogface greeted them in the driveway. The sheepdog barked happily, jumping up on Kermit, nearly knocking him to the ground.

"Shhh. Quiet, boy! Quiet!" Kermit cried, petting the dog, trying to stop his barks. "We don't want anyone to hear us."

Dogface gazed up at Evan — and got very quiet. The dog slumped across the driveway. It stared up suspiciously at Evan, panting hard, its stubby tail wagging furiously.

Evan's eyes darted up and down the driveway. No car. "Your mom isn't home yet, Kermit," he said.

"She must be working late," Kermit replied. "That's good news. This is our lucky day!"

Evan let out a bitter laugh. "For sure. Lucky day," he muttered.

Kermit and Andy hurried to the kitchen door. Evan started to follow. Then he remembered he didn't fit in the house.

"Wait right there," Andy instructed him. "Make sure no one sees you."

Evan nodded. "Hurry — please!"

He watched them disappear through the door. Then he sat down behind the house. He motioned for Dogface to come over to him. He felt like holding on to something.

But the big dog just stared back and wouldn't budge.

The whole town is looking for me, Evan thought unhappily. The whole town is looking for a *giant* me. But they'll never find the giant me. Because in a few seconds, I'll shrink back to normal size.

Then everything will be okay again.

He raised his eyes to the house. What is keeping Andy and Kermit? he wondered. Can't they find the bottle of blue liquid?

He took a deep breath. Don't panic, Evan, he instructed himself. They've only been in the house a few seconds. They'll be out soon. And everything will be okay.

To pass the time, he counted slowly to ten. Then he counted slowly to ten again.

He was about to start counting one more time

when the screen door flew open. Kermit stepped out, carrying the blue beaker. Andy followed right behind.

"Found it!" Kermit cried happily.

Evan jumped to his knees. He reached out eagerly. "Quick — let me have it."

Kermit stretched up his hand. Evan grabbed for the glass beaker.

It slipped out of his grasp.

It started to fall.

"Ohhh!" Evan let out a horrified moan — and caught the beaker just before it crashed against the driveway.

"Wow! Nice catch!" Kermit exclaimed.

Evan's heart had leaped to his mouth. He took a deep breath. He grasped the beaker tightly in his hand. "Close one," he murmured. The beaker was so tiny in his hand, like something made for a dollhouse.

They heard sirens in the distance.

The search for the giant Evan was still on.

"I — I hope this mixture works," Evan declared.

He raised the beaker. Tilted it upside down over his other hand. Waited.

And waited.

Finally, a tiny blue drop of liquid dripped on to Evan's palm.

Nothing more.

He shook the beaker. Hard. Harder. The way

he shook a ketchup bottle when the ketchup stuck.

Then he raised the beaker to his eye and peered inside.

A few seconds later, he let out a long, sad sigh. He tossed the bottle disgustedly onto the grass. "It's empty," Evan reported. "Totally empty."

# 24

"I knew there wasn't much left," Kermit murmured, shaking his head.

The empty bottle rolled under a shrub. Dogface walked over and sniffed it.

"I'm doomed," Evan muttered. Forgetting how strong he was, he angrily kicked a pebble down the driveway. The pebble sailed up into the air and disappeared over the house across the street.

"Be careful," Andy warned. "You could break a window."

"Who cares?" Evan snapped. "My life is ruined."

"No way!" Kermit cried. "You'll be okay, Evan." He started running to the house. "Be right back!"

"Kermit, where are you going?" Evan called glumly.

"To mix up another batch!" Kermit replied. "It will only take me a few seconds, Evan. I've got all the ingredients."

Evan could feel his sadness lifting. "Do you really think you can do it?" he asked his cousin.

"No problem," Kermit replied, flashing Evan a thumbs-up sign. "I think I remember what I put in it. I'll mix up more blue shrinking stuff and be back in a jiffy."

Kermit disappeared into the house. "I'm coming, too!" Andy called after him. She turned back to Evan. "I can try to clean up some of the lab while Kermit mixes the liquid. If Kermit's mom gets home and sees the basement, you'll be in big trouble."

Evan let out a weak laugh. *Big* trouble. Very funny, Annnndrea. You're a riot."

"Don't call me Andrea," she shot back, ignoring his sarcasm. He watched her hurry into the house.

Dogface got tired of sniffing the blue bottle. The sheepdog lumbered across the yard to inspect the fence that Evan had knocked down earlier.

Evan sighed. I wonder if my own dog will recognize me now? he thought. Trigger, Evan's cocker spaniel, had been the first to eat Monster Blood. The dog had grown bigger than a horse.

I wonder if Trigger ever has nightmares about that? Evan asked himself.

He knew he'd be having nightmares about today for a long time to come.

He glanced at his watch. Almost dinnertime. His parents would be getting home soon. And

Kermit's mom would be pulling up the driveway at any minute.

"Wow. She'll be surprised when she sees *me*!" Evan exclaimed out loud.

He turned to the house in time to see Kermit step out. He was carrying a fresh bottle of blue liquid. "See? No problem!" Kermit declared.

Evan carefully took the bottle from Kermit's hand.

Andy walked over, her eyes raised to Evan's. "Go ahead. Rub it all over," she urged. "Hurry!"

Evan carefully poured a puddle of blue liquid into his palm. Then he rubbed it onto his cheeks, his forehead, his neck.

He poured more into his hand. He rubbed blue liquid onto his arms. Then he raised his T-shirt and rubbed some on his chest.

Please let it work, he prayed silently. Please let it work.

He turned to Andy and Kermit. "See any change?"

# 25

Andy's mouth dropped open.

Kermit's eyes bulged, and he uttered a choking sound.

"Well?" Evan demanded eagerly. "Do you see any change? Do you?"

"Uh . . . well . . . uh . . ." Kermit sputtered.

"You turned blue!" Andy cried.

"Excuse me?" Evan demanded. He knew he hadn't heard her correctly.

"Your skin — it's bright blue!" Andy wailed, pressing her hands against her cheeks.

"My — what?" Evan shrieked. "You mean — HIC! —" A powerful hiccup made his entire body shake.

Evan stared down at his hands.

"They — they're blue!" he cried. "HIC!"

Another hiccup burst from his open mouth. His enormous body shook as if struck by an earthquake.

Frantically, he pulled up the T-shirt and stared at his stomach. His blue stomach.

His arms. His chest. All blue. Bright blue.

"HIC!"

*"I don't believe it!"* Evan screamed. "I'm bright blue, and — HIC! — I've got the hiccups!"

He glared down furiously at Kermit.

Kermit was so frightened, his legs trembled and his knees actually knocked together. "I — I can fix it," he called up to Evan. "N-no problem! I just mixed it up wrong. I'll be right back with another mixture."

He ran to the house. At the screen door, he turned back to Evan. "Don't go anywhere — okay?"

Evan let out a furious roar, interrupted by a deafening hiccup. *"Where can I go?"* he shrieked at the top of his lungs. *"Where can I — HIC! — go?!"*

The door slammed behind Kermit.

Evan let out another roar, clenching his blue fists and shaking his blue arms over his head. He paced back and forth on the driveway, hiccupping every few seconds.

"Try to calm down a little," Andy called up to him. "People will hear you."

"I — I — HIC! — can't calm down!" Evan complained bitterly. "Look at me!"

"But the neighbors will hear you. Or see you," Andy warned. "They'll call the police."

Evan replied with a hiccup that nearly knocked him off his feet.

Kermit came running out of the house. He raised another bottle of blue liquid to Evan. "Here! Try this!"

"HIC!" Evan declared. He grasped the bottle in his blue hand.

Without saying another word, he turned the bottle upside down. With quick, frantic motions, he splashed the blue liquid all over him. Over his cheeks. His forehead. His hands and arms. His chest.

He rolled up his jeans and rubbed the mixture onto his knees and legs. He pulled off his socks and sneakers and smoothed the blue liquid over his ankles and feet.

"It's *got* to work!" he cried. "This time, it's *got* to!"

Andy and Kermit stared up at him eagerly.

They waited.

Evan waited.

Nothing happened. No change at all.

Then Evan began to feel it.

"Hey — I'm tingling!" he announced happily.

He felt the same electric tingling he had felt before. The itchy feeling he had every time he was about to grow a little more.

"Yes!" Evan cheered. "Yes!"

The tingling grew sharper, stronger, as it spread over his entire body.

"It's working! I can — HIC! — feel it!" Evan shouted. "It's really working! I'm tingling! I'm itching! I can feel it! It's working!"

"No, it isn't," Andy murmured quietly.

# 26

"Huh?" Evan narrowed his eyes at her.

The tingling became a violent itch. He started to scratch. But pulled back his hand because his skin felt so strange.

"It . . . didn't . . . work. . . ." Andy said sadly, her voice trembling.

"Yuck! He looks so gross!" Kermit declared, making a disgusted face.

"Huh? HIC!" Evan replied.

He uttered a horrified gasp as he stared at his arms. "F-f-feathers!" he stammered in a high, shrill voice.

He checked out his arms. His stomach. His legs.

"Noooooo!" A long, low wail burst from his chest.

His entire body was covered in fluffy white feathers.

"Noooo — HIC! — ooooooooo!"

"I'm sorry," Kermit said, shaking his head. "I

don't know what I'm doing wrong. I thought I had the mixture right this time."

"You look like a big eagle," Andy commented. "Except eagles aren't blue."

"HIC!" Evan cried.

"And eagles don't get hiccups," Andy added. She gazed up at him with concern. "Poor Evan. That must itch like crazy. You're having a real bad day."

Evan frantically scratched his feathery chest. "It can't get any worse than this," he muttered.

And then he saw a police car pull up in front of the house.

# 27

"HIC!" Evan cried. He backed off the driveway and crouched low against the back wall of the house. "The police!" he whispered.

His throat tightened in panic. His feathers all stood up on end.

What should I do? he asked himself, pressed against the house, ducking his head. Should I run? Should I give myself up?

"One more try!" Kermit cried, leaping into the house. "Let me try one more mixture. I think I can get it this time!"

The door slammed behind him.

"Hurry!" Andy called from the driveway. "The police — they're climbing out of their car."

"How many are there?" Evan whispered. His feathers itched, but he was too frightened to scratch.

"Two," Andy replied, staring through the gray evening light to the street. "They look kind of mean."

A sudden cool gust of wind ruffled Evan's feathers. His huge body trembled.

"They're walking up the driveway," Andy reported. "They're going to be here in a few seconds!"

"I'd better make a run for it," Evan declared. He took one step away from the house and nearly fell. It was hard to run when your feet were covered with stiff, prickly feathers.

His entire body itched. He pressed himself against the house again. "I'm doomed," he murmured to himself.

"They stopped to check out the front door," Andy told him. "You've still got a few seconds."

"Hurry, Kermit! Hurry!" Evan urged out loud.

He turned to the kitchen door. No sign of Kermit.

Would Kermit get the mixture right this time? Could he get the mixture to Evan before the two police officers entered the backyard?

The screen door opened. Kermit burst out. He tripped on the back stoop. The blue bottle nearly went flying.

He caught his balance. He handed the bottle up to Evan. "Good luck!" Kermit called up to Evan. Kermit raised both hands. He had his fingers tightly crossed on both hands.

"Here come the police," Andy warned. "They're walking really fast now."

The bottle trembled in Evan's hand. He turned

it upside down. It puddled in his enormous, feathery palm.

Frantically, he began rubbing it over his feathers, over his blue skin. Splashing it wildly. Pouring it over his body.

Please work! he silently urged it. Please work!

He waited.

Kermit stared up at him hopefully, his fingers still crossed.

"They're here!" Andy reported from the driveway.

Evan gulped.

The mixture hadn't worked.

He hadn't changed. Not a bit.

The two dark-uniformed officers approached the back of the house. "Hello, there," one of them called to Andy.

# 28

Evan heard a loud POP.

He uttered a startled cry as he felt himself falling. Falling to the ground.

He reached out a hand and steadied himself against the house.

It took him a second or two to realize that he hadn't fallen. He had shrunk.

The two officers stepped into the backyard. One was very tall. The other was short and plump. "Sorry to bother you kids," the tall one said. "But we got a call from a neighbor."

"A call? About what?" Andy demanded. She cast a surprised glance at Evan. She didn't expect to see him back to normal.

"Did you kids see a giant in the neighborhood?" the short officer asked. He narrowed his eyes at them, trying to appear tough.

"A giant? What kind of giant?" Kermit asked innocently.

"A giant kid," the short officer replied.

Evan, Andy, and Kermit shook their heads.

"He didn't come back here," Andy told them.

"No. We didn't see him," Evan said. He couldn't keep a smile from crossing his face. His voice was back to normal, too.

The tall officer pushed his cap back on his head. "Well, if you see him, be careful," he warned. "He's dangerous."

"He's very dangerous," the short officer added. "Call us right away — okay?"

"Okay," all three kids replied in unison.

The officers gave the backyard one last look. Then they turned and headed back down the driveway to their car.

As soon as they were gone, Evan burst into a long, happy cheer. Andy and Kermit joined in, clapping him joyfully on the back, slapping high fives all around.

"Am I a genius or what?" Kermit demanded, grinning his toothy grin.

"Or what!" Evan joked.

They were still laughing and celebrating Evan's return to Evan-size when Kermit's mom pulled up the driveway. As she climbed out of her car, she appeared surprised to find them outdoors.

"Sorry I'm so late," she called. She hugged Kermit. "How was your afternoon?"

Kermit glanced at Evan. Then he smiled at

his mother. "Oh, it was kind of boring," he told her.

"Yeah. Kind of boring," Andy repeated.

"Kind of boring," Evan agreed.

Evan knew he'd have nightmares about what had happened to him. And that night, he had a really scary one. In the dream, he was a giant boy being chased by giant rats. The rats all looked like Kermit.

Evan sat up in the dark, shivering all over.

"Just a nightmare," he murmured, glancing at his clock radio. Midnight. "It was just a nightmare."

He sat up straight, wiping sweat off his forehead with his pajama-top sleeve. I need a glass of cold water, he decided.

He started to climb out of bed — but stopped when he saw what a steep drop it was to the floor.

Huh? What's going on? he asked himself.

He tried to click on the bedtable lamp. But it towered high above him, way beyond his reach.

He stood up on the bed. As his eyes adjusted to the dim light, he saw that his bed seemed to stretch on forever. A lump in the bedspread curled up over Evan's head.

I — I'm short! he realized. I'm as short as a mouse!

Kermit!

Kermit strikes again! Evan thought bitterly.

He made the blue shrinking mixture too powerful.

I shrank — and shrank — and shrank. And now I'm as tiny as a mouse.

"I'll pound Kermit! I really will!" Evan cried. His voice came out as tiny mouse squeaks.

Standing on the edge of his bed, staring down, down — miles down — to the floor, Evan heard a rumbling sound. Loud panting that sounded like a strong wind through the trees.

A big head popped up in front of him. Two dark eyes.

"No! Trigger! Go back to sleep!" Evan pleaded in his little mouse voice. "No! Trigger — down!"

Evan's squeaks had awakened the cocker spaniel.

Evan felt the dog's hot breath blow across his face.

"Yuck! Dog breath!" he squeaked.

Then he felt sharp teeth close around his waist. Felt himself tilted sideways. Felt the hot, wet saliva of Trigger's mouth as the dog secured Evan between its teeth.

"Trigger — down! Put me down!" Evan begged.

He was bounced hard now. The dog teeth tightened their grip.

"Trigger! Put me down! Where are you taking me?"

Through the dark hallway. The hot breath blowing over Evan's helpless body.

Into his parents' room. Evan gazed up to see his mom and dad getting ready for bed.

Mr. Ross leaned over the dog. "What have you got there, Trigger? Did you find a bone?"

"Uh . . . Dad? Dad?" Evan squeaked up at him. "Dad? It's me? Do you see me? Dad? Uh . . . I think we have a little problem!"